DEMON'S BLESSING

BY

SLOANE MURPHY

Demon's Blessing
The Shadow Weaver #3
Part of The Seven Realms Saga

Published by Hudson Indie Ink
www.hudsonindieink.com

Demon's Blessing/Sloane Murphy – 2nd ed.
ISBN-13 - 978-1-915118-06-6

Death is not the opposite of life, but a part of it

- HARUKI MURAKAMI

ONE

AZRIEL

They all thought I was dead.

I guess I'll show them.

You can't kill what never truly existed.

And I never did. I never got to live. But now I'm free.

I escaped Death's clutches, and while she tried to keep a hold of me, it's hard to catch what was never yours.

They won't even see me coming.

And her…

Well, she and I have some unfinished business.

TWO

MORGAN

"What do you mean, he escaped?" My shout echoes through the throne room, and Korrín winces from her spot before the dais.

"Just that, he escaped. I had him locked down the same as always but when I got to the part of the pits where we store lost souls before I transport them to Kavaraí, he was gone. I have no fucking idea how it happened. But I'm going to find him," she vows, almost as pissed off as I am. Except not quite, because she's not the one who has to tell Mara that the guy who tortured her favorite human is on the fucking loose and no one knows where the fuck he is.

"Find him," I bite out through clenched teeth, seething

with barely suppressed fury. I feel Caleb practically vibrating with his own anger beside me.

I shoot him a glance, gauging his anger. The same rage I feel is barely contained on his face. "We need to tell them."

"Yes, we do. You should go get Deacon. He'll want to know about this too."

"Mara is going to have fucking kittens," he mutters, shaking his head. My mouth twists into a frown. Talk about understatement of the century. "I guess I'll go get Deacon."

"Are you sure this is a good idea? Maybe we should look for him first?" Bryce questions. I'd almost forgotten he was still here. His quiet rage can be so unassuming.

Caleb grins at him, looking more excited than I've seen him in a long while. "Good idea. It's been a while. Let's go hunting, shall we?"

THREE

DEACON

Some of the worst things in my life have happened in this room, but this... I never saw this coming.

I don't want to make this about me. Not when the woman I love is trembling so hard in my arms that I'm not sure if I'm holding her up or if I'm stopping her from running away.

We've overcome so much to get here, but this could be the very thing that breaks us.

Which considering my life, and all the never-ending torment that's taken place in this fucking throne room, ending my one real shot at happiness would be par for the course. There's been so much fucking pain here, so much torment. I don't usually dwell on my past since nothing good can come from it. Considering all that's happened, though, it does seem only fitting that my world would crumble apart in this room just as I find happiness.

I don't remember a time in my hundred years when I ever felt so broken and helpless as I do now. I might be young, but I've grown up quickly. My father made sure of that. But even everything he did couldn't help the outcome of this one. My mother cries all the time, and he looks at me with such shame and disgust that I can't find it in me anymore to hate him for what he's doing.

My own self-loathing is enough. My twin sister is dead because of me. I wasn't strong enough to save her. I wasn't smart enough to find her. And now she's gone forever. She was the one part of me that was so bright it didn't matter how dark I, or our world, was. Scout could light up everything around her despite the circumstances, and she made me feel like maybe I could be good.

Now her light is gone.

Missing her is like missing the other half of my soul. My now black, shredded soul.

None of that matters now. How could it when I'm dragged in chains behind my father who leads me to my fate?

An existence of servitude to the Demon King. That is

what awaits me.

I shudder at the thought. The looming black palace is the thing of nightmares. Its tall black spires are topped with spikes that hold rotting heads. The statues of the Demon King's many pets line the wall like sentries on guard. Shadows and black mist move around the top of the palace like a living entity… The death mists—something I don't ever want to experience.

As I'm dragged down the path through the black gates and across the drawbridge, I find myself hoping for a swift death. I know that isn't something that the fates hold for me, though.

The giant doors to the palace are open as we reach it, and I shudder as we cross the threshold into the giant entrance hall.

"This way," my father jeers as he continues to drag me behind him. I lose track of where we're going; this place is a maze. The sounds of cheers bring with them the realization that we're close to reaching our destination.

The throne room.

I thought the palace looked terrifying, but it's nothing compared to the living nightmare of the throne room. The stone floor is black at first glance, but I quickly realize I can't tell if it's actually black or stained that way from so much blood. The walls are shiny and onyx, and it's all topped with a soaring, dark ceiling. It's literally like a pit of darkness. The cold of the room hits me, and I swear I can see my breath. There's a reason no one of reasonable mind wants to be here. It feels like the very room will suck my soul from my body.

The jeers of people just as sick and twisted as the King echo around the room, filling the few spaces that exist between the packed-in bodies. The King sits at the far end of the room, and I nearly gag as I notice the living statues dotted through the room like trophies. They're actual people encased in stone, still living, with their pleading eyes following me as my father pulls me along the marble floor.

I would save them if I could, but I can't even save myself.

"Father, please!" I know I shouldn't beg. It will only make his hatred of me grow, though I'm not sure it's possible for him to fish even another iota of hatred out of his heart for me. His eyes flare, red and full of disgust, as he sneers back at me.

"Do not embarrass me, boy. You will live to regret it." My head hangs in shame. I knew it was useless, but I had to at least try. I know that I deserve this. Scout is dead, and that's my fault. No punishment will ever be worse than her death, but this might be as close as I get.

The silver chains burn my neck, wrists, and ankles, but I savor the pain—the burn against my skin is something that could never compare to the constant burn in my gut. It distracts me from thinking about what my life will become. Stories of the King's cruelty are legendary in the Shadow Realm. Even on Level Six where I grew up, death parties, where the lower born are chosen as blood sacrifices, are thrown in his honor. I've never really been into the whole 'cruel for the sake of being cruel' thing, which is part of why my father thinks I'm soft.

He blamed my mother. Sometimes he blamed my sister. Usually, he blamed me. My entire life, he tried to beat me into the thing he most hoped for in a son. A cruel, vile beast that got off on the torture and screams of those on his table. More than once, he forced me to watch or to inflict pain on his victims to try and toughen me up.

I'm just not made that way. I might be a Demon, but I'm a Morph, so my animal side rules me more than most. I'd be happiest left to myself, out in nature, away from everything this kind of life brings with it.

I look up to find the King sitting on his throne, with his son Ares to his right and his daughter Morganna to his left, sitting on small thrones of their own. Their mother hasn't been seen at court for nearly thirty years. No one knows for certain, but rumors suggest the King had her killed. It wouldn't shock me. He is the Demon King, after all. He's the reason the Shadow Realm is the way it is. His darkness taints everything it encounters, all the way to the farthest reaches of this place. All Scout ever wanted to do was run away. To Earth, to the Sparkling Cities, to anywhere that wasn't in this place, to any place away from his grasp.

"I see you've come to pay your debts, Airon." The King's laughter booms around the throne room, and I can't help but wince at it. The sound is grating, tearing against the very sinew of my being, and I notice others around the room flinching and inching backward. I glance over to his daughter, who's not much older than me, and for just a moment, I think I see a look of pity on her face. It's gone in the blink of an eye, making me question whether or not it was ever even there. Ares is stone-faced, cold and hard, and I quickly realize that I won't find help from either of them.

My father grips my shoulder before shoving me to the ground, and white hot pain rips through my body as my knees smash onto the hard floor. I don't make a sound. Showing any kind of weakness won't help me here. I don't know what my father has arranged as my punishment, but I know nothing about it will be good.

"I always keep my word," my father responds with a slimy smile, and the King's laughter fills the room again, grating and awful. The only person who looks unaffected is Morganna. Every other person seems to be as scared as my father, shrinking away as far as they dare. Because no one is the King's friend. Not truly. And the reminders of

those who crossed him are on show all around the palace, living statues that ensure no one forgets. I heard he once encased a cook in stone for merely overcooking a steak.

The King's madness knows no bounds, and here I am, being sold to him as nothing more than a slave.

The King sneers down at me, and I cast my gaze to the floor. His attention is enough to make me feel as if I'll never be clean again. "He looks weak," he says, derision lacing his tone.

"He looks weaker than he is, but I'm sure he'll meet your needs, whatever they may be." My father's charming tone nearly makes me gag. I've never wanted to be someone's puppet. Yet here I am, chained like an animal, being handed over to the most feared man in our entire realm.

I can feel his gaze leave my kneeling form, the unclean feeling lifting only slightly as I stare at the obsidian-colored floor. "I'm sure he will. You should be more careful with your things, Airon. Soon you'll run out of bargaining chips."

My father drops my chains, and they land with a heavy thud next to my prone form. I remain where I am. What good would it do me to try to escape now? I've been traded into a lifetime of servitude. I will always have a master, never having the chance to be my own man. If I run now, the fate that awaits me is death... or something worse.

Because this life has shown me that there are things much worse than death.

With a snap of his fingers, the King's right hand man, Tenarious, appears. His bony fingers dig into my scalp as he grabs me by the hair, yanking me to my feet. I hiss at the pain, but he doesn't bother to look at me.

"Lock him up with the others. I'll have my fun later." The King waves his hand dismissively, and then I'm being dragged through a door behind the dais and away from the throne room. The smile on my father's face will forever haunt me.

I do not doubt he is glad to have found a reason to finally be rid of me.

As Tenarious drags me further down the hall, I hear them; and once he drags me through a door just around another corner, I see them. The cages. Lines and lines of them, stacked at least four high. Each with yet another tortured soul inside.

"This one is yours, boy," Tenarious snarls as he throws me inside one, locking the door with a nasty smile marring his face. I land on my front, and when I look up, for a second I think I see Scout. Then she's gone, replaced with another dark-haired girl who looks so much like her it's uncanny. Another glance tells me it's not her. There isn't a light in her.

Tenarious leaves the room, and I huddle in the back

corner of my dark cage. I'm glad I can only see out of the front, so at least there's only one other lost soul within my view. And while I know I deserve this punishment, I can't help but wonder how far they'll push me. What I'll have to do to survive. And that scares me more than anything else in the world.

I shake my head, forcing myself back to the present. It feels like the whole room is holding its breath. I can feel Fallon practically vibrating next to me, but I can't tell which emotion will win out. His eyes haven't left her, and I'm not sure if that's good or bad, but then she rips out of my arms and turns back to face Morgan and Caleb. Her gaze bounces back and forth between them and him.

"What the actual fuck is happening here?"

FOUR

FALLON

This can't be happening.

I can't breathe.

How is this *real?*

My knees go weak, and I feel Deacon's arms wrap around me again. His steadying support is the only thing keeping me standing. Anger flares to life within me, and my heart explodes in an irregular heartbeat as I stare open-mouthed at the sight in front of me. My stomach is a jumbled mess of butterflies, and the anger is softened with a touch of hope. The touch of betrayal, though… That's what keeps me going.

I blink, trying to convince myself that what I'm seeing

is real.

The whole room is silent, and all I hear are my own gasping breaths as tears run down my face.

He takes a step toward me, and the dam inside me breaks.

"Fallon…"

My name on his lips only makes me cry more.

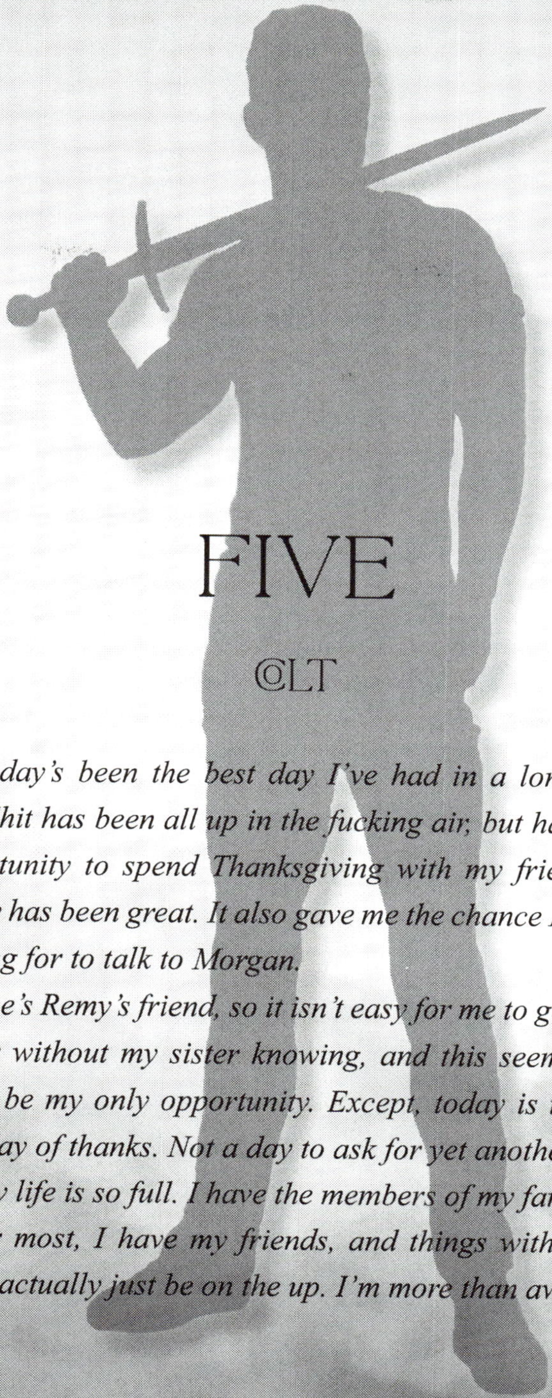

FIVE

COLT

Today's been the best day I've had in a long while. Shit has been all up in the fucking air, but having the opportunity to spend Thanksgiving with my friends and family has been great. It also gave me the chance I've been looking for to talk to Morgan.

She's Remy's friend, so it isn't easy for me to get access to her without my sister knowing, and this seems like it might be my only opportunity. Except, today is meant to be a day of thanks. Not a day to ask for yet another favor.

My life is so full. I have the members of my family who matter most, I have my friends, and things with my girl might actually just be on the up. I'm more than aware that most of my and Fallon's problems have been because of my stupid ass, but I'm determined to move past it.

I look around the table, at the crazy collection of people we have here, and I can't help but feel proud of Remy for bringing us all together. I just wish Bauer didn't look like he'd sucked on a fucking lemon. Guy needs to get with the program.

Nate clears his throat and stands, raising his glass. "This year has been one of the most turbulent ones I've lived in all of my lifetimes. I am happy and grateful that we can be here together, as a family, to celebrate this day. I know there are faces that are missing from the table, but I like to think they're still with us. Here's to family, and a quieter year next year."

Everyone raises their glasses in toast, and Nonnie hands the carving knife to Nate. He sits on the opposite end of the table from me and has somehow been crowned the designated speech giver and turkey carver.

Before this year, the honor always went to my dad. I try not to let the thought leave a sour taste in my mouth. It only seems right that Nate would be the one to carry that torch now as he's been a surrogate father to me in each life I've lived.

Once he finishes, it's like feeding time at the zoo. Everyone digs in, and the chatter starts, filling the room with happiness and laughter. Stories fly around the table as everyone gets to know each other a little better. Not going to lie, it's hilarious as hell watching Nate discuss Demon politics with Bryce, but he seems to be holding his own; and for the first time in a while, Fallon actually looks happy. Haunted still, but happy nonetheless.

I eat so much I think I might burst, pushing it to the point that the thought of eating anything else makes me feel like I might actually puke.

"You push it too far?" Nate asks with a knowing smile, so I just grin back.

"I never push it too far, old man." He laughs while Bauer scowls beside me. I am so sick of his bullshit right now, but this day is supposed to be about appreciating the good things in your life and family, so I'll just pull his ass up on it later.

Remy grins from the end of the table, running a hand over her belly. She groans before saying, "Nonnie, you truly outdid yourself. That was amazing."

"I hope you saved space. I made cheesecake," Nonnie teases, and I groan with Remy. Man, there is always space for dessert.

Maddie chuckles at our reactions, shaking her head as she laughs. "You two and cheesecake. I've never seen anything like it."

"What can I say? I'm one of a kind." Remy laughs, and the whole table joins in.

"You can say that again," Caleb teases from his spot near Morgan.

"Should we take this outside?" I ask, moving behind Fallon's chair and placing my hand on her shoulder. I've struggled to not touch her every second of every day since we got her back.

"Yes, let's get this party really started," Caleb says, standing too.

I lead our party outside, and Creek jogs ahead of me toward the gazebo. Music spills out of it moments later, and Fallon takes my hand, talking to her mom as we head into the gazebo. Not gonna lie, these guys sure know how to throw a party.

"DANCE OFF!" Caleb shouts pointing at me, and I grin. I never turn down a challenge, and while I might have two left feet, there is no way I'm going to change now.

The music changes from some slow jams to some absolute jams from a few years ago, and I see Bryce behind the deck grinning at us. "Unfair advantage!" I call out, laughing as I do.

"Of course there's an unfair advantage. I'm a Demon, not an idiot." Caleb smirks. I lose myself in the silliness of it all, and we dance until we're both laughing too hard to keep going.

"Let's call it a tie." I laugh before sucking down a bottle of water.

Caleb claps a hand on my shoulder, a grin on his face. "Deal!" he agrees.

"You got a minute, man? I need to talk to you... well, you and Morgan," I ask as we head off of the dance floor.

"You sound serious for once," he mocks, but when he looks back at me, there's a tight frown pulling the corners of his lips down. He considers me for a moment before continuing, "But sure, you're family."

He leads me to where Morgan sits with Killian and Malik, and catching the mood, they leave quickly, giving us some privacy. I have no idea how they manage the whole talking without words thing, but I guess a few thousand years together gives you those sorts of relationship dynamics.

"Colt." Morgan smiles up at me as I sit down and Caleb takes her other side. "What can we do for you?"

"Well, I usually wouldn't even think about it, but with the world being the way it is..." I trail off as I look over the two of them. I rub the back of my neck, trying to find the words to say without sounding like a total prick. I heave a sigh before continuing, "You guys might be my only chance..."

"I'm intrigued," Morgan says, raising an eyebrow. Fuck, she reminds me of Remy so much sometimes.

"So I'm sure you guys know all about the Hunter's curse being broken..."

Caleb nods. "We do."

"I'm not finished with this world or with this life, not yet at least. And I know that you guys helped Creek..." I trail off and roll my eyes. I hate how I sound right now. "Fuck me, I sound like such a bitch. Basically, I'm asking you guys that if I go too early—before I get chance to enjoy my fucking life if it's my last one—to pull my soul to the Realm. I want you to save me the way you saved Creek."

They look at each other, making a quick, silent exchange in the way that they do, and Caleb nods before Morgan turns back to me.

"Yes, we can do that. We would need to bind you to one of us. That includes a blood exchange, but it's a small ritual and nothing crazy," she tells me, and relief floods my body. I sag back in my chair. Relief isn't something I'm used to feeling, and it's definitely been a long fucking time since I've felt it on this scale.

"Thank you so fucking much," I tell her in a rush of gratitude. I bite the inside of my cheek hard, considering whether or not to go through with the next part. In the end, the rarely seen pragmatic side of me has his say. "I have one other request."

"Oh?" Morgan asks, an amused smile playing on her lips.

"I don't want you to tell my sister. Or anyone for that matter. I don't want them waiting around for me. I know

how long it can take a soul to cycle, and I also know how much Creek still struggles with his powers. I don't want them to see me suffer through that or to put their lives on hold for me. For all I know, it could be a lifetime before I'm ready to see them again."

They look at each other again, and I can tell that Caleb isn't happy with my request. Morgan pats his knee gently, squeezing slightly before turning back to me with an assessing stare.

"What is it with you mortals and your secrets?" she asks, but I don't have it in me to feel ashamed. All I've ever wanted to do is protect my family, and I won't have them suffering on my part. "But yes, we will do that. As Caleb said, you are family. I know what it is to wait and hope that the ones you love will come back to you. I also know what torture it is for the one who wants to return, knowing the burden and toll it will take on the ones they love. We will do all that you ask, Colt."

"Can we do it now? Quickly, so it's done? The last thing I want is to have someone attack tonight, and I die, and then I'm truly fucked."

Caleb roars out a laugh, shaking his head. "No soul is ever truly gone. Not unless the ritual is performed before it's salvaged. I forget how little information truly makes it to this realm. But yes, we can do it tonight. I will bind you to me since the two of us slipping out together will be less noticeable than you disappearing with Morgan. Let's go now, and then it's done."

He stands, and I follow suit. I nod to Morgan before turning back to him and muttering, "Thank you again."

"You have nothing to thank me for. You are my brother. And with what we're about to do, we'll be bound for eternity."

"Fallon…" I take a step toward where she's crying, standing next to Deacon. I can't tell if she's happy to see me or just really fucking angry. Caleb warned me this could happen when we did the ritual. If I'd known the Hunter's curse was going to be reborn, maybe I would've done things differently. But then again, maybe I wouldn't have.

I can't take my eyes off of her. Seeing her is the best belated birthday present I could've asked for, though I can't say that seeing her in Deacon's arms helps soothe the Demon inside of me. I've been here for six months, learning how to grapple with my Demon. It turns out being bound to one of the Four Horsemen really fucks with you when you're reborn. I have no idea how Creek did it so quickly, though I think it might be because he was reborn from Morgan's blood. Either way, if I said any of this had been easy, I'd be lying.

She pulls out of Deacon's arms, turning on the two people who have helped me more in the last six months than I remember anyone ever helping me in any of my previous lifetimes.

"What the actual fuck is happening here?" she shouts, and I take another step forward before her gaze bounces back to mine.

"Maybe we should give you guys some space," Caleb says before looking over at me. "Are you going to be okay?"

"Is he going to be okay?" Fallon yells. "He's supposed to be fucking dead!"

"Fallon," Deacon coos and pulls her into his arms, and my stomach clenches. Whatever he says to her seems to calm her down a bit, but I can't say that seeing it doesn't hurt something deep inside of me. Caleb warned me, telling me that they'd gotten together, but hearing it and seeing it are two very different things. I nod back at Caleb, letting him know I'll be fine. Regardless of what she's done in my absence, I would never hurt Fallon.

I can't say the same about Deacon. While I'll never be able to understand how she could forgive him for everything he put her through, I know that hurting him would hurt her. And so I'll do my best to keep my Demon under wraps.

Caleb and Morgan whisper away, though likely not too

far just in case, to give us some privacy. Deacon ushers Fallon into the chairs Morgan and Caleb vacated, and my stomach lurches again. I knew this would be a shock for Fallon; I had just hoped it would be a happier one. I expected her to be a little upset. I didn't expect the outright anger behind her tearful eyes.

"Fallon, please just give me a chance to explain," I plead, my heart breaking in my chest. I did this all for her, but I'll never tell her that. That's not who I am. I just hate that this happened when it did. She was so broken, and I can't even begin to imagine what she went through after I died. I don't know what happened, Morgan and Caleb explained what little they knew. I already know I'm going to have a hell of a time when it comes to explaining my decision to everyone else, but I needed to see her first.

I've been trying to see her since the day I woke up here six months ago; but because they didn't have my body, the process for me to become what I am now was different. It took longer apparently, and my soul was off in the ether for a while there too. Fuck knows what happened. The last thing I remember before waking up here was being in Avalon. I haven't asked the details of how I look exactly the same despite them not having my body, but I figured there were more important things I needed to wrap my head around. Like you know, controlling the Demon I awoke with.

Nearly decimating the room I awoke in isn't one of my highlights since being reborn like this.

My gaze never leaves the woman who still holds my heart as she sits down, hand clutched tightly around Deacon's. She won't look up at me, and though I don't understand it, I don't push it. I always knew this would be a huge shock for her, and the entirety of the reason I didn't want to tell her before I died hinged on me not knowing how long it would take for me to come back. I didn't want her waiting for me, putting her entire life on hold for a what-if. I'm thankful that I wasn't gone that long, but I was still gone long enough. Her whole life has changed in the two years since that day in Avalon.

"How is this even possible?" Fallon finally speaks, her gaze lifting to mine, and the pain shining in her eyes spears me through the heart.

"That is a long story," I start, moving closer to them. I sit at the table opposite to her when she doesn't object.

Deacon squeezes her hand, and my jaw clenches involuntarily. I hate the distance between her and I right now, but I know I created that distance. I'll just have to win my girl back. She looks at me, anger rising beneath her pain, and her lips go thin, pressed tightly together before she finally spits, "Then I guess you'd better start talking."

SIX

FALLON

"I'm not even sure where to begin."

I hear the words, and his voice shakes something deep inside of me. I'm angry. I feel betrayed. I can't believe he's actually real, that he's really here, in front of my eyes. Living and breathing.

At least I think he is.

This could all just be a dream. It wouldn't be the first one I've had where he came back to me. I honestly thought they'd passed. I subtly pinch myself, and fuck! Yes, it hurts. This is somehow real. I see Deacon's smirk out the corner of my eye, so obviously it wasn't that subtle, but I don't care.

I can't believe Colt is here.

Holy shit.

I take another deep breath, my gaze having barely left him. "Maybe start from the beginning?"

The bite in my tone isn't intended, but I can't seem to shut the anger down. I don't know exactly why I'm angry... Except maybe I do. Because this must have been planned, and if he'd just told me… So much pain could have been avoided.

A thought occurs to me, a wild desperate thought that sends another pang of betrayal through my chest. "Wait, does Remy know you're back?" I ask, my heart racing.

"Not yet. I wanted to see you first. But please don't tell her. I want to explain this to her myself," he says, and looks down at his inked-up hands. At least she didn't keep this from me too. It's a small silver lining, but over the last two years, I've learned to take every single silver lining I can find.

"Okay," I say, taking a deep breath, trying to make myself understand that he's actually here, that this is real, and that breaking down isn't the right way to handle it all. I steel my reserve, heaving a deep breath before asking him to start from the beginning again.

"It all started with the Hunter's curse being broken..." he begins, smiling at me sadly. My heart pangs within my chest, aching for him. I don't want him to be sad, but I really need to know how this happened, and knowing why the fuck he never said a word to me wouldn't hurt either. Maybe he couldn't tell me. Either way, I need to know.

I listen quietly as he explains everything. The curse being broken, his deal with Caleb, the curse being reborn and not knowing what would come to pass.

"I didn't want you to put your life on hold for me. I had no idea how long it would take for me to come back, or even if I would come back. With the Hunter's curse reborn, neither Caleb or I knew which way would win out in the end. It was only when he realized my soul was actually here that they took the steps to make me what I am now. Once I was back… let's just say it took a while to get the Demon side of me to a point where I could be in a room safely with anyone that wasn't indestructible. I'm still not totally good with everything that's changed about me, but I'm in control, and I couldn't keep waiting. I needed to see you."

The look he gives me practically screams regret, begging forgiveness, and that he's missed me almost as much as I've missed him. A part of me wants to get over myself. He's here now; he's actually here. But the other part of me, the part that guards my heart, that has been through so much pain these last few years, and it tells me that we shouldn't trust this. He lied to me, my heart has finally started to heal, and I've been happy.

I mean, what's the expectation? That I break down, rush into his arms, and welcome him back? Loss does strange things to people. Am I excited he's back? Of course I am, I never stopped loving him. But I don't dare to trust this.

Less than an hour ago, my world was spinning on its axis. I'd finally got my life back on track—at least mostly.

Now… Now I feel like I'm back where I was two years ago, and everything is spinning out of control again.

This just doesn't seem real.

"I'm happy you're alive. I really am. But… this is a lot, Colt," I say softly, and Deacon takes my hand again. He squeezes it gently, and I sap as much strength and calm from the gesture as I can.

"I know," he says, running a hand through his hair. It somehow looks exactly as it always has, which only sends me closer toward a tailspin. I watched his body burn on that pyre, so this is all just… It's so fucking much. Panic rises in my chest, and it feels like someone wraps their hand around my throat.

"I can't do this right now," I manage to sputter out as I climb to my feet. Deacon follows, his hand still clutching mine, and Colt zeroes in on where our hands join.

"Fallon—" Colt starts, but Deacon growls, interrupting whatever he was going to say.

"She said she needed a minute. Can't you see how much this is fucking with her already? After everything you've done, everything she went through to survive everything that was lost, the very least you could do is give her time to process this bombshell you just dropped on her. On all of us."

Colt's eyes go black, and Deacon tugs me behind him taking a protective stance. His voice is strong, authoritative, as he commands, "Control yourself!"

"You guys need to go," Colt says, though he doesn't sound like himself anymore. I can't see him where Deacon is shielding me, and I'm not sure that I want to. Not if he has completely changed. "I said go!"

The bellow makes my heart skip a beat. All I want is to go to him and soothe him despite everything that's going on. Before I get a chance to even speak, everything goes dark.

Deacon whispered us to his home, which has all but become my second home since we made this thing between us official. I spend just as much time here as I do on Earth, loving being able to spend time with Deacon in his home. I find comfort in the quiet here. But upon our arrival, we find that it's a hive of activity, and Deacon looks as thrown as I feel.

"Locke, what the fuck is going on?" Deacon calls

out to his new second. Apparently, he's a friend from his childhood, who just happened to show up here one day, begging refuge from wherever he was before. He's one of those hot nerd-looking types, but he's pretty quiet and stoic too. I've barely spoken to him despite the amount of time I spend here, because he seems to like to blend into the background. He's a Morph too, just like Deacon and a lot of the others he's moved to work inside his home. They're like their own wolf pack... at least I assume wolf pack since I know that's Deacon's Morph animal.

"No fucking idea. But two dead bodies showed up on the doorstep about thirty minutes ago, which wouldn't be such a big deal except they look like victims of The Carver." Deacon pales at the name, and I can't help but worry. Deacon isn't a pushover, so for a name to cause that sort of reaction? Well, it's pretty terrifying.

"Are you sure?" Deacon asks, and Locke gulps.

"Pretty sure. I had them taken to the chiller, but everyone's been pretty freaked out since, as you can see," Locke tells him and then disappears from the hall again.

"Who's The Carver?" I ask, though I almost don't want the answer. Knowledge is power, and this is an almost welcome distraction from everything that just happened. My brain still hasn't fully processed that Colt is still alive, and well, a Demon... Half Demon... I don't even know.

"The Carver is… Well, let's say he's not exactly the

kind of guy you want to come across. He was one of the Demon King's favorites. I thought he'd been killed back when Morgan took over…" he trails off, looking almost haunted. He shakes his head, as if clearing it of unwanted memories, and turns to me with a soft, yet reassuring smile. "I know you need to process everything that just happened. Do you need to talk?"

I shake my head no. I definitely need to talk, for him to help me put my world back on its axis, but I can tell he really needs to go to the chiller and see these bodies with his own eyes. He still hasn't told me a ton about his past. I get it—it's dark, twisty, and not so much fun to relive, but I have the feeling that however this links in, it's not pretty. He's been my rock so much over the last few years, so now it's my turn to step up, even if I don't know which way is up right now.

"Go, check it out. I'll just head to the nook. Come find me when you can." He leans down and kisses me, like he thinks he can right all of the wrongs in our world with just his kiss. I clutch his shirt as my toes curl from the heated contact. He might just actually be able to right all the wrongs if he keeps going the way he is.

"I won't be too long," he promises and then whispers away from me, leaving me in a room teeming with Demons. Most of them just ignore me, I am not their master—honestly I'm just glad that they don't fuck with me. I've had enough mindfuckery from Demons to last a lifetime.

Which brings me back to the whole Colt thing.

Fuck my life.

Talk about a mindfuck.

I make my way to the nook, passing by the kitchen on the way to grab some snacks, and curl up on the sofa. My mind whirs at about a million miles a minute, and I just can't focus. Not on Colt. Not on what I think about it. Not about how I really fucking feel about it all. Not about how it's going to likely blow up my life once again. There's too much going through my mind. The Carver. Deacon. The fact that I'm somehow fucking meant to *not* tell Remy that her brother isn't actually fucking dead.

So I turn the TV on and put on a mindless movie, something, anything to distract me from the emotions warring inside of me.

I stare at the screen, not really seeing it. I've managed to keep it together about this Colt thing, but it feels like there's a storm rising inside of me, and I can't keep it from surging over anymore.

The anger, the hurt, and the happiness collide, dragging me under a wave of emotion. I get lost in it, the undercurrents of pain mingling with joy pulling at me until I don't know which way is up, and I feel like I can't breathe. My vision starts to go spotty as the panic overwhelms me.

Why can't my life ever be simple? Why did Colt have

to die? Why didn't he warn me? At least try to prepare me? Holy shit, what must Deacon even be thinking about this all?

What the fuck do I do now?

I can't go home. Going back and not telling anyone he's alive is *so* not something I'm up for. Besides, I don't want to run away from this. Of course I'm happy he's back, but what does that mean for my life now? I love Deacon and I don't want to give him up, but I can't deny I love Colt too. I always have.

I have no idea how this is going to work.

What does he expect me to do, just run back to him like the last two years haven't happened? That isn't going to work. I'm not the same girl he knew back then. I was reborn through fire. Not only did I lose him after losing so much of myself, I lost my coven and my title. I had to rebuild my entire identity and purpose.

This is so fucked up.

I turn off the TV and put the bowl of popcorn on the table, since I can't eat or focus anyway, and focus on my breathing. Panic attacks are just another part of who I am now, but I haven't had one in a while.

I feel the bond between Deacon and I, and I know he can feel my panic. I don't want to tear him away from what he's doing, so I try to calm myself down. I look down at the ring on my finger, the very human gesture he offered me, and my heart slows a little as I smile.

We can get through this. We've gotten through so much worse.

I finish painting my lips red and stare back at my reflection. The past year has been a lot, but I made it through. I survived. And Deacon stood by my side every step of the way. It's been a year since I kissed him at the fair. Since he won me the giant black unicorn that sits in the corner of my room. Since he showed me his true self.

I feel so blessed to have him in my life. To be able to feel happy again when I thought after Colt's death that I would only ever feel numb.

"Fallon!" Mama calls from the sitting room. "Your... friend is here."

She hesitates on the word friend, and I roll my eyes. She's still struggling with the whole daughter dating a Demon thing. I mean, I get it I guess, but she doesn't judge Creek for being part Demon. And yeah, I get that Deacon isn't Creek, and she doesn't know him that well, but it isn't for a lack of trying.

I guess some things will just take time. Grabbing my jacket, I smooth my hands down my top one last time to make sure I look okay. Who would've thought I'd still have these kinds of butterflies after all this time?

For a little while, I worried that things would get weird after he asked me to move to the Shadow Realm with him and I said no. He pleasantly surprised me when he just took it in his stride. I kept waiting for the other shoe to drop, but that's not who Deacon is. He might be guarded and more than a little hesitant about delving into his past—which I get, he was Azriel's second for longer than I even want to think about, can you say age gap?—but he has one of the kindest, purest hearts I know.

Sure, he's done bad things, but that doesn't make him a bad person. Our past isn't exactly sunshine and roses, which doesn't help his standing with Mama, but if I can get past it, then she can too.

I find Mama in the kitchen on my way out of the house. "He's on the porch," she says through a tight-lipped smile.

"Thanks, Mama." I sigh, trying not to hold her prejudices against her because I know that she's trying. "See you tomorrow. Don't wait up."

"Okay, baby, have fun." She walks over to me and kisses my cheek before hugging me so very tight. "I love you, so much, baby girl. I just want you to be happy."

"He makes me happy, Mama," I tell her softly before pulling out of her embrace.

"Then I promise I'll try harder." I smile at her because I can't really ask for more.

I leave the house, butterflies causing chaos in my stomach, and find Deacon on the porch with the sun setting behind him, haloing him in golden light. He still takes my breath away.

"Hey, you," I say as I practically skip to where he's waiting for me.

"Hey, yourself," he grins before wrapping his hands around my waist and pulling me in for a kiss that leaves me breathless. I grip the front of his shirt, holding him close to me. I don't think I'll ever get enough of him.

"Are you ready?" he asks as he leans his forehead against mine, his lips brushing against mine with each syllable he speaks.

"Where are we going?" I ask, smiling. He's kept tonight a secret, which is odd for him, but I kinda like the idea of a surprise.

"You'll see when we get there. Shall we?" He offers me the crook of his arm, which makes me laugh out loud, but I loop my arm through his and let him lead me away nonetheless.

It doesn't take too long for me to figure out where we're going, and the smile stretching over my face almost makes my cheeks hurt. "The fairground?"

"It isn't fair to ask a guy to stay away from the Ferris wheel for so long, Fallon. I mean, really," he teases, and I laugh again which makes his smile widen. There was a long time where my laughter didn't come so freely, so I don't take any of this happiness for granted. Not even for a second.

The night passes in a haze of laughter, sugar, and Deacon's determination to win me a giant pink unicorn to go with the black one I already have at home. "This game is rigged," he grumbles, and I try not to laugh as he misses again. Considering his extra skills, I kind of have to agree.

It takes him another few goes, but Pinky is mine. I grin widely as the stall operator hands me the giant stuffed animal and Deacon lifts me off my feet, spinning me around. "I do love to hear your laugh."

He puts me down, and takes Pinky from me before clasping my hand in his. We wander around the fairground until we end up at the Ferris wheel. The night sky is black against the lights here, but the Ferris wheel almost looks like it makes the sky glow.

We wait in line in a comfortable silence, with his arm over my shoulders as I lean into him. I can't help but think about how lucky I am to have found love again.

The ride operator takes the unicorn for us, and when we climb into the Ferris wheel, I scoot under Deacon's arm. This time, there's no pretending there isn't something between us. Last time, I was so confused about what we were, guilty about what I was feeling, and I was just a general mess of emotions. This time I feel happy and secure at his side, knowing that he loves me too.

"This might be my favorite human pastime," he says before kissing the top of my head. The ride moves slowly, stopping every now and then as more people climb on, and I wait eagerly for us to reach the top. It's always been my favorite part. When we reach the apex of the Ferris wheel, I sigh, contentment filling my entire being as I look out over Salem's Bay. It's a lot more peaceful here now than it was before.

"Fallon," Deacon starts, pulling back from me a little and looking down at me. "Thank you for this last year, for forgiving me and seeing the man I could be, the man I am, behind the monster. I don't remember ever feeling this much joy and love in my entire existence. I know that we've been through a lot, but I don't see a day in my future without you in it." He reaches inside his jacket, and I swear to the Goddess that my heart stops beating for a second. "Fallon, I know that we haven't exactly had a steady road, and our journey hasn't been the easiest, but I wouldn't change any of it because it brought us here. Together. I want to be that way for the rest of time."

He opens a small black box, and a yellow stone sits in a bed of platinum, surrounded by a row of diamonds. "Fallon Laveau, will you make me the happiest man in all the realms and be my wife?"

Holy. Fucking. Shit.

He pulls the ring from the box and slides it onto my finger, but I still haven't even taken a breath.

"Yes," I gasp as tears start streaming down my face. I definitely didn't expect this tonight. The Ferris wheel starts to move again, and he kisses me with so much heat and so much love that I kind of wish we were anywhere but here, but this... This was perfect.

"This isn't the way of my people, but I know it is the way of yours, and I want to share that with you," he says once we finally break our kiss.

"What is the way of your people?" I ask, staring at the ring like it might disappear.

"We bond, not in the same way that you've bound yourself before. It is a link between us, a heart bond. One that means I can feel you, wherever you are, and the same in return. It links us in an everlasting way," he says softly, tucking an errant piece of hair behind my ear.

"That sounds beautiful."

"I would one day like that for us too," he smiles down at me softly. "But I understand after everything that's happened, you may not be ready for that yet. I am more than happy to wait, so long as you are in my life."

My heart skips a beat, and I realize that I don't want to wait. He's right, my last bond wasn't a happy one, but this is miles away from that one. So I squeeze his hand with mine and tell him my truth.

"I would be honored to be bonded with you."

SEVEN

DEACON

My father has been friends with the one they call The Carver longer than I've been alive. It doesn't surprise me that they're friends. They're both sadistic assholes, but I foolishly thought losing Scout might have changed Father for the better.

I was wrong.

If anything, he's worse than he once was. The last shred of decency he possessed was lost in her death. Selling me to the Demon King should have been my first hint. But tonight, sitting at the King's feet and being forced to watch the man I once looked up to torture some innocent girl with The Carver, really drove home the fact that the father

I once knew is gone. If he ever even existed at all.

The salted iron shackle around my throat burns. I can barely move, and if I do, the stinging flesh beneath the shackle nearly melts away. My wrists are raw from the struggle that erupted when they shackled me and dragged me to the throne room. Resistance, it seems, is futile. The Demon King has legions of assholes willing to carry out his every order without a blink.

But it could always be worse.

I could be that girl in the middle of the room.

Every single instinct in my body screams at me to throw my own life on the line to save hers. To take every bit of pain they can send my way in order to rescue her from the horrors that are in store for her. What she's experienced so far is horrific, but the night is young, and the Demon King demands entertainment. I don't know who she is, or how she ended up where she is, but her screams and tears will haunt me for the rest of my existence.

She looks way too fucking much like Scout.

How Father can bear to do the things he's so obviously reveling in is beyond me. Maybe that's why he calls me weak... but I can't ever imagine a scenario where I'd be broken enough to torture someone simply to entertain another person.

Then again, I never thought I'd be broken enough to sit at the King's feet like his fucking lapdog and watch another person be tortured like this either. Except the pain I've suffered in the last few weeks has been like nothing I've ever experienced.

What was worse was seeing Locke being sold off to the King too. His cage is opposite mine, and once they realized he was my friend... Watching them hurt him when I wouldn't scream the way they wanted me to was probably one of the worst things I've ever endured. I've never heard my friend scream like that before, and it's not something I ever want to experience again.

A shudder runs through my entire body at the memory, and I hiss as the metal shifts against my skin, burning another part of my neck.

I will never understand the depravity of men who enjoy this sort of pain and violence. How broken must you be to get off on someone else's screams? We might be Demons, but despite the humans' depiction of us, we're not all monsters. Just like every other race, there are the good and the bad—and I'm trapped with some of the worst for the rest of my existence unless I find a way to climb up the chain or buy back my freedom.

Both options seem out of reach because I refuse to become like the men I see in front of me. I will never hurt a woman just for the hell of it. I don't know that I'd hurt a woman even with a just cause, unless she was trying to kill me or someone I loved. I'm just not that guy.

Which is exactly why each of the girl's screams tear away another piece of my fucking soul. I've never felt so worthless in my entire goddamned existence.

"Should we carve up her pretty face?" The Carver grins, his black and yellow teeth on show as the girl sobs in the chair she's chained to. He looks to the King for instruction, and my father looks at me. The lunacy in his smile, an ugly, toothy grin as he sees how much this hurts me, breaks another part of my soul. I understand why he sold me, but why would he want to see me so broken as well? I'm his only living child. The others are all dead. Scout. Regan. Both of them paid for the sins of their father, and I guess I am too. Except I'm still breathing.

Well, for now anyway.

"Bring me her eyes." The Demon King's menacing laugh booms around the throne room, and the shouts of glee and encouragement from his sycophants makes me want to vomit. Only his daughter looks at him with disgust, though only briefly before her mask of indifference covers her ice princess face.

My father rubs his hands together as he moves behind the girl and then clasps her cheeks in his palms, holding her still for The Carver. Her screams pierce through me, and I almost fall back from my kneeling position as she begs them to stop. I try to look at the floor, unable to bear witness anymore, but I feel the chain around my neck tugged on like the leash it is.

"You will watch, boy. Otherwise we'll make her pay for your disobedience too." The King's snarls snap my neck upright. I have no choice but to watch the girl, who looks so much like my sister, as The Carver removes her eyes, laughing maniacally the entire time.

She passes out when the first eye is cut from her, but that doesn't stop the joy and hunger from building in the room. The entire group of them are monsters, nothing but black pits of evil all the way to their core.

"Is all of this really necessary, Father?" The ice princess asks, yawning from her throne. "I'm bored of all of this."

"You should be watching, Morganna, and learning how to keep these Demons in line. All of this will be yours one day," he says proudly, and Ares snorts from his seat. The prince's arrogance seems to know no bounds.

"Yes, Father. I know, but what's the point? She's not even conscious anymore." She glances over at me, and I see the truth of the anger burning behind the mask of her indifference. She wants to leave so she doesn't unleash in here. I understand that. The power that comes from her feels subdued, but only a fool would think that she is anything but the most deadly person in the room.

The King and her brother included.

"Fine, be gone. Take the fucking hound with you," he says, waving at the black hellhound sitting beside her with his fire eyes. It's creepy as fucking shit, but she pets him like anyone would pet their dog.

"That's fine, he needs a run anyway." She stands and leaves, the hellhound pressed to her side, and I drag my gaze away from her. I'm jealous that she gets to leave this behind, but I'm also mad as hell that she didn't do anything to even try to stop it.

Though, I guess we all pick our battles because it's not like I'm doing a fucking thing to stop this either.

I swallow the shame that threatens to make me vomit as the King tugs on my leash again. I clamp my jaw together, grinding my teeth as I'm forced to sit and watch them defile that poor girl. I'm filled with disgust, being in the presence of a room full of people who seem to be enjoying the show as much as my father and The Carver are enjoying ruining her. I'm glad she's unconscious, at least this way she won't have the memories of what they're doing to her.

When they strip her of her clothes and lay her face down on the floor, I can't hold it in anymore. I vomit all over the shiny black floor.

"Stupid fucking boy!" The King roars as it splashes on his shoes. "I should make you take your father's place!"

My face pales at the thought of it.

I could never.

I won't.

I just fucking won't.

"Father, he isn't worth the disruption," Ares says, his eyes flashing to full black as he looks at me properly. While he absolutely fucking terrifies me, I've never been more thankful for his willingness to speak up to his father. He's one of the few who can and still live. It's more than obvious that Ares is the favorite of his children.

"You're right," he sneers at Ares, as if he's pissed at having someone seem more reasonable than him and taking away his fun. "Take him back to his cage. Next time, you might find that it's you in that chair, boy," he seethes before dismissing me. I'm dragged away by one of his guards. I hate myself for the relief I feel in not having to watch what else that girl goes through, but I've never been so happy to be taken back to that tiny-ass cage.

At least there, the only nightmares that face me are the ones I've already lived through.

I spend way too long looking at the mutilated bodies laid out in the lowest level of the estate. I had never been down here before Azriel's death, but I feel like I've spent way too much time here already.

The way the bodies have been dissected definitely looks like The Carver's handiwork. But I was sure he was dead. I didn't personally see his body burn, so I guess there's always the chance that he body-jumped, but still…

The shudder that runs down my spine at the possibility of him being back makes my knees weak. I have my own scars from The Carver… some of which I see reflected in the etchings on the body that rests on the table before me.

If it's not him, it's someone who knew him well.

But why deliver them to my door? Who the fuck did I piss off now? I haven't done anything worthy of this… At least I don't think I have. I don't even recognize the bodies laid out before me, though that's not much of a shock considering the state of them.

I'm going to have to take this to Morgan. Hells, I hate feeling like I have to run to 'mom' every time something major goes wrong. Which is exactly what it feels like when I have to go to her with shit that feels outside of my control.

"Put them back on ice," I tell the guy who's been nervously hopping from one foot to the other the entire time I've been down here. He's another Morph. I've tried to surround myself with them here at the estate. A pack of sorts. Not every Morph here is a wolf like I am, but Morphs all have that same quiet need for a pack. I'm trying to give that to the people within my level because I don't want this to be a place where Demons have to fear their own shadows.

Those who fuck up, yes, I have no issues being the one to mete out their punishment. I learned a long time ago that without punishment, people that fuck up will just push further and harder the next time. That's not something I ever want to witness again, so I try to keep shit in line. The souls that land here, well, they're not my issue. Ferry leads them here and the lower level demons allocate them as required. All overseen by some of the higher demons here who keep that shit running the way it should.

I never claimed not to be a monster. Life is the way it is.

I shake my head to dispel the thoughts, and I feel the tug of the bond between Fallon and I. I'm such an idiot, disappearing on her like that after the bomb that was dropped on her. A giant fucking idiot.

I whisper back to her, feeling her location through the bond, and smile a little to myself about the fact that the bond even exists. I didn't think she'd say yes or that she'd be as open to it as she was; but then again, I never thought I'd get the girl either. Not after everything we went through. Everything that I did to her.

I became the man I swore I'd never be, and I vowed to her to never be that man again. I'll spend every day for the rest of my existence making it up to her.

Or at least for as long as she'll let me. With Colt back, everything could change. I swallow down the swell of fear that rises within me. She needs me to have my shit together while she deals with this, so that's exactly what I'm going to do.

I'm going to be every fucking thing she needs. I'm hers for as long as she'll have me and beyond that as well. I materialize in the nook and find her sitting on the sofa, staring down at the ring on her finger. My heart expands at the sight of it, just like it does every time I see it on her hand.

"I'm sorry," I utter as I step toward her. Her head snaps up, and in a second, she jumps up and bounds into my arms. I hold her close to me, breathing her in. I can feel my heart rate steady just at her touch, the ghosts of my past receding to the farthest parts of me.

"You have nothing to be sorry for," she sighs as she sinks into my embrace. "I'm just glad you're back."

"I'll always come back to you. I told you, our story is far from over," I tell her, and she pulls back a little. She looks up at me, those bright amber eyes of hers holding a lost look to them that I haven't seen in a while.

"Even with… today's revelations?" I lean down and kiss her forehead, feeling her melt in my arms despite the panic I can feel through our bond.

"Colt being back changes nothing for me, Fallon. I told you once a long time ago that as long as I have you, nothing else matters to me. If that means sharing you, I can do that, as long as I know that a part of you is still mine," I tell her firmly, and let her feel the truth of my words through the bond.

Sharing her isn't exactly how I saw our future, but I meant it back then, and I mean it right now. As long as a part of her heart belongs to me, I'll take it. I want her in my life, and it's not like Colt is someone new. I knew all about their relationship when we met, I experienced firsthand how hard she grieved for him, and I felt that loss with her. I also felt every single emotion she felt when she saw him standing there earlier today. I'm glad that the bond doesn't stretch between the realms well so she couldn't feel my anger before I got it under control when Caleb summoned me and told me about Colt.

Do I want to smash the guy's face into the floor for putting her through what he did? For not telling her? Of course I fucking do, but that would just hurt her more, so I keep that deep-seated desire locked down. Of course, if she wants me to beat his ass, I'd do it happily for her. I might be a monster, but at least I'm her monster.

"A part of my heart is always gonna be yours. I just feel so fucking confused right now, about all of this. I don't know what he wants, what he expects of me, or even if he expected anything at all. I feel like there's a shit ton of butterflies inside me, trying to burst through my skin." Panic flashes in her eyes, so I grasp her shoulders and take a step back from her, pulling myself up to my full height. "What if he wants to make this work?"

I reach out and grasp her chin, lifting her gaze to mine. "Fallon, if you want to be with him as well as me, I'm okay with that. If we have a set up like Morgan and Remy, I'm okay with that too. I'm also okay if you want to be with us both and me and him just have nothing to do with each other, if that's what you want. You tell me the plan, and we'll adjust. But I'm not going anywhere, do you understand?"

"Yes," she stutters, but I feel her spinning out of control, even with the relief that floods her.

"What do you need?" I ask, my voice dropping, and I feel her body practically melt at the tone. She sinks to her knees, giving me the control she now embodies in a way she never knew she needed. The wolf inside me purrs happily at her submission as she looks to the ground, and I grow instantly hard.

"I need you," she says breathlessly. I step forward and twist up her hair around my hand, pulling it so she has to look up at me.

"There's a good girl."

The shadows dancing in her eyes keep my blood boiling at an even level, but I take in a deep breath and focus on her lust. It's there, fighting the hurt and the confusion. By the time I'm done with her, those shadows will be non-existent. I'll make sure the only thing her brain can focus on is me and the pleasure I can give her.

"Show me how much you need me, Princess."

There's that spark, the one that glimmers in her eyes every time I pull her into this headspace. Because she no longer needs to make decisions. She no longer needs to be strong. She no longer needs to have control. She hands it to me like the gift that it is, and I carry the weight for her. I take her responsibilities and make them my own.

Her lithe fingers make quick work of my pants, pulling the zipper down then pushing the fabric to the floor as it pools around my feet.

Her gaze never leaves mine, and I know what she's seeing. The red-eyed Demon inside of me reveling in the thought of having her. Reveling in the sight of her kneeling before me. In the need etched over her beautiful features.

"Open your mouth. Let me see your throat before I fuck it."

And she does.

With her head back, her tongue resting on her bottom lip, I angle my rock-hard cock so it barely touches her flesh and rub myself up and down until I see her saliva pooling in her mouth. It's heady as fuck to know that her mouth is literally watering at the feel of my dick.

"That's a good girl. I can see how much you want me. But tell me, Princess, how wet is your pussy for me right now?"

She doesn't respond. Mostly because she can't since

I'm holding her tongue hostage, but also because she doesn't have my permission to speak. Everything I say is rhetorical until I expressively tell her to answer me, and she knows it.

"Show me."

Without breaking her position, she reaches down, slipping her hand under her pants and sinks two fingers inside herself before bringing them up so I can see her juices dripping from them. My dick twitches at the sight, knowing, with everything going on, that she still wants me this badly is a balm to my soul.

"Hmm, spread it on my cock so you can taste yourself while I fuck your mouth."

Again, she does as she's told, and just as she's spread her desire over my skin, I place both of my hands on either side of her head and sink slowly into her mouth. I push until I feel the back of her throat bumping against the tip of my dick.

I take a second to enjoy the velvety heat of her mouth around my cock before I pull out slowly. I thrust back in with a little more demand.

She mewls, the sound dancing along the length of my dick and caressing my tight balls.

"Do that again." I sound possessed, and I guess in a way, I am. I'm possessed by my need for her, by her very presence.

I'm a slave to her pussy and her mouth, all the while dominating every inch of her.

I hit the back of her throat three more times before I stop and look at her.

"You are the most enchanting, stunning woman I've ever met. More so when your mouth is full of my cock. When your eyes are shimmer with tears each time I bump the back of your throat. Absolutely gorgeous."

I fuck her mouth a couple more times then pull out. I have no interest in coming just yet. I want to take her savagely against the wall, to let her know she can trust me to take her mind off her troubles.

"Stand up, Princess. Strip for me."

In one fluid movement, she's on her feet, with her shirt ripped away and falling to the ground. I reach out and tweak one nipple, then the other, making sure I give her the bite of pain she craves.

Bringing my other hand to her shoulder, I run the back of a finger up along the column of her delicate neck before placing my palm right under her chin and closing my fingers just enough to make her breath hitch.

Then I kiss her like a man starved for her touch.

Our lips collide, our tongues tangling in a dance of love and devotion. We bite and suck and lick, the only sound around us our need for one other.

When I pinch her nipple again, I taste her gasp in my

mouth, and it fuels my desire for her.

"Turn around, hands on the wall, ass in the air."

Once she does what I ordered, I rip the remainder of her clothing off and sink two of my fingers inside her pussy. I'm met with her overflowing juices dripping down my palm and wrist. She's primed for me. Who am I to deny her of pleasure?

With my fingers dripping wet, I push one inside her ass and pump a couple of times before sinking my ridiculously hard cock inside her pussy.

"Fuck, you feel so good, Princess."

I fuck her with my cock, with my fingers in her ass and the other hand holding her hip, trying my best to not slam her against the wall. Fallon uses her spread legs as an anchor, taking my thrusts like a good girl, and I slap her ass, loving her groan at the sting. The mix of pain and pleasure she's grown to crave over our time together.

My eyes are red as my need for her grows even more heated. I don't need to see them to know this, and neither does she. She can feel my Demon possessing her very soul.

"Fuck. So. Fucking. Good."

I pump out a couple more thrusts before I tell her to hold on for dear life. She looks back over her shoulder at me and bites her lip when she sees me. I barely contain myself at the sight of her.

With her palms bracing against the wall, I let my hand

on her hip slide to her clit. I fuck her pussy, pump my fingers in and out of her ass, and rub her clit in perfect unison until I hear the symphony of her cries as she comes undone, clamping down on my dick as she falls over the very precipice of euphoria.

On a cry that can only be described as primal, Fallon melts into my arms, her legs no longer capable of holding herself up.

I pull myself from her, lifting her into my arms with her back against the wall, and enter her once more, her gaze on mine as I build her up again. I lean forward, lavishing her nipples with attention and biting down, her cries encouraging me not to stop.

My girl enjoys the sharp bite of pain with her pleasure.

I move to the other and pay it just as much attention before kissing up to her neck and biting down on the soft skin there as she comes all over my dick again, dragging me over the edge with her.

I pull out of her again, her entire body pliant, and walk her into the bathroom, turning on the shower.

“I hope you’re not done yet, Princess, because I haven’t had anywhere near my fill of you yet.”

EIGHT

FALLON

I know I need to deal with Colt being back, but I'm such a fucking mess of emotions. Deacon helps me so fucking much, giving me a space where I don't have to think about everything, but I know this isn't something I can ultimately hide from.

Hell, it isn't something I *want* to hide from. I just have no idea what to do now. Am I glad he's back? That's the stupidest question in the fucking world. I just don't know what this means for me, for us, for him.

And the only way to know is to pull up my big girl pants and talk to him. Which is exactly why I'm standing in the throne room this morning, nervous as a kid on her first day of school, waiting for someone to arrive so I can ask how to find Colt.

Goddess, I feel so fucking awkward right now. Deacon offered to come with me, but I feel like I need to talk to Colt one-on-one. Colt was never Deacon's biggest fan, and I'd rather just have him speak openly with me. I don't want to risk him holding anything back.

"Fallon, fancy seeing you here," Caleb smirks at me as he swaggers into the throne room. "Looking for a certain lost love?"

I roll my eyes at the Demon. When we first met, I was a quiet mouse, terrified of all four of the Horsemen. Now I know them properly, I know he's just a pussy cat—unless you piss him off—then he's just fucking terrifying. Luckily, I've never pissed him off, but I've heard enough stories to know that I never want to be on the bad side of any of them.

"Pretty much," I shrug, trying to act way more nonchalant than I feel. I know he doesn't buy any of it based on the giant smirk on his face.

"Lover boy is in his room. You want me to bring him here? Take you there?" he asks, and I just wring my hands trying to decide. Everyone's going to be here, eating, having family time, doing whatever it is they do. But going to his room almost seems too personal almost. Though, I guess that's better than having this conversation with an audience.

"Would you mind taking me to him?" I ask, and then bite my lip. Why am I so fucking nervous right now?

Stupid question, Fallon. Of course you're fucking nervous. Your first love just came back from the dead; and when you saw him, you freaked out, got angry, and then left. It would be more ridiculous if I wasn't nervous.

"Sure thing." Caleb strides across the room to me and takes my hand, whispering me away to wherever Colt is staying. We materialize in a hall I recognize… I look at the door and realize it's the room next to the one that I've always stayed in if I was here. "This is him. He'll already know you're here, Demon senses and all that. But I'm sure he's going to be a good fucking Demon and be a gentleman," Caleb all but shouts, and I can't help but laugh softly.

"Thank you," I say to him, and he squeezes my shoulder once before whispering away out of sight. I take a deep breath and knock on the door. I hear Colt's footsteps as he crosses the room. I'm sure he did that for my sake, and I'm not upset about it. It gives me a second to prepare myself to see him again.

I spent months wishing that I'd see him, and now here I am, terrified of doing so. Stupid mortal brain. My hands start to tingle, and my heart races as the anticipation builds at seeing him again.

The door opens, and it feels like my heart stutters to a stop. I can't breathe. Everything I didn't feel when I saw him yesterday floods through me in a tidal wave. The sheer joy, the wonder, the love.

He's actually real.

I almost forgot just how much taller he is than me.

Almost.

I reach forward to touch him, but stop myself less than an inch from his chest. I know Deacon said he's okay with whatever happens and I trust that he really is okay with it all, but what if Colt isn't? I can't just let myself fall into this without talking it all out first.

I don't get a chance to overthink it as Colt moves forward, and his hands clasp my face as he lowers his lips to mine. I melt under his touch and lose myself in his kiss. I gasp as he pushes me back against the wall, his tongue sliding against mine, battling for dominance as I hang onto him.

When he pulls back, I'm panting. He smirks as he rests his forehead against mine. "Fuck, Fal, I missed you."

"I missed you too," I tell him honestly, but push against his chest. Not that it does a thing, the immoveable asshole. "But we should probably talk."

"Do we have to?" he groans. "This is much more fun."

I can't help but laugh. He hasn't changed at all.

But I have, and I don't know if he's ready for that.

"Yes, we have to talk," I tell him, trying to be as firm as I can with the hard planes of his body pushing against mine.

"Okay," he says, taking my hand. "Let's talk."

He leads me into his room, closing the door behind me as I move further into the space. The room is so very Colt. There are weapons all over the place, a workout station, and a giant TV. I look back at him, and he rubs the back of his neck, almost looking awkward. "I needed ways to keep myself busy while I was trying to learn how to control myself."

"I see," I say, not truly understanding. I know he said he was learning how to control the Demon side of himself, but it seems from this image that he's had plenty of spare time. Could he really not have reached out to any of us to let us know he was alive?

"Fallon, I really am sorry I didn't let you know sooner. Caleb… he was against it, and because of how I'm back, there's a weird tie between us. I quite literally can't disobey him yet. I'm not strong enough. It's like a Demonic failsafe to make sure I can't hurt anyone I don't mean to. Luckily Caleb isn't an asshole about it, but he's super protective of Remy, especially with my nephew being so young." His voice cracks at the mention of Raziel, and my heart hurts for him. He's missed a lot. He clears his throat and then says, "And well, he didn't want me anywhere near the mortal realm until I had my shit under control, which it mostly is now. But I couldn't wait anymore, that's why he and Morgan had Deacon bring you here."

I nod, not really knowing what to say again. I understand it, but that doesn't make it hurt any less. Even with my swollen lips throbbing, the memory of his body against mine... The hurt of him not telling me before still stings. Even if my heart hurts for him as well as myself.

"Okay," I say, after what feels like the longest, most awkward pause ever. "But what happens from here?"

"What do you want to happen?" he asks, taking a few steps toward me, but stopping just beyond arm's reach.

"Colt, I need you to answer my question. You saw me with Deacon yesterday, and that isn't something that's going to change. I thought you were dead. I grieved for you. It nearly fucking broke me, but I let you go. And now…" A tear slips down my cheek, and he rushes toward me, wiping the tear away with his thumb.

"I am so sorry I hurt you, Fallon, and I'll be sorry for the rest of my existence. I just want the chance to make it up to you. A chance to be what we were meant to be."

"Colt, you can't expect to come back and think everything is just going to go back to the way it was," I say, my heart breaking all over again. I need him to say that he wants me, even with Deacon in the picture.

"Fal, I love you. We can work the rest of it out later."

He captures my mouth with his again, and all thoughts of what we were supposed to be talking about leaves my mind. He takes me over, body and soul.

With his soft lips and his tongue demanding entrance, I can't help but open myself up to him. It's like no time has passed between us, like the two years that separated us were a mere figment of my imagination. A painful, soul-destroying figment.

"Don't think, baby, just feel me. Feel us."

His words reassure me that this is all real, and not just another dream where my mind floats toward the things that could have been.

His heat, his hard body pressing up against me, it's all there. All real. And I'm helpless to its demands.

He walks me backward until the cold press of the wall hits me from shoulder blade to ass, and the contrast with his infernal heat at my front doesn't escape me. He's here, back in my life, and I don't know how I'm supposed to handle it at all.

"Look at me."

I do as he asks; and when my eyes rise to meet his, my body relaxes with the sight of him. Here, alive. With me. Touching me in ways I'd shoved to the back of my mind.

"Colt…"

With one hand on my throat, his fingers pressing dangerously at the sides of my neck, his other hand slides down my arm, causing my skin to pebble under his touch.

"Say yes, baby."

I want to. Oh Goddess, how I want to, but what happens after that? After this? What am I supposed to do after I give myself to him? We should probably talk before we do this, but I don't know if I want to talk anymore. Maybe I should just savor this while I can and figure the rest out later.

I feel the tug of war waging inside me between my heart, my soul, and my body. It hums, begging to get closer to him. My need to touch him is so great that resisting him would be futile.

"Say it, Fal." His words are on my lips, his breath speaking to my soul, begging me to give in to him. My heart cries out to surrender to his demands, as it always had in the past.

"Yes." I don't actually speak, the word is a sigh that comes from deep within me as though the Goddess herself ordered it out.

Colt doesn't wait for me to reiterate. He's there, his cock hard and pressing against my belly. We both pant, but neither of us moves, memorizing this moment, taking in every breath. Every sound. Every touch. His lips are gliding from one end of my mouth to the other as his fingers lace through mine, squeezing with reassurance.

"Yes," I repeat, for no other reason than to remind myself that this is Colt and refusing him is more than I could ever handle.

In one smooth move, my jeans are off, and my legs are around his waist. My arms automatically wrap around his neck as our mouths melt together like liquid gold.

“Fuck, Fal, you taste divine, but I need your pussy on my tongue, now.”

With all four limbs wrapped around him like my entire body is afraid he’ll disappear, he turns and carries me to his bed. The massive four-poster bed dwarfs me as he lays me down gently upon the comforter like I’m an offering to the Goddess. Standing at the foot of the bed, he takes me in, his heated gaze running from the tips of my toes to the length of my legs. His gaze lingers hungrily on the vee between my thighs, and he licks his lips with unabashed hunger. I shift under his demanding gaze, resting on my elbows to watch him reveal his body to me after two years of being deprived of its beauty.

Slowly, he reaches over his shoulder, reaching for his shirt and pulling it off in one fell swoop before throwing it to the side. Every muscle in his chest and abdomen ripples with mass and power. He’s a force of nature, a storm that could bring armies and women alike to their knees. My mouth waters at the sight of him. The sight of the work of art he calls his body. It’s my turn to lick my lips, and his stare follows the path from one corner of my mouth to the other. If the growl that follows is any indication, his level of lust is running as high as my own.

"Do that again." The command is barely contained, his words coming from between his teeth. The sound comes from deep within his chest.

I comply. Of course, I do.

And within seconds, he's naked and on top of me, his tongue licking the same path mine had. Like he's tasting my tongue. Owning my lips. The metal of his tongue bar is an added sensation against my skin, making my body heat even more.

"Spread your legs, Fallon. I'm hungry."

I sigh, my legs falling open across the top of his mattress as he grabs both sides of my bra, ripping it in two and exposing my pebbled nipples to the cool air of his room. I pant with the need for him to touch me.

His tongue wets his lips before he engulfs my nipple into his mouth and flicks the hard nub with the tip of his piercing, making me mewl with want.

My hips shoot up off the bed as he sucks what feels like half my tit into his mouth before moving on to the other.

My teeth sink into my bottom lip as I try not to scream from the pleasure he's offering me.

"Fuck, I've missed the feel of you, Fal. This is where I belong. Right here with you."

And then his mouth is on my pussy, and the world as I know it stops spinning.

His hands circle my thighs, feeling twice the size that they used to. His shoulders invade every inch between my legs, his mouth kissing, licking, biting, worshipping my core. It's been two years.

Two years since I last felt his touch. Since I last felt his love and lust mixed together. Two years since his love for me was this real and poignant.

The realization washes over me as I lie back on my elbows and stare up at the ceiling. My body trembles with pleasure over his pussy-eating talents.

"Oh Goddess, of all that is—" He cuts me off with a growl as his tongue spears inside me, and his hands clutch at my ass cheeks trying to pull me closer still. I'm nothing better than a ragdoll in his arms. I'm his buffet, and he intends to devour every single morsel of me before the day is done.

Oh, how I've missed this. Him. Us.

"Colt…" I don't know what else to say. His name on my lips feels like a dream, one that I held onto for so long until I gave it up and let myself live again.

"Fuck, you taste so fucking good." His words are whispers across the soaked skin of my pussy, and I can feel his breath on my lips, worshipping every inch of my skin.

When two of his fingers sink into me, I can't control the cry that escapes me. He's fucking me with his mouth and fingers, and it's almost too much. Too good. Too intense. My fingers sink into his hair, tugging insistently, but I have a hard time caring that the pressure might be too much. It just doesn't seem to matter in the moment. His teeth grate against my soaking pussy, and the sound of my juices against his lips is the most erotic sound I think I've ever heard. I writhe against his comforter, nearly ready to beg for mercy when he curls his middle finger and touches the deepest, most sensitive part of my core, and everything explodes into a million pieces. Behind my closed lids, the world is one gigantic storm of fireworks. Color exists everywhere, light splashing from one neuron to the other.

My breath catches in my throat, and I struggle as I try to drag oxygen inside my deprived lungs.

It's only when I feel his mouth on mine that I can breathe again.

"Breathe, baby. Breathe with me." My taste on his lips and tongue drives my own hunger back to the forefront. The orgasm sapped the strength from my limbs but not the lust from my core.

Taking both of my wrists in one of his big hands, he pins them down above my head. With a devilish look on his gorgeous face, he offers me the full wattage of his charming grin.

"I'm going to fuck you hard and deep, baby. So hard your pussy will never be able to forget me."

I don't tell him that he's already tattooed on me, on my

mind and soul.

Before I can manage a comeback, his cock slams into me.

My breath hitches, my gasp likely heard throughout the many dimensions of our universe.

“That’s it, feel me. Feel my cock, Fallon. I own you, and I always have.”

With one hand holding me down and the other on my jaw, he pushes his thumb inside my mouth, fucking me in tandem with the movement.

His entire body coils like a snake preparing to strike, his cock pistons reverently inside of me, hitting its mark like a professional sniper. Over and over again, I can feel his Jacob’s ladder rubbing against my walls, driving the sensations to a whole new level.

“You need to come, Fal. I can feel the way your pussy grips my dick. You need this, and I’m going to give it to you.”

And he does. He thrusts inside me like he’s a god of orgasms. He pushes inside me as if he’s the only reason I could possibly feel pleasure. And maybe he is because I can’t stop the rush of adrenaline that courses through my body on his last push.

I’m done for.

My entire body tenses for two seconds as I take a deep breath, praying I don’t pass out from the pleasure he’s pouring into me. When his lips fall on mine, I cry into his mouth, my pleas mere growls and grunts as he swallows them for his own.

When he stills, his entire body shaking with pent-up pleasure, I know he's coming right along with me. His seed coats every inch of my pussy, desperately trying to own me as he did before.

I don't know what's going to happen, but one thing I do know is that a part of my heart is still his.

NINE

COLT

I bounce on the balls of my feet before attacking the punching bag again. Nervous energy has flooded my system since Caleb okayed today's trip home.

The trip to tell my sister that I'm not actually dead.

Though, I'm a little worried I might actually die before she's done with me.

I might be more scared to face my sister than I was Fallon, and that's saying something. Because I was fucking *terrified* of seeing my girl again. Afraid that she'd reject me, that she'd never want to see me again. That she'd truly moved on. I mean, things aren't exactly settled with us right now, but at least she didn't outright turn me away.

I don't remember another time in all of my lives that I've been this nervous; and thanks to Caleb, I now have every memory from each of my lifetimes. Go Team Demon, I guess?

"Are you nearly ready to go?" Caleb asks from the corner of the room. I didn't see him whisper in, but considering that's the only way into this particular gym, I know he did.

"Yeah, I guess," I tell him with a shrug and gulp down the water in my bottle. "She's going to fucking obliterate me."

The fucker laughs and shakes his head. He knows Remy as well as I do, so he knows she's going to go nuclear. "Just tell her about the bond and then she can be angry at me. I'll be there to make sure nothing gets too out of control anyway. Can't have you hurting my favorite Angel."

"I wouldn't hurt her," I grumble. I've worked my fucking ass off to make sure of it. It's the only way I could get him to agree to let me see my family again. It's part of why it took me so long to even be able to see Fallon.

"I know you don't want to hurt her, but you also haven't been attacked outside of a safe space. Your power will be dulled in the mortal realm; but if she comes at you, your instincts will automatically kick in. You've worked hard, but I'll be there just in case." I nod, understanding his reasoning even if I don't like it. Anything could happen, and I wouldn't be able to live with myself if I hurt Remy. If I hurt any of them.

"Okay, let me go grab a quick shower. I'll be good to go in twenty?"

"Sounds good. I'll grab Deacon and Fallon, and we'll all head back to Earth together," he says, smirking as I grumble about Deacon having to come. As if it isn't bad enough that he has my girl right now, he gets to encroach on this moment too. I don't care if everyone else has accepted him as part of our mishmashed family, they've had over two years to get over what he did. I don't know that I'll ever be able to forgive him for what he did to Fallon.

I was there when she came back from the Shadow Realm. I'm the one who got her back to herself, but even then she was never the girl she was before she was taken. I take a deep breath, trying to control the wave of anger that washes over me. I feel the shift as my Demon rises, and the tips of my fingers extend to claws and turn black.

"Colt," Caleb shouts my name just as the dark haze comes over my vision. "Calm your fucking shit down."

He yanks on the chain of my Demon, and it subdues. Maybe I don't have quite as much control as I'd like to believe. But man, Deacon really is a weak spot for me.

"Maybe going today isn't such a good idea," Caleb muses, and I glare at him.

"I have it under control. I'm going back, Caleb. You

can't ask me to keep this from Remy any longer, and I won't ask Fallon to lie to her, either."

"Yeah, I'm not exactly looking forward to telling Mara we kept this from her either. You mortals and your fucking secrets. Though, I guess you're not mortal anymore... Anyway, get yourself ready and meet me in the throne room in twenty minutes. If you're late, I'll cancel all of this. And if you can't control your shit around Deacon, I'll nix it too. Understood?"

"Yes. Asshole," I grumble, but he barks out a laugh and disappears from the room. Thank fuck I learned how to whisper early on. I got stuck in here more than once after I came back, and Caleb has a very sink-or-swim learning style. He can be a giant jackass, but I can't find it in me to be anything but grateful. Even with the Hunter's curse reborn, with its unknowns, I'm glad that the deal we made won out. Now I just need to work out how to win Fallon back and then make her immortal too.

But first... I have to face my sister's wrath.

I wake up disoriented, with a hangover bad enough to rival any I've ever had. Considering the states I've managed to get myself in before, that's saying something.

"What the fuck?" I groan as I roll over, reaching for

my bedside table to find my phone. I grab nothing but air. I open my eyes, and it takes a minute to adjust to the darkness in the room. It's then I realize I'm not in my room.

Where the fuck am I?

I push myself up on shaking arms, and my entire body aches. I blink, realizing I can see way better than I should be able to.

"Colt." My head turns faster than I intend, searching for the person who called my name, and I groan at the pain splintering my mind. "You need to calm yourself."

I feel a darkness rise inside of my body and mind. My vision grows a little darker, though everything gets sharper. What the fuck is going on?

"Colt! Calm the fuck down!" The words are like a bucket of ice water over my body. The darkness recedes, and my mind clears. I spot Caleb standing at the end of the bed. How the fuck did I miss him?

"Caleb? What the fuck is happening?" I ask, trying to piece shit together, but I can't remember anything which just makes me panic more.

"The deal we made became a reality," he says, his tone somber. I lean back in the bed and realize I'm bare-ass naked under this sheet. Why that occurs to me, I don't know, but it really doesn't help the current situation.

"I died?" I gulp, realizing what his words actually mean as he nods. Shit.

Shit.

Fallon.

"Is Fallon okay?"

"She's doing okay now."

"Now?" I ask. "Wait. How long ago did I die?"

"You've been gone about eighteen months in the mortal realm. You died in Avalon, in battle. I didn't feel the tug of your soul once you passed..." he says softly, and I can almost hear the apology even though it's obviously not his fault. "We figured the Hunter's Curse had overruled the deal we made, so we kept it quiet from the others just like you asked. But about a week ago, I felt the bond between us spark to life. Since your body was burned in your memorial, we had to work some shit out to bring you back. Don't worry your pretty face, we brought you back exactly as you were, but it means that you're not just half Demon. It means you are *a Demon. One of mine."*

"Holy shit. What does that even mean?" I ask, trying to take this all in, but it's a lot to handle all at once.

"You probably can't feel it yet because you're in shock, but there's a bond between us. You won't be able to break it until you're stronger, but it means that you literally can't disobey me. At all. It's a failsafe of sorts. To make sure you can't hurt anyone. Just be thankful you didn't tie your soul to a different, not so nice Demon." He smirks, and I shake my head.

This is actually real.

I know it was my idea, but I clearly didn't give it much thought. I didn't think I'd go like, full Demon. Not that I have an issue with it, but I feel more than a little shocked.

"Can I see Fallon? Remy? Ah, man, I missed the birth of the kid! Shit, they're going to kick my ass for being gone so long... Also, where can I get some clothes?" I ask, all of my thoughts and questions rushing out of me at once, and Caleb laughs at me.

"You're still so mortal it's funny. Nudity just isn't something we ever really think of," he says, and with a snap of his fingers, clothes appear in front of me on the bed. "The room has everything you'll need, but if there's something missing, just ask. This is your home now. As for seeing the others, it's not safe yet. We need to make sure you can control yourself first."

"Control myself?" I ask, shrugging into the t-shirt before pulling on the boxers and jeans.

"Yeah, you might not feel it fully yet, but you're a Demon, Colt. A baby Demon in the body of a fully grown one. We don't know what power you're going to have yet or how strong it's going to be. Considering you're the only Demon I've ever made, it's likely not going to be a drip of power. I'm not letting you anywhere near the mortal realm, or near the people I consider family, until I know it's safe to do so."

"Come on, Caleb. That's horseshit. I would never hurt my family."

"You'd never mean to, but we don't know what you're capable of yet. Imagine losing your shit and hurting your sister. Or your nephew. You wouldn't be able to live with yourself. You might be a Demon, but your soul is still yours. You'll still feel the guilt you would have felt before. But that guilt mixed with the power of a Demon? That's not something I'm unleashing on any world."

"Can't they come here? Or you come with me?" I feel like I'm begging, and that feels like shit. I want to be able to see the people I love, though. It might've been a while for them, but time hasn't changed for me.

"Colt. You've been gone a while. Some things have changed… You'll be here until you can control your Demon power. End of story" he says forcefully, and I feel that darkness rise back up inside of me. I force it down, not letting it break through like it did before. See, I've got this shit.

"What do you mean things have changed?" I ask, registering his words.

"They thought you were gone. We all did. Fallon… she's moved on. It took her a long time to grieve your death, but she's with someone else, man," he says, obviously sorry, and I go still.

I knew it was a risk when I made the deal with him. It's

part of why I didn't tell her what I did. I knew I might not even come back in her lifetime, and I didn't want her to put her life on pause for me... but motherfucker, that hurts.

"Who?" I ask, not really wanting the answer, but I need to know.

"She's with Deacon."

The world goes dark with his words, and the darkness grows tenfold. Of everyone it could be, it had to be the guy who fucking tortured her? What the actual fuck?! I let out a roar that is the least human sound I've ever made and unleash the pressure building up inside of me.

"Control yourself, Colt," Caleb says, but the request barely registers in the hurricane of emotion I'm riding. All I see is red. I am anger embodied.

"Colt!" Caleb shouts. "Stop!"

The command is like being doused in ice water again. The pressure, the power, recedes, and I blink as the world comes back to focus.

"This is exactly why you aren't going fucking anywhere."

I whisper into the throne room to find Caleb already there with Fallon and Deacon. Her hand is in his. I look away because I can't afford to lose my shit about that whole situation right now. I want to see my sister and my nephew. I don't know that a time will ever exist when I'm not pissed that she moved on with the guy who fucking tortured her. I don't see myself ever getting over it.

"Finally," Caleb grins, but I can feel his worry through the bond. Last time I saw Fallon with Deacon, my anger was overridden because I was so fucking excited to see her. It didn't exactly go as planned, but I held my shit. But now that I've tasted her again and felt her skin against mine, the possessive asshole that I am is angry that she's standing with him and not me. My Demon is like a caveman in my mind screaming 'mine'. "Let's get this show on the road, shall we?"

"Sure, man, let's do this." I nod at him, and I feel him accept that I'm not going to lose my shit right now.

"Okay, I think Fallon should head inside the manor, bringing Remy and everyone outside. We'll post up out there so there isn't any danger to their home. Who knows how this shit is going to go."

"I'm good with that," Fallon says quietly, and her concerned gaze bounces from Caleb to me. Deacon squeezes her hand. I growl quietly at the gesture, and I know he notices even if she doesn't because his eyes flash red at me.

Asshole.

"Let's go then," Caleb says, clapping his hands together,

controlling the whisper of us all back to the mortal realm. The feeling of someone else controlling my movement now that I can do it myself is weird as fuck, but it only takes seconds to materialize at the manor.

I hear my sister's laughter, followed by a childish squeal and giggle, and my heart pangs. I've missed so much already. I was right to fight Caleb about coming here so soon. I don't want to miss anything else. I'd have been here six Earth months ago if I had my way.

Fallon takes a deep breath and walks away from us, leaving me flanked by Caleb and Deacon. I'm not sure what Deacon thinks he can do that Caleb can't, and just having him there as if he's protecting my family from me pisses me off. I take a deep breath and let it go, which is made easier by the childish laughter that rings out as Fallon opens the door that leads to the kitchen.

"Hey, guys! I er… I need you to come outside. But I need you to prepare yourselves," I hear Fallon say, standing in the doorway.

"Hey, Fal, what's going on?" I hear Creek's voice, and then I feel a roll of power that can only be from Levi.

"You should probably just come outside," Fallon says nervously, but she manages not to look back at us. A storm of fucking bats takes flight in my stomach as my heart hammers against my chest. I'm excited to see Remy, but I'm not looking forward to how badly she's going to tear me a new one for not keeping her in the loop.

"Fallon? You're freaking me out. Kain, take Raze?" Remy's voice is exactly as I remember it, though the love in it when she says the kid's name is like a kick to the junk. I should have been here for all of this.

My gaze doesn't leave the back door, so when Fallon steps aside, I see my sister easily. It's like the world tips sideways.

"Surprise," I croak, knowing she can hear me even though I'm not very loud. Caleb chuckles beside me as Remy screams and runs toward me. I meet her halfway as she jumps into my arms, and I spin her around. "Hey, little bit."

"How is this even happening right now?" she asks, crying as she pulls back. "You're really here?"

Power ripples from Levi, who's standing by the kitchen door watching me closely. From the corner of my eye, I see Caleb nod to him, hopefully letting him know I'm not a Demon he needs to smite. Fates please be on my side right now. The others are standing with him, but Remy pulls my attention back to her as she tries to stop her tears.

"It's a long story…" I trail off, not sure how exactly to convey everything I need to her, so I opt for the shortest version possible. "I'm a Demon now, thanks to Caleb."

"Oh my Fates…" she says, covering her mouth with her hand. She's shocked, but I see the minute the anger takes over, and then I can't breathe.

Motherfucker, she punched me in the throat. I drop to my knees, trying to suck in air and failing miserably.

"Remy," Creek says as he joins us, almost as if scolding her. I can feel Caleb get closer, making sure I have my shit on lock down. Creek steps forward and holds out a hand, helping me back to my feet once I can breathe again. He pulls me into a hug. "I missed you, man."

"I missed you too," I tell him, feeling way more emotional than I thought I would. He's been my best friend forever. I knew seeing Remy would be a lot, but I hadn't factored in how much I'd missed him too.

"Well, now I know he's not going to hulk out on you all, I'll be off. Colt, make sure your ass is back tonight," Caleb says, pulling Remy in for a quick hug. He whispers away before I have a chance to even try to object.

"What was that all about?" Remy asks, looking confused.

"I'll explain everything, I promise; but first, can I see my nephew?" I ask, and her face softens. A sly smile pastes itself on her face. I don't know what she's thinking, but I'm a little scared of her and her devious mind sometimes.

"Of course you can, he's inside. Come on."

"We should maybe leave you guys alone," Fallon says, standing back with Deacon.

"Don't be an idiot, Fallon, you're family," Remy says,

before looking back at me and over to Deacon. “Oh, right. Uhm, well yeah, it’s up to you guys. You can stay, but it’s cool if you go too. I’ll see you again soon, right?”

“You will,” Fallon says with a nod.

“See you guys soon,” Deacon says, and whispers the two of them away as I clench my hands into fists.

“You’re taking that better than I thought you would,” Creek says, clasping my shoulder.

“Not really,” I tell him, my voice lower than usual. He startles when he sees my eyes. I close them and take a deep breath, getting myself back under control. “I’m fine. Where’s my nephew?”

“He’s here,” Remy says, walking toward me slowly with a little dark-haired boy waddling along beside her. His hair is as black as night, and his eyes are a bright violet. There’s no doubt who his mom is, that’s for sure. “Colt, meet Raziel. Raze.”

I drop down into a crouch, and he smiles as they pull to a stop right before me. “Hey, buddy!”

“Raze, this is your uncle Colt,” Remy says, crouching down with us and waving his hand.

“Hi, Untle Tolt.” My heart melts at the garbled words, and I scoop him up into my arms. Caleb had nothing to be worried about. This little guy is someone I could never hurt.

‘Family’ my Demon growls in my mind, and the

protective feeling for this little bundle of joy grows tenfold.

We had nothing to worry about at all.

She grins at me, and then tips her head backward, motioning toward the kitchen door. I see Roman appear, with a sleeping little boy in his arms. Roman looks like he'll tear my throat out if I so much as move, so I remain as still as possible.

"Holy shit," I utter. This can't be happening. I missed two of them?

"This is Maddox," Remy says softly as Roman walks toward me. I reach forward and brush some of the little guy's hair from his head, and he gurgles in his sleep. He looks just like Roman too. My heart leaps in my chest, and I can't help but feel overjoyed for my sister and the family she's growing.

'Family' my Demon growls again, and I can't help but smile.

Even if nothing else, meeting these guys was worth everything I've been through.

It feels like no time has really passed at all, but the sun has set, and I can almost feel the command from Caleb like an itch under my skin. The night is still young, and I'm not ready to leave yet. Roman and Levi disappeared a little while ago, but I was too wrapped up in my nephews to register where they went.

This day has been so fucking amazing. I don't want it to end, but I know it's coming. I can't go against Caleb's command yet. But I'm looking forward to the day when I can.

"Okay, I'm going to put this little guy down and then hit the hay. I know you have to go back tonight, but come back and see me soon," Remy says as she takes Raze's sleeping form from my arms. She's adapted to being a mom so well, not that I ever really had any doubt that she would. She's good at fucking everything. "And maybe don't miss the birth of your niece."

She grins at me, and Kain looks proud as shit. "You're pregnant again?"

"That she is," Kain says, placing a hand on Remy's stomach. "Our little princess."

I jump up and hug her gently, with Raze between us. "Congratulations, I swear I won't disappear again."

"You better not. Explanation or not, I'm still not sure if I need to kick your ass or Caleb's," she laughs, and I shake my head. Here's hoping for Caleb. The throat punch earlier was enough, thank you very much! "I'll see you soon."

She turns and leaves the room with Roman, leaving Creek and I in the kitchen. He grabs us both a beer before sitting back down at the table with me. I take a swig from the ice cold bottle and smile. "First beer in my new life."

"Well cheers to that, and to you being back in time for my birthday, even if we did miss yours," Creek says, tilting his bottle to me and taking a swig himself. "How are you doing, really? Adapting to the whole Demon thing?"

"Honestly?" I lean back in my chair, mentally trying to prepare myself for this conversation. If anyone is going to understand, though, it's him. "I'm doing okay. Sometimes, that darkness inside of me is fucking terrifying, more because it feels so… welcoming. Other times, it's terrifying because I haven't really explored just how deep down that pit of darkness goes."

"I get that," he says, nodding. "It feels so natural sometimes to just embrace that darker part of yourself, but it's scary how easy it is to let that part take control."

"Yeah. I've just been focused on locking it down so I could see you all sooner, but I still have a long way to go. Caleb said it'll be harder for me because his power is a different line than Morgan's, that it's more primal. But we've only barely touched on using it properly. I've mainly been working on not letting it win when it comes out."

"I get that, but maybe in a safe space you need to let it out fully, just so you can see what you're dealing with. Ask Caleb to take you to the pits. Bryce did that with me, and as terrifying as it was, it made me feel better after. I knew what I was working with, what I was capable of."

"I might do that. He mentioned it once or twice, but like I said, I just wanted to get back to you guys. Exploring all that power is still on my to-do list. I just want to get my life back," I say, running a hand through my hair. I mean the words, but I know that I'm never really going to get my life back. At least not as it was. I can feel how draining being on Earth is even after only a day.

"How do you manage it?" I ask. "The constant drained feeling?"

"It's not the same for me," he says with a shrug. "I guess because I'm a hybrid, my Hunter side is the one fully in power here. If I was in the Shadow Realm, my Demon side would prop up my Hunter side. But I guess, since you're not a hybrid, it's going to be harder for you. I'm sure once your power grows it won't be so bad, but again, talk to Caleb. He is literally the best source of knowledge, and you have him at your constant disposal."

He watches me as I process his words. Of course it's easier for him. His eyes narrow, and I can already tell I'm not going to like wherever this conversation is going next.

"How are you coping with the whole Fallon thing?" he asks, and I clench my fists, taking a deep breath.

"I'm not. Not well, anyway. She said she still loves me and that will never change, but I don't know where we go from here. She obviously loves Deacon too… don't even get me started on that mindfuck."

"He was there for her in a really dark time," Creek says as he stands and grabs a bottle of whiskey and two glasses. He pours us both a shot and downs one before pouring another. "After you died, she retreated. Hard. Even Remy couldn't really reach her, but Deacon pulled her back from that. I know it's not what you want to hear, man, but if he hadn't been there, I don't even want to think about what would've happened. Especially when the coven took her crown."

"Took her crown?" I ask, and he goes wide-eyed.

"I guess you guys haven't spoken all that much about what happened after… But the Witches' council revoked her place as heir. She's essentially cast out of the coven, and Rebel took up the mantle as heir. She's pretty much a lone Witch now. I think she's adjusted and is okay with it since it gives her more freedom over her life, but yeah. You missed a lot."

"Tell me about it," I say through clenched teeth before taking a shot myself. Fallon and I need to talk some more. I can't let my dick take charge again. I just need to get her alone.

Fuck my life.

"I'm sorry, man, I know it's probably not what you want to hear."

"None of this is what I wanted." I sigh. "I did all of this

to give us a second chance once the Hunter's Curse was broken. But of course my soul is an asshole and floated around for too long before deciding to let Caleb know we were around. I just want shit to go back to the way it was."

"That ship is long gone, my friend. It's time to carve a new path," he says, taking a shot of whiskey before pouring me another.

I take the shot, embracing the burn, but it doesn't touch the burn of my anger. "Don't I know it."

TEN

FALLON

This week has been fucking insane. Between Colt coming back, taking him to see Remy, and explaining to Mama everything that's happened, I feel like I've aged a thousand years. That's all before I even begin to think about what my reality is supposed to look like these days, and so I'm heading to Remy's today. I am in desperate need of a girls' night and tequila; and it's her birthday, so win-win.

After last year's fiasco, doing the tradition at the restaurant with a baby and a toddler, and the chaos that ensued, she decided not to go there this year. I get it, but I'm not sad about it as long as there's tequila. So. Much.

Tequila.

I finish painting on my lipstick, and call out goodbye to Mama before portaling through to the manor. I knock loudly before opening the door to find myself facing a screaming, butt-ass naked toddler shuffling toward me with his daddy chasing him with a towel.

"Raze! Get your cute little butt over here." Levi sighs, while laughing. "Hi, Fallon, Remy's in the kitchen."

"Thanks." I smile as I crouch down and scoop up the light of my life. "Hey, you, are you running away from bath time?"

"Ya!" Raze squeals, squirming in my arms to avoid going back to his dad, and I can't help but laugh.

"Thank you," Levi says as he takes the squirming toddler from my arms. Raze squeals as Levi tickles him and walks back into the depths of the large house. I head to the kitchen to find Remy sitting at the island. Nonnie is there pouring blended margaritas, and Emrys is sipping on a glass of whiskey. Everyone is laughing in here, and it fills me with the warm feeling of contentment.

Remy looks up when I enter the room and jumps up to hug me. "I know this was meant to be you, me, and tequila. Since I can't drink, I thought Nonnie and Emrys could help us with the boy bashing and birthday joy."

"Hey, it's your birthday, invite who you want…" The full meaning of her words hit me, and I laugh. She grins slyly. "You can't drink? Holy shit! You're actually pregnant again! Who's the daddy?"

"Kain," she says, practically beaming.

"Well now I almost feel bad about the boy bashing since you have so many awesome ones." I laugh, and she shakes her head.

"Oh no, let's boy bash, especially since we get to boy bash on my idiotic brother. As happy as I am that he's alive, I can't help but keep thinking about what a fucking idiot he is. He definitely went about it all in the wrong way. Plus, I love you, so let's bash away. Call it my birthday treat, I rarely get to boy bash anymore." She drags me over to the island, and Nonnie hands me a shot of tequila, which I throw back instantly in the second before she hands me the margarita.

After a little prompting and a lot more tequila, I explain everything that's happened since I found out that Colt was alive. Including Deacon's admission that he's okay with sharing me, and the fact that I accidentally fell on Colt's dick.

Oops.

Remy laughs and gets just as grossed out as she would have if she was drinking. It's refreshing, the normalcy of it all. Plus, I can't deny that Emrys and Nonnie's input on jackass men has me doing anything but crying with laughter.

"So, what are you going to do?" Emrys asks once we've all managed to get a grip on ourselves after one of Nonnie's tales from her youth about the stupid things she did to get the D.

"I have no idea. Deacon invited me to move with him to the Shadow Realm about a year ago, and I've been hesitant because of Mama. With them both being there… Nope, I still have no idea," I say, shooting back another drink, hoping maybe the answer will appear in the bottom of my glass.

"I mean, maybe move there for a bit but don't make any commitment to stay to see how it goes?" Emrys offers as she pours herself another drink.

"But what if Deacon takes that as me deciding to move there just because Colt's there now too? I was already thinking about moving now that Rebel's a little older, and Mama has more than enough shit going on to keep her busy, but still…" I groan and drop my forehead onto my forearms. I'm such a whiny bitch right now, but I don't care. I'm in this amazing, yet crappy place, and I don't know what to do about any of it.

"Deacon doesn't really seem like that kind of guy," Remy says with a shrug. "I say go for it. It's not like you're just jumping into a relationship with them both. You'll still be living with Deacon—you'll just be able to see Colt a bit easier. Have you talked to Marie about it?"

"No, I haven't dared. She didn't take the Colt news all that well, and you already know how much she isn't a fan of Deacon's," I tell them, fully embracing my current pity party for one.

"You need more fire in your belly," Nonnie says, pouring out more shots. I think if I tried to actually keep up with her drinking, I'd legit die.

"I think she might be near her limit of belly-fire," Remy says, laughing as the older Dracul scoffs.

"Women don't have limits for fire in their bellies and veins!" she insists, and I can't help but laugh. I really needed this tonight. I haven't laughed this hard in a while, and even though I have no idea what to do with my dumpster fire of a life right now, I know that the night with these ladies as my sounding board is exactly what I needed.

"I guess I should speak to Mama," I tell them before taking another shot. I know I'm going to regret it tomorrow, but why the fuck not? I'm going to need all the courage I can get to even consider broaching this subject with Mama.

She's going to lose her fucking mind.

I've spent three days going back and forth and trying to make a decision about what I'm going to do. Now that I've made my decision, I've spent the entire morning trying to psych myself up to talk to Mama about what I'm doing.

Goddess help me. I'm sure this isn't going to go well.

"Will you stop pacing your room like a kenneled dog and just come talk to me about whatever has your tail in a knot?" Mama yells from the living room, and I can't help but jump. She knows me so well. Too well sometimes.

I take another deep breath and yank open my door before heading toward the living room. I wring my hands as I try to find the words that I've been searching for all morning. When I find Mama sitting at the kitchen island with a mug of coffee in front of her, and another in front of the other stool, my mind goes blank all over again.

"I'm moving out," I blurt out before slapping my hand over my mouth. She raises an eyebrow at me and takes a sip of her coffee.

"Care to elaborate?" she asks, and I swear to the Goddess I feel like I'm going to hurl. I'm a grown-ass woman who can take on Demons, Hunters, and other monsters without so much as breaking a sweat. But telling my mama I'm moving out? It's like I'm a kid all over again.

I take a deep breath and sit on the stool before taking a sip of the dark wonder that is Mama's coffee. "I'm moving in with Deacon temporarily…"

"Because of Colt?" she asks, her eyes never leaving mine. I swear I'm sweating bullets under her gaze.

"No, Deacon asked me to move in with him about a

year ago," I pause, watching her frown deepen, but she doesn't say a word. "But I wasn't ready yet, and since I was thinking about doing it even before Colt came back, I think I'm finally ready. That you guys are ready. Colt being around doesn't affect my decision, but me being there might make things easier for him, at least, while he's still getting used to what he is."

"I don't know if that's a good decision, baby. I understand it, but you're still dealing with the after-effects of what happened with Azriel. Don't you sit there acting like you don't still get echoes of his memories. I know it was bad after Colt died, and I know it's gotten better; but I think being in the Shadow Realm so much with Deacon hasn't been helping. I don't think being there permanently is good for you. Plus you'll be completely disconnected from your magic. From our entire way of life." I sigh at her words because I knew this was coming. Mama accepting that I'm dating a Demon is one thing, but her coming round to the fact that this isn't just some fling is another thing entirely. With Colt being a Demon too? Yeah, she's digging in her heels.

Unfortunately for her, I'm as stubborn as she raised me to be.

"Mama, I understand your concerns, but this is happening. I'd like your blessing, and as much as I love you and don't want to piss you off or upset you, this is my life. I'm not the heir anymore, so I'm free to travel whichever road I choose. This is the one I'm on right now. This is my decision," I say, sounding a hell of a lot more confident than I actually feel.

"Fallon," she says with a huff, and I raise an eyebrow in challenge. There's no time to back down now. "I obviously can't stop you, but I don't want to see you get hurt."

"Mama, Deacon will never hurt me. He'd rather wipe himself from existence than do that. And if you can't trust him, trust that I know him and the kind of man he is."

"He's no man. He's a Demon."

"Would you say the same about Colt?" I challenge her, and she rolls her eyes.

"That's different."

"No, Mama, it's not different at all. I get it, and I know it's a hard adjustment. Demons are meant to be evil, but nothing is that black and white, which you should know better than most. Demons, like humans, are a mix of good and bad. No one person is inherently one way or the other." I feel the fire inside me lighting, as if having this conversation with her has completely solidified my decision to follow the path to my own happiness. I've spent my whole life doing stuff to make everyone else happy. Enough is enough. It's my turn now.

"It's your life, Fallon, and I do trust you. I just worry. You've been through so much—"

"I have, Mama, but I survived it all. I'm stronger now than I ever was before. Sometimes I still question myself, but I'm learning to trust myself and my instincts. And those instincts are telling me that this is what's right for me."

"He's making you a different person," she argues, and my ire rises to the bait of her comment. I slam my mug down on the counter.

"Mama, I love you, but he's done nothing but give me the room to grow into who I'm meant to be. You can be on board with this or not, but it's happening either way." I stand and calmly leave the room despite the whirlwind of emotions swirling inside of me, threatening to pull me under.

At least that went about as well as I thought it would.

ELEVEN

DEACON

I have no idea where the last few weeks have gone, but between dealing with bodies appearing on my door at random times, trying to stop Fallon freaking out about the Colt thing, and helping her move in… Well, it's been chaos, that's for damn sure. But Fallon is finally settling in here, Colt has avoided me entirely, and things are finally calming back down.

I head down to the dining room where Ellis will have breakfast waiting for us. I've tried to create a family type feel here since I took over, which is why I have more Morphs around the estate. I try to do dinners once a month for everyone, and Locke joins us most days for breakfast.

Slowly but surely, everyone's getting more comfortable and less terrified that I'm going to skin them alive if they fuck up.

I'm not Azriel. I don't work by his rules, and I never will.

Not that I'm saying I don't have my own ways to keep people in line, but I think respect is a much better way to earn loyalty than fear. I'm less likely to have my food poisoned this way too. Plus, Morphs need to be around others like them. We're similar to Lycans in that way. Pack mentality is a real thing. We feel more joy when we're around others of our kind.

I enter the dining room and find Locke already sitting in there with Fallon, talking to Ellis. I pause at the door and smile. It's nice to feel like I'm finally building a family of my own since my own never truly wanted me... or those who did want me died so long ago. I haven't had a true family dynamic since my twin died. Scout was the light to my darkness. She would've liked Fallon, I just know it.

I shake myself mentally, not wanting to go down that particular rabbit hole, and bring myself back to the present. As I enter the room fully, Ellis jumps when he sees me and scampers from the room. I guess he's not quite as relaxed around me as I thought.

"He's just grabbing your breakfast," Fallon says, a small smile playing on her lips. Once I reach her, I kiss her chastely before taking my seat. I'd like to do a lot more than that, but I already had a taste of her this morning when we woke up. If I focused on her as much as I'd like to, this level would go to absolute shit.

"I guessed since he looked like someone just lit a fire under his ass." I chuckle softly, and Locke shakes his head.

"They'll come around eventually. They just need to get to know you some more. I think everyone's waiting for the other shoe to drop. Azriel… well you know he ran this level in a very different way than you plan to. I don't think they trust the adjustment yet. Especially since you were his right hand man for so long. Just give them some time, they'll come around." He smiles reassuringly, and despite the fact he was trying to make me feel better, I actually feel a little worse. I was Azriel's right hand from necessity, not because I wanted to be. I'm holding onto a lot of guilt from the things I did while I held that position... and the things I did to get there.

Once upon a time, I refused to be that guy; but then self-preservation kicked in, and I lost myself. A lot. Until I found Fallon. Seeing her was like a kick in the balls and a slap on the face all at the same time. She reminded me of the man I once was, and the shame and guilt over everything I'd done hit me like a ton of bricks.

She makes me want to be a better man, and I won't let her down. The only reason I'd ever revert to my old ways would be if someone hurt her or tried to take her from me.

If a person ever crossed me like that, all fucking bets would be off..

"Erm, Sir… I mean, Deacon…" I glance up to find a young boy standing in the doorway looking like he's about to shit his pants. "Tex sent me to find you. There's a parcel for you downstairs."

"Why didn't you bring it up?" Locke asks, and the boy jumps again.

"It's fine," I say, waving it off. "I'll come down once I've eaten."

"Erm, okay, I mean... we didn't bring it up because the box is, well… it's… it's bleeding, but I'll tell Tex what you said, Sir." He stammers over his words, and I groan. What is it with dead shit being delivered to my door? This never happened when Azriel was around. I'm starting to think someone is trying to send me a message, though if they are, I have no idea what it could be. Maybe they need to start being a little more fucking clear with their meaning.

"Maybe we should go down now?" Fallon offers, pushing her plate away. I guess her appetite disappeared too. I make a mental note to gut whoever is sending this shit. She already doesn't eat enough as it is.

"I think you're right. Locke, can you let Ellis know that I'll eat later? Meet us in the chiller when you're done?" He nods at me and I stand, taking Fallon's hand as she stands as well. “I guess we better go see what delightfulness awaits us. What’s your name?” I ask the boy.

“Kevin, sir.”

“Okay, Kevin, lead the way.”

We make it to the foyer to find a small crowd of people around the table in the middle of the room. Tex has his trademark cap in his hands, scrunching it like he’s nervous. One day these people will understand that I’m not going to lash out at them, but I know it’s going to take time. I swallow down my annoyance and smile at the people idling in the foyer.

“I hear we have another mysterious package, Tex?” I ask as we reach him. Fallon says hello to a few of the others, exchanging the pleasantries she’s so easily adopted since she first started coming here. Fallon’s practiced decorum leaves me free to focus on the bleeding box that’s currently dripping all over my hardwood floors. “Let’s take it to the chiller before we open it up.”

“Sounds good to me, boss.” Tex nods, gently lifting the box.

“I’ll get this cleaned up,” one of the other guys says as Kevin hands me an envelope.

“This came with the box, sir.”

"Thank you, Kevin." I smile at him, trying to seem a little less menacing than his shaking hand insinuates I am. I wait for Fallon to say her goodbyes and then follow Tex down to the chiller. I've been here way too fucking much lately. I've had at least twelve carved-up bodies dropped on my doorstep over the past few weeks. Some I've recognized, though most I haven't. They don't usually turn up in boxes, which makes this entire situation more than a little concerning.

When I notice the seal on the envelope, my heart stutters in my chest. My family crest. My father always took so much stupid pride in it that I'll never forget it.

"Are you okay?" Fallon asks, her gaze bouncing between mine and the letter in my hand.

"I don't know." I take a deep breath and open the letter, peeling the wax carefully to leave the seal intact. I almost hold my breath as I pull the card from the envelope, the bright red ink reminding me of blood.

Deacon,
Happy Birthday,
here's something you've always wanted. Your parents won't bother you again.

There's no signature.

"Open the box," I demand, my voice steadier than my

hands at least. Tex opens the box just as Locke enters the room. Tex tips the box out, and Fallon immediately looks like she's going to puke.

"Is that a heart?" she asks, and I can tell she's fighting the urge to gag.

"It is," I confirm before moving closer to the contents. The severed head is distorted with lacerations, but when I lift it, I know who it is instantly. I drop it as if it burned me.

"I guess my parents are dead," I say callously, not really processing the fact that my father's head is looking back at me from the table. The heart is the wrong color to be his. He wasn't a Morph, he was one of the Shadowed. He quite literally had a black heart.

"The head of my father and the heart of my mother," I say, my tone icier than I expected. I feel numb. I didn't expect to feel anything when they died, but I also didn't expect to find out quite like this.

"I'm so sorry, Deacon," Fallon says as Locke scoops up the parts and puts them in one of the many chiller drawers we have down here.

"I guess I'm the only one left now," I say with a sigh, pinching the bridge of my nose. Fuck, if I'm the only one left, I'm the one who will have to sort out all of their bullshit. Fantastic.

"Deacon..." Fallon's voice trails off, but I shake my head.

"It's fine. I haven't seen or spoken to either of them in hundreds of years. My time with them before that wasn't exactly joyful, so don't feel sorry for me," I say to her before walking from the room. I make my way back to the main level of the estate before heading to my study. It's only morning, and I'm exhausted already.

Luckily for me, there's an entire level of Demons waiting on me to handle their shit. My head thrums from the stress of it all. I have more than a little bit of politics to worry about.

All of that is on top of the constant worry that Caleb and the others still haven't tracked Azriel yet. It's like he disappeared into thin air. If him disappearing like that was actually possible, I'd maybe worry less, but the only way a Demon's life is truly destroyed is with Shadow Fire or Hell Fire. It's why Remy made so many people so uneasy. Even in her life as Amantara, she held the power of Shadow Fire, despite the fact that only a few Shadow Walkers in history have possessed the ability to wield it. It's not exactly a common power for Demons to hold either. Other than Morgan, Caleb, and a literal handful of others throughout history, I don't think anyone else has had the ability to wield Shadow Fire.

I'd really like all of this shit to just be tied up in a neat little bow. I'd also happily hand over the reins to this level in the realm to somebody else if I thought they'd take it.

I just want a life with my girl. I never wanted all of the bullshit that comes with being a higher Demon, yet here I am.

My father would be proud. You know, if his head wasn't in a box in my chiller.

Fuck my actual life.

Of course this would happen on my birthday. Not that birthdays mean that much when you've had a few hundred of them, but still. It's the note that bugs me more than anything. It feels almost like whoever sent it thought they were killing my parents for me. But the only people who give a fuck about me don't know my parents, and they definitely didn't kill them for me.

Just another thing to add to my ever-growing to-do list.

Look into my parents' murders.

This has been one long-ass day. By the time I practically crawl back to the nook, I find it empty with a note on the door telling me to head to the kitchen.

I sigh, because as much as I'm looking forward to seeing my girl, I just kind of want to curl up on the sofa with her and chill out. I head to the kitchen to find her dancing around in little shorts and a crop top, with her hair piled up on her head as she sings to the music she's playing while she cooks.

"Well, isn't this just a sight for sore eyes," I say as I lean up against the doorframe, chuckling softly as she jumps and turns to face me. She sticks her tongue out at me before practically skipping across the room and jumping into my arms.

"Happy birthday." She grins before planting a kiss on my lips. I lift her slightly, squeezing her ass. "Now put me down. I've been cooking for you, and you can't have dessert until after dinner." She winks, and I laugh as she slides down my body. I just manage to stifle my groan at the feeling of her tight little body on mine. We've adapted to this whole living together thing pretty well. There haven't really been any issues, other than the Colt-sized elephant in the room but when he's ready to man up and talk to me, we'll deal with that. Until then, my girl is here, making this space ours, and I can't remember a time when I was happier.

"I am definitely looking forward to dessert," I say, nipping at her bottom lip before I let her walk away from me. "I was thinking… Do you think it would be easier for you if Colt moved to the estate instead of being at the palace?"

She startles before turning back to face me. "Erm, maybe?"

"You don't sound too sure about that," I say, raising an

eyebrow at her.

"Well, I know you guys aren't exactly best buds." She shrugs, and I move over to her, wrapping my arms around her waist.

"Baby, I know you've been struggling with what's happening between you guys. I can feel it. I just want you to be happy; so if having him closer is what makes you happy, we can offer the invitation. And you guys become a thing again, I'm still good with it. As long as it makes you happy."

"What would make me happy is if you guys could get along," she says, letting out a huff. "And I'm very aware that's more on him than it is on you. But thank you for the offer. Now, let's not think about anyone else for a while, okay? It's your birthday, and whether you think it's special or not, I do. I cooked, and I baked, dammit. We're gonna have fun, or so help me..."

She puts her hands on her hips, and I can't help but smirk at just how southern she gets when she's worked up. I do love that fire of hers.

"Okay, baby, let's do this birthday fun thing of yours. I'm so ready for it." I grin down at her as she leans up on her tiptoes and kisses me quickly.

"Go sit that fine ass of yours down, dinner is served."

I laugh and salute her. "Yes, ma'am."

I move around the kitchen, pouring from the wine

bottle that she's put on the table and then sit back, enjoying being able to watch her in her element. She loves to cook; and if I wasn't a Demon, I'd be scared about becoming that comfortable guy who gets a dad bod because his girl loves to feed him. I take in the view, laughing as she shakes her ass at me while she stirs the pot and sings into the wooden spoon.

I don't remember a time when we were this carefree and so easy to laugh.

I never want this to change.

But that nagging voice in my mind reminds me of Azriel. Of the bodies and body parts that keep arriving at my door. I'm convinced they're not linked, which almost makes it worse because then we have more than one person fucking with us. I chug down my glass of wine and pour another. I'm going to need something stronger if I maintain this train of thought.

"Dinner's up!" she exclaims as she puts a plate in front of me. It smells spicy as fuck, and my stomach rumbles in response.

"What is this deliciousness?" I smile up at her and pull her into my lap, kissing her neck.

"Down, boy, this is my grammie's recipe. Jambalaya. It's one of my favorites, and I figured you'd probably never had it. After you liked the low country boil so much, I thought you might like it."

“Baby, I love everything you do.” I grin, and she rolls her eyes at me. “I love everything about you.”

“Okay, sweet talker, if you say so.” She laughs and kisses me again. I lean into the kiss, deepening it until she squirms in my lap. “Boy, you need to put me down otherwise we’re not having dinner. And Grammie will haunt my ass to the grave if we waste her jambalaya.”

“Then I guess we better eat,” I say, smirking at her. “But later, I get to eat you.”

TWELVE

FALLON

Deacon's birthday hasn't exactly gone as planned, but I'm determined to finish it with a bang.

Literally.

He's in the shower, making this the perfect time to sneak away and prepare myself. Red is his color, so I found a lace and silk lingerie set in black and red especially for tonight. The set came with bandage wraps as well as wrist ties.

I'm excited just thinking about how much he'll enjoy it all. I want him to realize that I'm in this with him for the long haul, no matter what else is going on in our lives. Part of me wants to submit to him fully. I think I crave it as much as he does, and with so much craziness going on around us, I can feel how on edge he is through our bond. If I can make him feel better, I am absolutely on board for that. I want to offer a night where neither of us has to focus on anything but each other.

I strip quickly, slipping into the lingerie and taking care with the bandage wraps as they crisscross over my chest and stomach. Once I'm dressed, I fluff up the curls in my hair and retouch the red on my lips. I can still hear the shower running, so I decide to paint my nails and toenails in the matching red too and pop them under the UV lamp Deacon procured for me. There's nothing quite like going all out.

If you're going to do something, you might as well do it right.

I swear to the Goddess that the anticipation of all of this has me so freaking excited I'm already wet.

The shower shuts off just as I finish binding my wrists, and I drop down onto my knees, head tilted forward with my gaze on the floor, waiting for him.

My breath hitches when the door opens, I can't see him, but I feel the shot of excitement through our bond. This was absolutely the best idea.

"Such a good girl," his voice lowers when he speaks, and a shudder runs down my spine. I love when he gets primal and possessive. I remain silent. This is his show, and he'll ask me to speak if he wants me to, so I stay still and let the anticipation build as he watches me kneel for him.

He circles around me, and I know he's assessing me from every angle—playing out the scene in his head and anticipating my submission. When the pad of his finger slides from one of my shoulder blades to the other, every inch of my skin erupts in goosebumps. His low chuckle tells me he sees it just as he stops in front of me.

I don't move. I don't speak. Anticipation of all the delicious things to come keeps me rooted to the spot. I love this part, the mind game, just as much as the things I know will follow.

"You did all of this for me?"

I nod, causing a few strands of hair to fall from my shoulder and tickle my lace-covered breast.

"The red, the bindings, the pose. Such a good girl."

Without warning, he sinks his fingers into my hair at the nape of my neck and closes his fist, pulling my head back so he can look at me. The move has me as pliant as a kitten, and the hold is akin to a lover's caress.

"Is there something you want to say to me?"

He crouches, not releasing my hair. With my face just inches from his, I keep my eyes down and realize he's not wearing a towel. He's not wearing anything. His dick is hard and resting just below his navel, angry with desire.

It makes my mouth water, my pussy wetter still, and my mind forgetful.

"Answer me, baby girl. I don't like repeating myself."

My eyes travel the length of his taut, waterdrop-ridden body and finally reach his red, lust-filled eyes.

"Happy Birthday—"

I don't even have time to say his name before his mouth is on mine, bruising my lips. His tongue demands that I part and allow him entrance. And I do. Of course, I do.

When he's finished fucking my mouth with his tongue, he pulls back just an inch and whispers, "I'm going to destroy you, pretty girl, in the most delicious of ways."

I almost come right there. His words are like fingers fucking my pussy, like a tongue teasing my clit. I'm so wet it's almost embarrassing.

Almost.

"My first birthday wish is your mouth on my cock. Can you handle that?" I nod, licking my lips. I love the taste of him, so this isn't exactly a hardship. None of it is.

With praises pouring from his lips, he brings his hand to the base of his cock and pushes the shaft down just low enough to tease my mouth. His pre-cum paints my lips, and that alone has my nipples hard and aching with want for him.

"Open."

I don't hesitate at his command. I loosen my jaw

muscles, sticking my tongue out a little and giving him the space he needs to push the head of his dick inside my waiting mouth. Deacon doesn't immediately thrust inside me. Instead, he teases me with a long, lingering push until he reaches the back of my throat.

Breathing through my nose, I hum my satisfaction as he lingers there a moment, whispering encouragement, before he slides back out and starts the process all over again.

"Such a good girl."

"Your mouth is so hot, so perfect for my hungry cock."

"I can't wait to see you cry. You're so beautiful when you cry for me."

He's going to fuck my face until all I see is the blur from my tears, and I can't wait. There's something so fucking serene about handing him this power over me. It makes me feel lighter than I've ever felt before.

Letting my hair go, Deacon brings his hand to my jaw, caressing my cheek before he cups my chin and digs two fingers into each of my cheeks, making sure my mouth is hollowed out properly.

Then he pushes his dick back inside my mouth and fucks me with abandon. I feel the soft skin pushing in and out of my mouth, and the thick head bumps at the back of my throat with every thrust. His eyes never leave my own as he takes what I'm more than willing to give.

His look alone tells me I'm beautiful and that I'm the most desirable woman to ever exist. His look urges me to take him deeper, to choke on his cock like the good girl he knows I can be. He pushes just a little bit deeper, and I almost gag but remember his simple rules. Concentrate on him and breathe through my nose. Getting my reflexes under control, I let him bottom out; and when he does, I'm blessed with the most enthralling vision of all time. Tears fall down my cheeks, and I love that my body obeys him instinctively. His face is a mask of pleasure. His top teeth dig into his bottom lip, and his eyes are as red as rubies as his lust kicks up a notch, unveiling his Demon to me. He keeps his control on a tight leash, but I want him free. I want to see that side of him completely.

I want him to show me his power in all the delicious ways he knows how. So, I do what no good girl is ever supposed to do. I top from the bottom and inch a tad closer to him, forcing his cock into my throat, inhaling the scent that is entirely him, almost getting high on it.

He growls and pulls out of my mouth with a look that tells me he's far from happy about what I've done, and a thrill runs down my spine. Poking his beast would be terrifying for most, but it excites me. I let out a squeak as he pulls me by the hair and forces me to stand, my knees trembling with anticipation and the excitement at it all.

His chest heaves, his nostrils flaring with his pent-up

need. It's heady, and I know that whatever punishment I'm going to get will be worth the pleasure a thousand times over.

"What were you expecting with that little stunt, hmmm?" His eyebrow rises, and I can see the barely contained restraint as his hand shakes. I bite down on my lip to keep from smiling, but I'm pretty sure he sees it. He growls low in his throat, like he's a predator and I'm his prey, and my entire body shivers as goosebumps take over my skin. Deacon crashes his mouth against mine, his tongue exploring me with a possessive sort of passion before biting my bottom lip hard enough to break the skin a little. The coppery tang that lands on my tongue is proof that his control is waning which means, in a small kind of way, I've won.

But he doesn't need to know that.

"Get on the bed, face down, ass up." His words make me shiver, but the tone is what gets me wetter than I could have imagined possible.

I don't hesitate. I rise with his taste still on my tongue, and I can't stop the smile from spreading across my face. I make my way to the bed, where I do exactly as he asks.

First, I place one knee followed by the other on the mattress, and then I lower the top half of my body, keeping my ass up.

Behind me, I hear him moving around, opening and

closing drawers, and the anticipation builds in me.

I can feel my juices running down the insides of my thighs in this position and knowing just how turned on I am for him makes me even wetter.

When Deacon returns, he rests his hand on my ass, running a thumb down the crease between my ass cheeks. He pushes the fabric of my lingerie against both my pussy and my ass.

“What should I fuck first?” he muses, playing with me like the prey that I am.

“Should I use a butt plug while I destroy your pussy with my cock?” He pushes two fingers inside me, and I struggle not to moan at the feel of him. The sensation of him inside of me mixed with his words is enough to push me too close to the edge already.

“Or,” he takes in a deep breath, pausing to build me up even higher, “I could shove a dildo in your pretty little pussy while I fuck your ass.” He pulls the fabric out of his way and slowly pushes one finger inside my ass.

In a moment of lusty forgetfulness, I squirm, my thighs rubbing together to alleviate the need that courses through my body.

The punishment is immediate.

The sound of his hand connecting with my right ass cheek echoes throughout the room a second before I feel the red-hot pain it leaves behind.

I mewl from the sensation it creates within me. The feeling of belonging to him. Of being at his command.

"You know what, I've changed my mind."

I panic for a second, thinking he's going to stop. I'm almost afraid I've pushed him too far—that he could leave before we've really started—until another slap across my ass snaps me back to reality.

"Don't you dare ever think that. It will never, ever happen, and the fact that you would even feel that I could leave you pisses me off."

I don't know when he got it, but the sharp sound of a belt rings through the air before it slashes across both of my cheeks. I cry out in pain, but the moment I feel his hot tongue licking across my new marking, I feel whole again.

"I like what you're wearing, but it's in my way." I recognize the feeling of his silk ropes as he makes quick work of tying them on my arms and legs. With my wrists bound together, he secures me to the headboard. He spreads my thighs wide, and I feel completely exposed. Because I am. My pussy is on full view, and my ass is as well. Every bit of my body on display for his visual pleasure.

Once my ankles are attached to the bottom posters of the bed, I know things are getting real. The snip and snap of my black and red lingerie being torn apart almost makes me cry in protest. Dammit, I really loved that underwear. But now it's in pieces.

"I love seeing you like this. Tied to our bed. Naked and waiting for me. Open for my eyes, my mouth, my fingers, my cock. At any moment, I can fuck you anywhere I want. More than once, if I want. And there is my dilemma, my sweet. I'm torn between fucking your pussy with my tongue first or fucking your ass raw."

Goddess, that mouth of his. I bite down on the pillow to hide the groan as a shudder runs down my body from his words.

When his tongue spears me without warning, I cry out. It's sudden and delicious and everything I needed. My body is on fire from him playing around with me, the teasing and his dirty talk. His suggestive moans and the mere fact that he's been doing it all completely naked stokes the fire burning in my belly.

He's quite literally in his birthday suit, offering me the most carnal of pleasures.

I try not to squirm, but it's nearly impossible, and he knows it. I'm sure he's counting on me breaking all of his rules just so he can have an excuse to land a spank or ten on each of my cheeks. And I do. I break all of the rules, reveling in the feel of the sting. Each slap makes me hornier than the last, leaving me writhing and panting until I practically fuck his tongue. He promptly stops all movement.

I bite the inside of my cheek to avoid crying out in

frustration, nearly making myself bleed with the effort.

"Such a good girl trying so hard not to be naughty." His breath tickles across my skin, and I want to demand more.

He moves languidly, pushing two fingers into my pussy and fucking me leisurely. My core clenches with hot desire when I feel the first drops of lube coating my asshole. Linking my fingers together and squeezing them, I avoid the urge to push into him. To make him go faster. My fingers are so knotted together that the pain erases the sting on my ass.

"I hope you're ready, because I've barely even gotten started with you. I've fucked your mouth. Now, I'm going to fuck your pussy while I prepare your ass. Then, when you're nice and ready, I'm going to fuck it until you break for me. Until you cry with the need to come. I'm going to make sure this night is imprinted in the pleasure center of your brain for all of eternity."

My mouth is dry with the need to taste him. My entire body sweats with anticipation. The only sound around us is of him touching me and my barely stifled moans. He fucks me with his fingers, spreading the lube and my juices around my asshole to make sure I'm prepared for what he offers. I'm a raging fire of need, and he's pouring gasoline on top with his filthy imagery.

Then his cock is inside me to the hilt. He's not gentle;

he's not making love. He's fucking me like the birthday present I am. He's taking his pleasure and teasing mine out of me. He gives just enough to make me soar but stops in the moments before I come. My clit throbs with my need to come.

"Such a good girl waiting on me to give you permission."

It's only when I feel through our bond that he's satisfied with my obedience, that he leans down and whispers in my ear. He slowly pistons his cock, slowly bottoming out with each syllable he speaks. It's mind numbing. "Come all over my dick, sweet princess. I want to feel your orgasm coat every inch of me."

His words are the only signal I need to let go.

I fly. I cry out as if I'm in pain even though this is nothing but pleasure. Deacon pounds my pussy as he pinches my clit, creating an inferno of pleasure that licks every inch of me. My fingers are raw, and my thighs shake, barely keeping me up. And just when I think I'm done, he slides a dildo into my ass and alternates his thrusting.

"Fuck, you feel so good. So tight, with both your holes getting a good fucking. This is the best fucking present in the world."

When I drop back to the mattress, after coming so hard I think I may have blacked out, I first feel the dildo exit my ass before his fingers reverently caress it. "Keep pushing out, baby. Don't let it close up. You're so beautiful with your ass completely open for me. Begging me to fuck it."

Deacon pulls out of my pussy and swiftly pushes into my ass, groaning like he's been through hell and back. Something drops on the floor, probably the dildo, and then I feel another toy push slowly into my pussy giving me the same sensation of complete fullness.

"It's the new glass one, baby girl. How does it feel?"

Panting, my chest heaving with each lusty breath I take, I try to answer. All that comes out is a bad rendition of the words, "So good." Deacon chuckles at my lack of control before he takes off, pounding into me in earnest again. One hand fucks my pussy with his new glass dildo, and the other pinches my nipples while his cock pistons mercilessly in and out of my ass. With each thrust, I'm pushed closer and closer to the headboard, my bound ankles the only thing keeping me in place. The movement of my body doesn't stop him. He merely continues on his quest to tattoo his cock inside of me. I feel the tale-tell flutter of a release building in my core.

"Fuck! Do. Not. Come. Not now."

I obey. But damn, it's so hard.

When I feel his fingers leave my nipple and latch onto my hip, I know he's about to come. He's going to lose all his control, and I can't wait to feel it.

Roaring through his orgasm, Deacon shoves the dildo deep into my pussy and keeps it pushed inside there while he loses his utter mind on my ass. He's not fucking me, he's destroying me, pounding me until I know I'll be bruised all over. They're bruises I welcome.

It's so fucking hot, but it makes it so difficult to not come with him.

He stills once he's milked himself dry of his pleasure, and I feel like I'm going to explode. He only rests for a second before he pulls out, throwing the dildo somewhere across the room and unbinding me faster than the speed of light.

In mere seconds, he has me flipped over. With my wrists still bound, my arms cross over my head, and he buries his face between my legs. His fingers bruise my thighs, and with his tongue imitating the thrusting of his dick from moments before, he devours my pussy like a starving man coming home from battle.

"Fuck, this is better than birthday cake," he mumbles between his assault on my pussy. "Come for me now, baby girl."

His words are all I need to send me over the edge and into the waiting chasm of pleasure. I let go, knowing that his mouth drinks every ounce of my ecstasy, leaving nothing behind. The orgasm takes over every one of my senses, and I swear I see the fucking stars.

I almost pass out from pleasure, my body shaking with tremors long after he pulls his face from between my legs.

He slides up my body and kisses me with so much love and devotion that tears burn my eyes.

"I love you." Such simple words after such an intense experience.

"Happy Birthday, Deac."

I woke up this morning sore, but happy. I had a revelation of sorts too.

I've been going around in circles for the last few weeks trying to figure out how to do this whole thing with Colt since he came back. When I woke up this morning, it was like it came to me in my sleep.

I love Colt.

I love Deacon.

I didn't think it was possible for me to love more than one person, but here we are, living with this level of complexity binding us. I don't want to lose either of them, and if other people in our lives can manage poly relationships, then why can't we? I know Deacon's on board, he's been so open about it all. He's also been super understanding about everything. I mean offering, on his freaking birthday, for Colt to move into the estate with us for me. Even though Colt's been nothing but a giant jackass to Deacon.

There's no freaking way I'm giving Deacon up.

Which means really, the decision lies with Colt. I've been agonizing over this all for almost no reason at all. I mean, yes I'm still angry at Colt for lying to me—to all of us. I'm pissed that we all went through what we did when we lost him. But I also understand. Well, kind of.

It doesn't stop the hurt, though.

But for now at least, I have a plan.

Talk to Colt. Tell him where I stand, where Deacon stands, and what I'm willing to accept. If he doesn't want to get on board, I'll be devastated, but I'll also understand. I get that this isn't what he signed up for, and love only goes so far sometimes.

Love can't save everything and everyone. No matter how much we might want it to.

And I'm simply not giving Deacon up.

Don't get me wrong. If Colt had never died, and none of this had ever happened, I would have been happy as a clam to have stayed blissfully in love with Colt and Colt alone. But that isn't how any of this happened.

He died.

He didn't tell anyone what he'd done.

And I grieved for him.

I went to a place so dark that I sometimes wonder just how close I came to losing myself. But when I was there, it was Deacon who pulled me out. It was Deacon who brought me back and showed me that life was still worth living.

So I'm not just going to drop him because Colt is back. No matter how much I love Colt.

I love Deacon too.

Colt needs to accept that if he wants to be a part of my life. He can't just keep being a jackass about Deacon. We all have shit we regret in our past, but I've forgiven him, so Colt needs to as well.

I just need to work out exactly what the fuck I'm going to say, in hopes that he jumps on board. So I'm going to talk to the one person I know I can ask anything, the person who has a firsthand idea of how the hell to make all of this craziness work.

So I'm dressed, the necklace from Caleb is fastened around my throat, and I'm ready to face this day. I already said goodbye to Deacon this morning, and after last night I was amazed my body could take any more, but take more I did. I swear to the Goddess, that man knows exactly how to make my body sing.

So now I'm psyching myself up to go and talk to my bestie about how to make her brother see sense and live a ménage life with me. Goddess save me from myself.

I close my eyes and palm the stone on my necklace, picturing the manor. I don't know that I'll ever get used to traveling this way. It feels like my body is pulled apart and put back together so quickly that it doesn't even hurt.

It leaves a tingling sensation over my entire body. Before I can even really register it, a cold breeze hits my face as I land in the backyard of the manor. The sun is only just rising, and if this had been a few years ago, Remy would've killed me for being here this early. The light in the kitchen shows me her silhouette, cradling little Maddox.

She really adapted to being a mom so well. Better than she ever imagined she would anyway, but I always knew deep down she'd be fine. She's always looked after us all.

I open the door to the kitchen quietly, and she barely even looks up before asking, "What did my dumbass brother do this time?"

I snort a laugh before shaking my head. Only Remy could ask that question while coo-ing over her kid.

"I mean, I could just be here to see you," I say, grabbing a mug of coffee for us both when I spot that hers is almost empty. I hand her the steaming mug of goodness and sit opposite of her at the table. Thank the Goddess for Angel coffee and being allowed it while pregnant.

"You could, but you're not. Your energy is all over the place."

"I forget you can do that now." I sigh before taking a sip of the coffee. I love this angel coffee they get. There's really nothing else like it. Maybe I shouldn't tell my Demon boyfriend that, though.

"Well I can, and the kids are going to hate it," she

smirks. "But it does come in handy more often than not. If only it would work on my guys. I don't know how they worked out how to lock their shit out, I'd put money on Levi working some juju, but anyway. Spill it."

"I want to date both Colt and Deacon," I blurt out, and her eyebrows rise before a grin splits across her face.

"Those fuckers are going to owe me money." She fist pumps before doing a mini dance with Maddox. "I knew you'd see the light."

"Oh, I saw the light…" I start, but trail off and she sobers up.

"But my brother is a stubborn macho idiot, right?"

"I haven't exactly mentioned it to him yet, but yeah. I don't anticipate it going too good. I wanna know how you managed it. None of your guys are the sharing type, but y'all seem to make it work." I shrug and down more of the coffee now that my word vomit has spewed.

"It wasn't easy. Not to start with anyway. Roman and Creek *hated* each other, past life bullshit and all that. Roman and Kain had a weird alliance thing in the beginning, but Kain has always been way more open about sharing." She blushes a little, but Maddox lets out a string of gibberish and distracts her from it. "Levi… well, he just wants me to be happy, so he made it work himself. I never really had to put my foot down too much. I was just really open with them about not wanting to lose anyone. I never had just a one-on-one with any of them in this life either, so I think that made it easier."

"So I'm screwed," I groan, dropping my head into my hands. "Of course it was easy for you," I grumble, and she sticks her tongue out at me. She might be a mom of two and pregnant again, but she's still Remy.

"I think if you're bold and upfront with Colt, he'll come round. He loves you, and he doesn't want to lose you. Just don't beat around the bush to try to appease him. If this is what you want, take that bull by the horns and own it."

"I think it's going to be easier said than done."

"Everything worth doing or having is. You just need to decide if you're really willing to lose either of them. If not, and they don't want to lose you, you'll all make it work."

"You make it sound so easy."

"Everything is pretty simple at the fundamental level. We have lived and died for each other far too many times to sacrifice what we have now. There's something about knowing that everything you have can be ripped away in a moment that makes treasuring it that much easier." She shrugs and starts bouncing Maddox in her arms. It's almost soothing watching him fall asleep.

"Thank you," I say, though I'm still not feeling that much more resolved about what I need to do. At least the path is clear.

"You've got this. You've survived too much to lose

what means the most to you because my brother is too pigheaded to see past his own dick."

I snort a laugh again, but stifle it when Roman appears, taking Maddox from Remy. He basically melts when he holds the little guy, and the sight of it warms me all the way to the core. "Will you guys please stop discussing dick with my kid in the room?"

Remy laughs at his grumble and kisses his cheek. "You don't seem to mind when I'm talking about your dick."

"Well, that's different," he grumbles again before leaving with Maddox, shaking his head the entire way.

"Glad to see some things never change," I chuckle, and she winks at me.

"Men are easily led by their dicks. And I'll acknowledge that this is super gross since we're talking about my brother, but maybe just start there."

THIRTEEN

COLT

I've been a testy, cranky asshole for weeks to the point that I'm even pissing myself off. I hate that I still don't have full control of my power or even an idea of what I'm capable of once I've harnessed my full power. I hate that I have no idea where I stand with Fallon. And I really fucking hate that this is all turning me into a whiny-ass bitch.

Even Caleb is starting to get pissed at me, and that guy has the patience of a freaking saint. Which is hilarious considering, you know, apocalyptic figure and all that. He's taking me down to the pits next week. Apparently that's where I'll get to see what level of power really resides within me, and despite wanting it, I can't help but wonder if that's what I actually need.

Do I want to see just how dark that pit inside of me really is? Do I want to see just how much I'm not who I always thought I was?

A knock at the door of my room pulls me back from spiraling down the rabbit hole, and I open it to find Fallon standing there, looking like a fucking vision. She's wearing little booty shorts and a white tank top with her hair piled on her head. She has these little work type boots on, and she ties it all together with a long cardigan thing. She looks good enough to fucking eat. My cock springs to attention as I take her in, but when I reach her eyes again, some of my excitement dies.

Down boy.

"Can we talk?" she asks, and I wave her into my room. She wrings her hands, and I don't know if I've ever seen her look so uneasy in front me. She was always just fine, even after I broke things off with her when I had my head up my ass. She was a raging storm, but I guess everything that's happened in the three years since we started fooling around has changed her more than I realized.

"What's up?" I ask once I've closed the door. She takes a deep breath and sits on the edge of my bed. She seems nervous, so I keep my distance, trying to respect the obvious space she's put between us even though it kills me a little inside.

She lets out something that's half a laugh and half a huff. It makes me antsy, but I keep myself planted in place despite my Demon screaming at me to protect her, even if it's protecting her from me.

"This. Us. All of it." She shakes her head, and I nervously flick my tongue bar around my teeth while I cross my arms. It's more to keep myself from fidgeting because I get the feeling I'm not going to like what's getting ready to go down.

"What do you mean, exactly?" I ask, trying to not sound as frustrated as I feel.

She stands and paces before turning on me, one hand on her hip. A flicker of my old Fallon shines through. "What I mean, you giant asshole, is that the ball's in your court."

I can't help but smirk as she comes alive before my eyes. "Ball's in my court, huh?"

"Yes, I swear to the Goddess." She rolls her eyes, and my stupid heart skips a beat. My Fal is still in there, even with everything she's been through. I know she's been wary of me but seeing her like this gives me some hope. "The ball's in your court. I want you. I want to be with you, but I'm not giving up Deacon and what I have with him either."

"And what exactly does that mean?" I ask, raising an eyebrow, because she's going to have to lay this out for me.

"It means I want you, and I want him, you big jacked-up dummy. I love you both, so I'm asking you to not make me choose, Colt. A part of me died when you died. Deacon helped bring me back to life, and what I have with him is something I'm not willing to give up. But that doesn't mean I don't love you too."

"So you want what? The three of us to be a big happy family?"

"That's exactly what I want. Deacon is on board…"

"Of course he is," I grumble, and she huffs at me again.

"He even invited you to move into the estate with us," she finishes, and my eyes go wide.

"You're living with him? Here?" Her admission knocks me on my ass a bit, taking the wind out of my sails. She nods, and it's like a junk punch. Even with everything she'd said before, the fact that she wasn't living here kind of felt like she wasn't all-in with him. But if she's here, and she's asking for this…

"I don't understand how you can even stand to look at him after what he did to you, Fallon. You said he helped bring you back to life, but he fucking *broke* you too. I put you back together after what he did to you!"

"You broke me too, Colt!"

"I fucking died, he *tortured* you!" I feel my Demon climbing to the surface, despite the leash I have him on.

"Colt, you need to move past it. I have." She sighs and drops back down onto the bed. "This is the only option before us, and the choice is yours."

"I don't want to lose you, Fallon, but I won't ever be okay with Deacon."

I throw a jab at Caleb, and he rolls away from it, laughing as he goes. The miss followed by his laughter feeds the ever-growing anger that's been burning inside my gut since my conversation with Fallon first thing this morning. Caleb hits me with an uppercut using nothing but his power, and I end up sprawled out on my ass, staring at the ceiling while he laughs his ass off.

"What has you so distracted? You haven't been this sloppy since you first woke up half-crazed," he asks as he offers a hand and pulls me back to my feet.

"Fallon," I grumble. "She came to see me this morning."

"Ah, the power of pussy. That'll do it every time." He grins, and I wanna wipe the thing off his face, but I know he's been going easy on me, and he could probably rip my soul from my body without so much as a second thought.

Always good to keep reality firmly in check when dealing with the Horsemen.

"What did she say?" he asks, trying not to laugh while

I grumble under my breath.

"That she loves me and wants to be with me."

"I don't see why that would get your panties in a bunch," he interrupts, shrugging.

"Yeah, well she also told me she loves Deacon and isn't giving him up. She put the ball in my court. Her fucking words."

"Oh, man," he bursts out laughing, and I can't help the small smile that tugs at my lips. The guy is just too charismatic. "She hit you with the ménage bomb, did she?"

"Something like that. And I have no fucking clue what to do. I love her, I did all of this for a chance to be with her, but Deacon… I fucking hate him. After what he did to her when she was here… I just can't get over that."

"I mean, I get that. I totally do, but he's also the one who risked everything to come to Morgan and the rest of us to save her. He didn't have to do that. We would've found her eventually, but it could've taken a lot longer, and Hell knows what Azriel would've done to her if he hadn't have come to us when he did."

"Yeah, I guess," I grumble. "That doesn't forgive everything else though."

"Maybe not, but if she can get over it, maybe you should Demon up and do the same. If you really love her, you'll find a way. Especially if this is what she wants and what will make her happy."

"How did you guys do it?" I ask, hoping for some small nugget of wisdom.

"Man, that feels like so fucking long ago, but it was a whole different thing for us. I've known Morgan our entire lives. Then Malik came along, and it wasn't long before Bryce worked his way into her heart. Killian was the last to join, but at that point, he just kind of completed the circle. It's not like we ever really discussed it. Demons are different from humans. We don't see relationships the same way you have your entire existence. Things are pretty fluid here, which is why the Dracul are the way they are. They come from us, it's why they're way more open when it comes to relationships. But I'm getting off track. There isn't a magic pill for making this sort of thing work. You just need to open yourself to the possibility. The biggest thing to think about, really, is are you willing to live this existence without her? You're a Demon now, that's a long fucking time. And since she's bonded to Deacon, her life span will last at least as long as his."

"They're bonded?" I ask, another dagger hits my heart with that little bit of information.

"Yeah, I thought you knew. Sorry. But that's what I mean, man. She's not going to just give him up because you say no. A bond is no joke. You saw how she was after we broke her bond with Azriel, who we still haven't found by the way, but anyway, yeah. It literally shredded her soul. Twice. She's healed now, but once a bond is made, breaking it has consequences. She would've known that going in."

"Fuck." I thread my fingers behind my head and try to process everything. Fuck doesn't seem to quite convey the vortex of suck going on inside my chest right now.

"Something like that. So like I said, can you really see yourself living without her?"

"No, but I also can't see how I'll ever forgive Deacon either."

"Well, I guess you better find a way. Otherwise your own stubbornness will be your downfall." He claps a hand on my shoulder and gives me a tight smile.

"Yeah I guess. Also, how is it even possible that Azriel has evaded you guys this long?"

"We're not sure, which pisses me off. Tracking Demons isn't really hard, but tracking a soul is a little different. We have Korrín and Ferry on it though. Malik is staying on top of it, but rest assured, the minute the asshole surfaces, we're burning him. We won't make that mistake again. I'll use fucking Shadow Fire if I have to."

"Wait, you have Shadow Fire too?"

"Yeah, Mara isn't the only one with fancy secrets." He grins like he knows something I don't. "Now enough of this, you ready for me to beat your ass some more? I want you to try and use your power the same way I did when I knocked you on your ass. I don't want you to fight with your fists. Use your power instead. This is a very small part of what you're able to do, but I don't want to take you to the pits until you're able to defend yourself properly against what's down there."

I scoff at his words but jump back in the ring. "I can handle myself. I might be a baby Demon, but I've been a Hunter a long fucking time."

"I'm hearing a lot of big talk. But you've yet to land a hit, so let's do this until you do."

I laugh as he climbs in the ring, and I bounce on the balls of my feet, ready to unleash some of the rage churning inside of me. "Bring it on, old man."

After burning off most of my rage with Caleb, I feel a little better. I ache to feel more like myself, and I know exactly what will help with that. I need a dose of happiness, so I'm going to see Remy and my nephews. The boys need some Uncle Colt in their lives. Everyone needs a fun uncle to teach them bad habits, right? I might've missed out on some big moments already, but I don't intend on missing any more. Plus, I want to check in with my sister. I missed her birthday, so I want to show my face to prove I'm not just a giant let down.

I whisper to the manor without too much effort and I'm so fucking glad that's one of the first things Caleb taught me how to do, along with the ring he gave me that holds a stone which allows me access between realms. Apparently coming here once and not blowing shit up earned me the trust to have my own stone, so I can move at will.

I know if I fuck up, he'll revoke it fast enough to make my head spin. When I emerge at the manor, it's the middle of the day. In an instant I hear a squeal and then see my nephew running toward me. I crouch down and catch him as he launches himself at me, giggling as I spin him around. "Untle Tolt!"

"Hey, buddy!" My grin practically splits my face in two as Remy jogs over to us, shaking her head. "He's really not shy, is he?"

"Not with people here, no. He's a smart little sh… cookie. He knows when people are here that they're approved by the wards we have set up, so they're good people. And while he's young, he loves with his entire heart." At her words, Raze squeezes his arms around my neck, hugging me tighter.

"That's cause he's one of us." I squeeze him back, and he squeals before wriggling to get down. I hand him over to Remy who kisses his nose before popping him on the ground. He runs back toward the manor.

"So what brings you here, brother dearest?" She loops

her arm through mine, and we stroll back toward the manor.

"Do I need a reason to come and see you, little bit?" I grin at her, and she swats at me.

"No, but you probably have one. You might be reborn, Colt Bennett, but some things never change." I let go of her and stumble, pretending to take a knife to the heart, and she laughs at my dramatics. "I did miss you, though."

"I missed you too. And I'm sorry I missed your birthday."

"It's all good. We didn't really do much this year. Last year's antics at the restaurant with a baby and a toddler were enough to teach me a lesson. And with this little madam coming so quickly after Maddox, I have a feeling we'll skip next year too. And then I'm putting a lock down on the babies for a minute. I love my kids, but I am so sick of being pregnant." I laugh at her exasperation as we walk into the kitchen, and I scoop Raze up as we cross the threshold. He squeals and giggles, summoning Levi into the room with us.

"Colt, good to see you." He nods at me, and Raze wriggles, holding his arms out to Levi. It's weird as fuck seeing this big bad Archangel of War turn to mush with his kid, but I also know Levi would literally end worlds for his family. I can't think of anything better for my family. I hand the wriggling toddler over, and Levi kisses Remy's cheek. They communicate without even speaking—it's always both awed me and creeped me out when they do that—but then Levi leaves me with Remy, who grabs me a beer and herself a cup of coffee.

Some things never change.

"So, you're here to talk about Fallon?" she asks as she sits opposite me at the island, and I laugh before swigging down half the bottle.

"She already talked to you, I'm guessing?"

"She might have mentioned she was going to talk to you, and I'm guessing since you're here, you acted like a total asshole about it?" she says, pinning me with that stare of hers that I swear I almost missed. My little sister really doesn't like bullshit. She never has.

"Something like that," I say with a shrug. "I just don't get it."

"You don't have to get it, you idiot. All you're doing by acting like a twatwaffle about it is pushing her away. I'm pretty sure that isn't what you want."

"You know it's not," I say, exasperated. "But how did everyone just forgive what he did to her?"

"Because we love her, you giant dumbass. She's a big girl who is more than competent enough to make her own decisions and judgements about people. Deacon isn't the bad guy you've built him up to be. He's risked a lot for her, probably more than you even know about, because Fallon doesn't want to push him on you. But if you love her, you need to trust her. That means trusting her decisions. If she's decided he's a person she wants in her life, you need to trust that she's made a sound decision. You don't have to like it, but if you want to be in her life, you do need to accept it. So accept it or let her go. It's not good for either of you being in this weird limbo."

I drain the rest of the bottle, letting her words sink in. I hate it when she makes sense and it isn't what I want to hear.

"So, how do we do this? You guys make it look so easy, and Caleb had about as much advice as a bag of nails."

"You take baby steps. Starting with you telling her you're willing to try. Even if you're not around Deac to start with. But you do need to accept that he'll be a part of her life, even if he's not a part of yours."

I let out a deep breath and run a hand through my hair.

When did life get this fucking complicated?

I've been a wreck for two days. I need to see Fallon and not fuck things up by running my stupid mouth. I've wanted to reach out to her for days, but I've had no idea what the fuck to say. She hasn't tried to reach out to me since our last conversation, and I can't really blame her. There's been a lot going on, and I'm still not sure where I fall on the whole being with her while she's with Deacon thing.

Despite Caleb and my sister both telling me to just give it a go, I don't know that I'm the sharing type. I pace around in the gym. The hours I've spent here working out haven't gotten rid of the restless feeling that's consumed me since I last talked to Fallon.

As if I summoned her with my mind, she whispers into the sealed gym and squeaks when she sees me. "Sorry, I didn't know you'd be here. Killian said I could work out here, but I can go."

"No, wait." I take a step toward her but then hold myself on the spot. "You don't need to go."

"Oh, okay…" she says but stands there looking as awkward as I feel.

"Fallon," I sigh, running a towel down my face. When I look back at her, she's biting her lip. Her sports bra and tight leggings accentuate every fucking one of her curves. The thigh material is like a second skin. I glance up from my slow perusal of her body, and I can't help my smirk as she stares at my sweaty chest and arms. I was working out in just sweatpants, and with the way she's looking at me, I definitely don't regret the decision. "Maybe I should go."

I make the offer, hoping she doesn't ask me to leave, but I will if that's what she wants. The last thing I want is for her to be uncomfortable, and since I don't seem to be able to think of the right words to take the discomfort away, I'll go if that helps.

"No, don't," she says quickly as her gaze rakes over my body. I move toward her, knowing I couldn't stop myself even if I wanted to. She moves at the same time, and we slam into each other. I twist her ponytail around my hand as our lips clash, and her hands roam over my sweat-slicked skin.

Our tongues tangle, fighting for control, which won't do at all. As I squeeze her ponytail harder, she melts into me like a kitten held at the nape of her neck, and it makes my dick so hard it physically hurts.

Her submission is beautiful, and I want more of it.

With one hand on her face, I pull back and groan with regret as soon as our lips no longer touch. How can I miss her when I can still taste her on my tongue?

I have more important things to think about... like where will I fuck her first?

Without letting her go, I let my gaze sweep around the room, assessing every plausible surface where I could fuck her. Where I can taste her slowly and thoroughly.

"Colt…"

Fuck, the need in her eyes, with her breathy moans just against my lips, is everything right now.

My gaze zeroes in on the weight bench, and I know it's the best thing I'll find for what I have in mind. It won't be the most comfortable, but at this point, I couldn't give two fucks. I just need to see her come and feel the wet warmth of her pussy on my dick.

"Come here, baby."

With a searing kiss on her lips, I let her go and take her hand instead, leading her to the nearest bench. It hasn't been used, thank fuck, so it's not covered in my or any other fucker's sweat.

"Are you sure, Fal? Because once I taste you, I'm not sure I'll be able to stop," I ask, because after how we left things before, I want to hear the words. I can see her answer in the way her eyes devour my naked chest but when she settles on a nod, I know I can't accept that.

"Words, baby. I need to hear you say it."

"Yes, I'm sure. I want you so badly right now, Colt." I can't deny the truth, it's written in the fire dancing in her eyes. I can't wait for her to burn me.

Once we get to the weight bench, I pull her yoga pants down all the way to her ankles, leaving a path of wet kisses along her golden, silky skin. I keep going until I get to her hidden pussy and decide to rip the remaining underwear right off.

"What is it that is so offensive about my underwear?" she mumbles the words, but I can hear the humor behind them.

"It's in my way."

"To what?" She knows what, the little minx, but I'll

play along.

"It's in my way to your sweet, deliciously drenched pussy. Your pussy is mine, and I fucking want it, so the underwear has to go."

"Oh."

I sit down and spread my legs so she has space to sit facing me. Placing a clean towel where her ass will rest, I pull her thighs on top of mine and let her legs hang behind me. The heat of her pussy is proof of her need for me.

"You're so fucking beautiful, Fal. Fates, I can feel your heat, and it's making my dick even harder than it was."

And as much as I want to just bury my cock inside her, I need to taste and touch her first. As though she can read my mind, she lifts her arms and gives me a sly little smile, telling me to pull her bra off.

Making sure I don't hurt her, I slip my fingers under the bottom band of the bra and pull it up and over her sun-kissed breasts, exposing the perky buds of her nipples. My mouth waters at the sight. My need to suck on them is just as strong as my need to sink to the hilt inside of her.

When her bra reaches her wrists, I tie it in a knot, binding her instead of pulling it off. I loop her arms around my neck, leaving her vulnerable to my every whim.

"But I can't touch you like this."

"Sure you can. Use your imagination."

Leaning her back as far as her bound wrists allow, I

latch onto her hard nipple and lavish her with my tongue. I wet the perky bud just enough so I can suck and bite and make her moan just the way I love it. She makes all the sounds I dream about at night when I wish I could feel her naked body against mine. It's even better than in my dreams. Here, I can feel her flesh heating beneath my touch. I can smell her heady scent as she rubs against me, wanting me, needing me.

"Hmm, does your pussy need some relief, Fal?"

"Yes, please, Colt. I need—"

"I know exactly what you need. You need to do as you're told and let me finish worshipping your tits. That's what you need."

Throwing her head back in abandon, she gives me complete access to her flesh. Her nipples are so hard they're practically begging me to sink my teeth into them.

So, I do.

Hard.

When she cries out in the sound mixed of pleasure and pain that she makes when she wants to protest but she wants more, I know it's time.

"Lock your legs around me."

I don't have to repeat myself. Her ankles lock at the small of my back, allowing me to slide backward, lifting her arms up over my head and giving her room to lie back down.

Her pussy is exposed, completely open to me and my watering mouth.

I trail heated kisses down the length of her calves, and then her thighs, before pulling her legs up to my shoulders and grabbing her ass cheeks. Within seconds, my mouth is on her pussy, eating her like she's my last meal.

The room is completely quiet save for her moans.

"Oh Goddess, Colt." She writhes on the narrow bench, but I've got her. I'm holding her steady as my tongue bar works its magic on her pussy. "So, good. So fucking good, Colt."

"I've missed your taste. It's been too fucking long. Any day without you is too fucking long."

Squeezing her ass cheeks just enough to cause her a little pain, I almost come in my fucking sweats when she tells me to fuck her in that throaty voice she has when she's about to come hard for me.

"Christ, Fal." My chest heaves with my need for her, but fucking hell, I haven't quite had enough of her taste on my tongue.

Fucking choices.

With one last, lingering lick on her clit, I suck that hard nub until her body begins to shake. As soon as I feel her start to climax, I push two of my fingers inside her and curl them just enough to caress the magical spot that has her mind spinning if her moans are anything to go by. Her orgasm is beautiful, and loud, and magnificent to watch. My tongue bar continues wreaking havoc with her clit as my fingers play with her innermost pleasure point, and I watch as she loses complete control of herself.

Fuck, she's the most incredible thing I've ever seen.

When she begins to come down from her high, a high that I gave her, I kiss her pussy before placing her feet back on the floor.

"I miss you, Fallon." My words are honest and heartfelt, but what I really want in the moment is to feel her all over me. To control her with my dick. To make her come all over again.

As she tries to pull herself up, I quickly strip out of my sweats and boxers before picking her up and sitting her on my waiting dick.

"Time to ride my cock, babe. You'll feel every single fucking ridge of my piercing. I want to watch you come all over me, to feel your juices running down my shaft."

Taking both of her wrists in one hand, I untie them and pin them at the small of her back. I drop another hand on her hip, guiding her as she rocks against me gently. I clench my jaw, fucking her with complete and total abandon.

She starts out slowly, tentatively sliding up and down my shaft. But when I bite one nipple and then the other, she speeds up, her moans getting louder by the second.

"Do you feel that? Do you feel how much my cock

needs you?"

Her "yes," is just a breath, a puff of air as she sinks on my dick and rubs her clit over my groin.

"That's it, beautiful. Fuck, you look so fucking good." I groan as she takes control, but I don't even care. "Ride me, Fallon. Fuck me hard, baby."

I can feel my eyes getting darker and darker with my rising desire. I need to come so fucking hard I'm afraid I might hurt her.

Christ, her pussy is a fucking glove. It's tight, wet, slippery, and hot as fuck. I could live inside her and would never have to think twice about it.

"I'm so close, Colt," she moans, but I already know she is because her walls just squeezed my dick so hard I lost my breath.

"Come for me, Fal. Come all over me."

At her first cry, I let myself go. I couldn't stop myself even if I wanted to. With her head thrown back, her mouth dropped open, and her eyes closed, she looks like a fucking Goddess.

My fucking Goddess coming all over my fucking cock.

It's the most beautiful sight in the world.

FOURTEEN

FALLON

I look myself over in the mirror and take in the shimmer of the amber dress. It's one of many gifts from Deacon, despite the fact that my birthday isn't even here yet. It brings out the golden hue of my skin and the amber of my eyes. My shiny black hair sits in waves down my back. I look fucking good if I do say so myself.

We're going to dinner with Colt, Morgan, and the guys. I'm hoping Colt and Deacon can at least be civil, especially after my conversation with Colt the other day. I'm still more than a little heartbroken about how he left it, but all I can hope is that he comes around. He certainly didn't seem to have any issues when I was riding his dick, but then, when does any man complain about that?

I slide my feet into the black stilettos decorated with nude lace and red soles. I don't know how Deacon got these pretties, or how he always seems to find something I love but would have never bought for myself, but he did.

Every. Single. Time.

It still amazes me how easy my transition to living here has been. The knowledge that, despite turning twenty-three in a few days, I'll pretty much be twenty-one forever since I'm bonded with Deacon doesn't hurt either. Easy to see why so few of these guys celebrate birthdays. I imagine once you hit a few hundred, it gets kind of old.

For me though, this is still fun, so I'll take our quiet pre-birthday dinner. Especially since I finally get to meet little Ares tonight. I understand why Morgan and the others have kept him squirreled away; a baby Demon can't be easy to tame power-wise. But also, considering who they are, there has to be more than a little risk. He's about the same age as Raze, so he'll be just so squishy and delicious, and I can't wait.

I put the finishing touches on my face with a swipe of mascara and a little lipstick and smile back at my reflection.

"Well, don't you look good enough to eat. Maybe we should skip dinner." I jump at Deacon's voice and turn to find him leaning against the doorframe in black suit pants and a white shirt that seems to only just contain the delicious planes of his muscles underneath. The wolfish grin on his face as he runs his gaze over me widens, and my skin erupts in goosebumps. I'm definitely in favor of his plan, but my manners won't let me. My mama would have my hide if she ever knew I skipped an engagement for sex.

"As much as I want to say yes and let you eat me instead of dinner, we should go. Plus, Ares," I say, grinning, and he shakes his head, holding out a hand to me.

"If that's your wish, it's my command, my love. But don't think I'm not going to enjoy you later."

"I wouldn't expect anything less," I say, almost breathless as he leans toward me, eyes heating with barely contained lust. He captures my lips with his own, kissing me with so much heat that I want to change my mind about leaving the estate.

"You really do look beautiful," he says as he pulls away. I smile, but before I get a chance to respond, he whispers us to the Shadow Palace. We emerge just outside of the throne room with the huge doors looming before us. They open as we approach, and we find everyone else already in here.

"Happy Birthday!" they shout as we enter the room, and I grin so hard my cheeks almost hurt. I didn't expect Remy and company to be here too, but I am definitely not sad about it. We make our way over to everyone and say our hellos. The guys move to one end of the table, leaving Remy, Morgan, and I at the other.

"So where is this little bundle of squishy joy that I've been dying to meet?" I ask Morgan, looking around the room but only seeing Raze and Maddox with their dads.

"He's with Mireya and Kaos. They'll be here in a minute." She smiles.

"The hell's Kaos?" I ask, and Remy chuckles softly. Before Morgan gets a chance to answer, a giant—I don't know if I'd call him a dog? He looks like a giant fucking Doberman with eyes of flame as he enters the room with Mireya at his side. A miniature male version of Morgan sits on his back.

"This is Kaos," she says as the hound moves toward us, very much a protector as he takes in every person in the room. As he nears, Morgan holds out her hand, and he dips his head so she can stroke between his ears. I swear he almost smiles, but his teeth are nearly as terrifying as his eyes. "He's my hellhound, well, one of them. He is the pack leader, and my oldest, dearest friend."

The hound, whose shoulders come up to my freaking chest, snorts back as if he understands, smoke tendrils coming from his nostrils. I almost dare not move. Morgan takes the happy cooing bundle from his back, and Mireya darts off toward Caleb and the others. "And this is Ares."

"He's so stinking cute," I gush as he pulls on her hair.

Kaos makes his way to the dais at the back of the room and lies beside Morgan's throne, watching the entire room. I daresay if anyone managed to get in here, he'd leap the table before anyone else could even blink.

Morgan places the squealing bundle of joy in Remy's waiting arms, and when his eyes light up with literal flames, she just laughs. "He really is his mother's son."

"Holy shit," I say softly, and Morgan laughs.

"Yeah, baby Demons are… well, work. Luckily he's been pretty chill. He just gets overly excited sometimes. Not that Caleb helps, of course. He loves working him up."

"Men," Remy says, rolling her eyes, and I swear every single member of the penis parade looks over at us. "Yes, you massive group of assholes."

"Can I hold him?" I ask Morgan, and she nods. Remy hands over the little ball of adorableness; his skin is almost as sun-kissed as mine, which leads me to think that Malik might be his dad. Not that they never talk about it, because they're all his dad. It's the same with Mireya, if I remember correctly. They each provide power to help create the child, but I guess Malik offered a little more with this little guy. His dark hair is curly and his eyes, when not made of flames, are a dark brown. He's so stinking cute, I swear it almost makes me want one of my own. All of my friends having babies is bad for my ovaries, but I don't even know if kids are a possibility now.

I should probably sort out a stable relationship base first, though.

Mireya stops and stares at Colt, tilting her head as she studies him. “You were in my dream.”

Everyone goes quiet, and Caleb moves over to her, crouching beside her. “He was, we already talked about this, remember?”

“I remember,” she says nodding, “but I dreamt about him again. He died, there was so much death, so much blood. It’s strange seeing him as if he’s a ghost, but he’s not. That’s why I was so scared when I saw him the first time. I thought he was here to hurt me.”

“Colt would never hurt you, sweetheart. He’s Mara’s brother, which means he’s family.”

“So he won’t try to steal my body, like the other man tried?”

“No, sweetheart,” Caleb says, but looks back over at Morgan with a worried frown. “Nobody is ever going to hurt you.”

“Okay,” she says with a smile, and then skips over to where Kaos is sitting and plonks herself down beside him.

Everyone stays quiet, just watching her, and I get a horrible sense of foreboding. It doesn’t take long for everyone to shake it off, and I lose focus of the conversation while I play with Ares. When he starts to fuss, Malik appears and takes him for a feeding. With that, everyone shuffles around, and I end up sitting at the other end of the table between Colt and Deacon. Despite the obvious tension between them, thanks to everyone else being here, it's actually an amazing evening.

Time flies by in a whirl of food and laughter, and I really do laugh so hard I cry at times. Plus, watching Mireya with the other kids is just adorable. Raze looks at her like she hung the moon. But him and Ares are also fast friends while Maddox snoozes in a sling on Roman's chest.

I'm so full I could burst, but then Morgan snaps her fingers and a giant cake appears with more candles than I want to count, and I smile wider than I thought possible.

"Happy Birthday, Princess," Deacon leans over and murmurs in my ear before kissing my cheek. I can feel Colt's eyes on me, but when I turn to face him, he's smiling. I'm grateful he's not being a dick about me being here with Deacon.

They sing happy birthday to me, and I laugh the whole way through, trying not to look as embarrassed as I feel. The joy on Raze and Ares faces as they get their cake makes my entire night. Malik and Killian end up taking their two to bed, while Bryce heads out after saying he needed to check in on something. Remy and the others leave to get theirs down too, leaving me with Morgan, Caleb, Deacon, and Colt.

Interesting crowd.

"You want a drink?" Colt asks, and I nod. He pours me a tequila sunrise from the bar in the corner and brings the bottle of whiskey over with four glasses for the rest of them.

"Thank you for tonight," I say to Morgan and Caleb, who both just wave me off.

"It was fun. I love getting everyone together." Morgan smiles at me as Caleb pats her leg.

"She's right, she loves having the excuse." He grins as she leans on his shoulder.

Deacon shifts in his chair looking serious all of a sudden, and Caleb straightens in response. "What's up?"

Deacon sighs and rubs his chin before throwing back a shot of whiskey and then pouring another. "You guys killed The Carver, right?"

"Woah, there's a blast from the past," Caleb exclaims while shadows fill Morgan's eyes.

"We did. Why?" she asks, her voice much colder than it was before.

"We've had a few… deliveries at the estate the past few weeks. They look like his handiwork. I also had my father's head and my mother's heart delivered to me. We're looking into it, but I wanted to check with you guys because I was sure he was dead," Deacon tells them. Colt stays quiet, but he looks almost as serious as Caleb. I can tell he's angry from his clenched fists.

"Well, I mean, you know who his apprentice was… and we've not found him yet," Caleb says, and it's like a bulb lighting in my mind.

"Azriel?" I ask, and he nods.

"Yeah, The Carver had a few, but that's how Azriel ended up in the position he was in. The Carver was legendary when my father ruled here. He was my father's favorite torturer. By the time I got around to dealing with him, Azriel was firmly established as his second in the level. He wasn't such a giant dick back then, so it made sense for him to take over the position under the ruling that he would no longer practice The Carver's ways," Morgan says, and I swear my blood turns to ice. I know that Azriel had escaped Korrín, and I know that the hunt is ongoing, but the thought that he could be the one behind the mess those bodies were in… just no.

"Surely we would've noticed if he'd reformed?" Caleb mutters, and Morgan shakes her head.

"It depends on whether he got himself a new body or latched onto someone else the way he did with Fallon. He's a parasite, in every sense of the word it seems, so either could be possible," she says, with a frown. "We're going to need to start a sweep."

"That's going to be a big job," Caleb muses.

"What can I do to help?" Colt asks, and we all look at

him. "If he's out there, alive, and threatening Fallon, then I want to help. Really, I'd like to tear him to shreds, which I'll happily do if I find him. I want to help."

"I'll loop you in. We need to speak with Korrín, Ferry, and Malik. We'll sort it tomorrow," Caleb says with a nod, and I chew on my lip.

"Is there anything I can do to help?" I ask, and both Deacon and Colt object almost instantly.

"I don't think so," Morgan says with a small smile. "But if I think of something that you can do to help coax him out, since I imagine the bodies are more to do with you than Deacon, despite his parents' appendages, then I will call on you."

"Thank you," I say, half relieved. Having dealt with Azriel once already, I don't fancy facing him again. The fear of him attaching himself to me the way he did before is very real indeed.

"We won't let him get to you again," Deacon says fiercely, and Colt agrees. The shock of them actually agreeing on something almost overtakes the fear of Azriel managing to fuck with me again, and Morgan just smirks.

I guess birthday miracles do happen.

ONE YEAR AGO

"Fallon, it's your birthday. You can't just not celebrate it. You already missed two in the chaos of everything that's been happening the last couple of years. One, you were kidnapped for, and the other you just lost your heirship. I get it, but this year, you need to celebrate it. Even if not just your birthday, but everything you've overcome in the last few years." Deacon tries to persuade me, almost exasperated. I accepted his ring a few months ago, and we bonded not long after. And then he realized it was my birthday. He spoils me every day as it is, and now he wants to do something big for my birthday. He's right, I've kind of ignored the last few. They haven't exactly been great, so I didn't want to remember them so much.

"Deacon, I don't need or want to celebrate my birthday. We didn't celebrate yours a few weeks ago."

"Fallon, I'm older than dirt. My birthday has kind of lost its sparkle, but you're about to turn twenty-two. You finally got your emergence; and even if it wasn't all that you hoped for, it's still a big deal. There's a lot to celebrate. Plus, you said yes just after my birthday, so we celebrated plenty." He grins, and I can't help but laugh and shake my head at him. My emergence was just an empathic skill that had already started showing itself. Though I spend so much time in the Shadow Realm these days I don't really notice it anyway. He grins as I continue to laugh. Of course he takes that as a win.

Men.

"I have everything I want already. I have you, and we're happy. Nothing disastrous has happened in like nine months. Let's not jinx ourselves by getting too carried away." I smile wryly as he takes my hand as we walk along the beach. It's so early in the day there isn't another soul in sight, and it's just beautiful here.

"Well then, I guess I'm just going to have to come up with something to do myself, and then you're just going to have to take everything I throw at you." He waggles his eyebrows at me, and I can't help but laugh at his silliness.

"You know I can take any and everything." I wink back at him, and he grabs me by the waist and spins me around. I laugh through my squeals for him to put me down, but he throws me over his shoulder and runs along the beach despite my lame protests. We reach a small alcove, hidden from sight, and he whispers us back to his estate in the Shadow Realm.

He sets me back on my feet, and it takes me a minute to process the sight before me. "Deacon… you didn't have to do this," I gasp, eyes wide. There are so many fucking wrapped presents around the room and a table set up with a candlelit dinner for two, with soft music playing in the background and it's just… it's a lot. Tears spring to my eyes.

"I know I didn't have to. But you are my world, Fallon, and I wanted to show you just how much I treasure you and your happiness. If it's within my power, then I will grant you any wish I can. This is just a small show, mostly little things I've seen you admire or things you've mentioned. Mainly, I want you to know that I'm yours, now, forever, and always."

"Oh, Deacon," I sigh happily and kiss him, pouring every drop of emotion that threatens to overwhelm me into it. I know he can feel it through our bond too. "This is all too much."

"This is nothing in the grand scheme of things, Fallon. I love you, and I can't wait to show you every day for the rest of our existence just how much." He tucks my hair behind my ears and cups my cheeks. "Happy Birthday, Princess."

"Thank you," I say, breathless. He's spoiled me beyond anything I've ever known, but that isn't why I love him. I love him because he made me whole again, and he shows me every day just why this life is worth living for.

"Now sit, I had Ellis make your favorite." He grins as he leads me to the table and lifts the silver plate cover once I'm tucked in, and I can't help but laugh. Mac and Cheese, steak, and a red velvet cupcake. The man has me figured out, that much is obvious. "This is just for starters. We

have so many tasting plates coming, so I hope you brought your appetite."

He sits down opposite me, and his grin matches my own. I almost feel guilty about being this happy, but I've learned that life is too short for that, so I just cherish these moments as much as I can.

"I definitely brought my appetite," I say, teasing him, and his eyes flash.

"Oh don't worry, pretty girl, you'll get plenty full later on too."

FIFTEEN

DEACON

I've almost lost count of the bodies that have turned up at the estate at this point. Between Locke and I, we've managed to keep most of them from being found by the rest of the household, including Fallon. After our talk with Caleb and Morgan, I'm more than a little worried about the possibility these are either gifts or threats for Fallon.

If it is Azriel who's doing this, it makes no fucking sense to me how no one has sensed him. I also don't know why he'd go about it in this way either. Is it gross and weird? Yes, but Fallon doesn't know about my history with The Carver, so the resemblance would mean nothing to her.

I can't wrap my head around any of it, and it's beginning to piss me off. I want whoever is sending the carcasses to my house to be found and dealt with. This is not how I wanted to start off our lives once Fallon moved in here.

I have enough to worry about with her, this level, and now Colt, without worrying about the bodies and the threat of Az too. I'm almost at the point where I just fucking want to burn the bodies and ignore it. The bodies are little more than a nuisance, but it's still fucking annoying that I don't know *why* they keep arriving.

I recognize a good amount of the Demons that arrive with their faces intact, but I wouldn't say I knew them. Some are part of the Demon King's court, some were my father's friends, but others I have no idea about. Which is why I'm not totally convinced that it is Azriel or expressly about Fallon. Because none of this relates to her. Not really.

I groan and rub at my temples because all of this bullshit is giving me a goddamn headache. I lean back in the chair in my study, trying to clear my mind, when I hear the door open and scent Locke.

"Is now a bad time?" he asks, and I already know what's coming when a piercing scream echoes through the halls of the estate.

"Fallon!" The growl comes from my chest, and I move faster than I ever have to get to her. The bond between us pulls me in her direction, but it still feels like I'm not moving fast enough. I find her in the main hall and discover both Fallon and what Locke was obviously coming to get me for.

The main double doors to the front are open and lining the walkway to the house are at least a dozen bodies, each hung from a lamp, each mutilated, and even with their faces it's impossible to know who they are. I move to stand in front of Fallon and wrap her in my arms so she can't see anything but me.

"Locke, get them down," I snarl, and he moves quickly, with Tex hurrying along behind Once they're outside, I slam the doors closed with my power.

"There were children," she says, her voice cold and empty. "They mutilated children."

I curse under my breath because I hadn't even really paid attention. I just wanted to stop her from seeing the very real horrors of living in this place. Which is why, despite me wanting her to move here, I didn't push her when she said she needed time. There's a lot about this place that isn't really acceptable for human sensibilities.

"I'm not sure if they were really children. Demons come in all shapes and sizes, but you should've never had to see that. I'm sorry. I'm going to ramp up the security because that shouldn't have been possible," I tell her, lifting her chin to look her in the eyes.

She looks so haunted, and I genuinely feel helpless and

so fucking angry all at the same time. She's been through so much already, and this isn't something I ever wanted her to see. There's a reason I've kept most of my past to myself. It's beyond fucked up, and that's not something I ever want her to have to experience.

It's bad enough that I lived it, but with this shit happening here, I'm questioning whether it was a good idea to have her move here. I hate that I'm doubting it due to outside reasons because I love having her here. Hopefully, if Colt does take up the invitation I extended, and I get the security increased, I can shield her from most of it. I know she can handle herself, but this is our home, and it's meant to be her safe space.

I know she talked to him about it, but beyond telling me that, she hasn't spoken much about the two of them to me. Well other than letting me know that they're working things out, and that she gave him the option to move in. Though she did explicitly tell me that I have nothing to worry about because she isn't going anywhere. I didn't even realize that was a worry until she said something about it and a weight I hadn't known I was carrying lifted from my shoulders.

What I'd like to do is clear the air between him and I because we both have some fucking issues. Mine being mainly how badly he broke her when he died without explaining what he had set up. He might've thought it was a good idea, but he didn't have to see the aftermath of it. And that gives me an idea…

"They were children," she says, rage lacing her voice, pulling me from my drifting thoughts.

"Then whoever did this will pay," I tell her, and she nods tightly.

"Yes, yes they will."

"Are you sure about this?" Fallon asks as I slide on a pair of sweatpants.

"I'd be offended if I thought you were worried about me, Princess. But yes, I am sure about this. Colt and I have some issues to work out. Both of us need to air some shit out, and this is the best way I can think of for us to move past everything."

"Are you positive you don't want me to come?" she asks, and I smile, turning to her and rubbing my hands up and down her arms. I offer her as much comfort as she'll accept because she looks totally skittish.

"I'm sure. I want you to do something fun, not spend your time worrying about Colt and I for a change. Let us boys sort this out for once." I drop a kiss on her forehead and wrap her in my arms. She sinks against my chest, wrapping her arms around my waist.

"Please don't kill each other," she mutters softly, and I smile.

"Don't worry. Caleb and Malik will be there to make sure we stay in line."

"Oh yeah," she snorts. "Having Conquest and fucking Death there with you makes me feel so much better."

"It should. They enjoy killing, not watching it. And they won't want to piss Remy off. Pretty sure letting me kill her brother would piss both you and her off, and pissing you off will enrage Remy more." I smirk, and she swats at my chest. "Plus, despite everything, neither of us wants to hurt you. I'm very aware that killing him would hurt you; so while I'm definitely going to enjoy beating his face in, I promise to leave him pretty-ish for you."

"Such a man," she chuckles.

"You know it, babe." I grin, and she shakes her head before rising up on her tiptoes and kissing me softly.

"Just be careful, please."

"Always," I tell her before pulling out of her arms because I know if I don't, I'll end up never leaving. I just want this shit over and done with. We have too many things piling up that we need to focus on, and this is just splitting my focus.

I want to find out who's fucking with us and why they sent me my parents' body parts, which are still in my fucking chiller. While I'm worried about this shit with

Colt, and how Fallon's coping with it, I'm not giving it my full focus. I know that Malik is working with Ferry and Korrín to try and find Azriel, but not having control of it myself is making me antsy. As soon as I'm finished with Colt, I'm going to talk to Malik and get shit sorted out.

But first…

"I'll see you later." I kiss her forehead again and whisper from the room down to the gym in the Shadow Palace, where I know the others will be waiting for me.

When I arrive, I find Colt already beating the shit out of a punching bag while Caleb and Malik chat next to the ring in the center of the room. As soon as Colt senses me, he stops and turns toward me, a hard look on his face.

I guess I was right. This will be the best way to clear the air. We're both born from violence, so it makes sense that this is how we'll try to sort through all the bullshit. I smile at the thought of making him pay for the shit he's put Fallon through and head over to where Caleb and Malik are waiting.

"Afternoon, gents. Lovely day out," I say, and they both laugh.

"Lovely day for blood sport," Caleb grins as Colt joins us and nods.

"Are we doing this?" Colt asks, his voice low. It's obvious his Demon is close to the surface. I'm not sure exactly *what* he is. I just know he's borne of Caleb, which could mean fucking anything for all the power that man holds. This will likely hurt if he gets any decent power hits in, but I'm hoping the centuries I have on him will count for something.

"I'm ready when you are," I say, stretching my neck from side to side before climbing in the ring. I don't bother with gloves, that's not how we've ever done things down here. When Colt notices, he takes his off.

"Try not to kill each other, please," Caleb requests, but we both know he won't let it get that far. "I don't want Mara down here kicking my ass because someone died on my watch… again." He looks pointedly at Colt who shrugs before looking at me, and I nod.

"Well then, let's do this." A bell sounds, and Colt and I bounce around each other for a minute, waiting to see who will strike first. When I see his attention dart over my shoulder, I strike. A quick one, two, landing decent enough blows to make him unsteady on his feet.

Destroy my wolf says in my mind, but I push him down.

We're not here to destroy. Just to teach the pup a lesson.

There's a corresponding grumble in my head, and while I'm distracted, Colt takes advantage and comes at me. He gets in a few good blows before roaring as his eyes go dark. "You fucking son of a bitch, moving in on my girl. Ruining all of my fucking plans."

He bounces back away from me, and I spit the blood from my mouth from his uppercut. "Well, maybe if you'd told her your fucking plans, she'd still be your girl, but now she's mine," I shout back, and from the corner of my eye, I see Caleb shuffle to see us both more clearly. "She's giving you the opportunity to be with her, and you're fucking it up."

"I don't share!" he growls, and I bark out a laugh.

"Stop being such a whiny, stick-up-the-ass human," I say, before shooting forward. I rain down blow after blow until his Demon breaks through in a burst of power, and I fly backward out of the ring. I crash into the wall.

Little fucker

"Get a hold of yourself!" Caleb commands as I climb back to my feet. Colt's control is instant, and his Demon retreats. He glares at me from where he pants in the middle of the ring.

"Maybe I should have told her, but what would that have achieved? What if it hadn't worked, and I'd never come back? Would you have wanted her just to wait for me forever because I told her I was maybe coming back?" Colt practically spits at me, and I can't help but roll my eyes.

"What I want is for you to stop being such a whiny prick about our current situation. She loves you, and you're making her fucking miserable."

"She didn't look miserable riding my dick the other day." He smirks, and Caleb jumps up and smacks him around the back of the head.

"Don't be a cocky shit."

"I know all about it," I tell them all, while Malik watches everything calmly from the sidelines. "Fallon and I have no secrets, and I trust her. I value her happiness above all else. You think I'd want you in my relationship otherwise? Fuck off.

"But she loves you, and I love her. If she wants you in her life, I'll accept that and go with it. So I suggest you Demon the fuck up, work out what you're willing to do and sacrifice for her. And if she isn't worth sacrificing your petty fucking ego, leave her the fuck alone."

The time in the ring could have gone better, but I did get a chance to speak to Malik. Thankfully, he gave me his blessing to track where the bodies are coming from, and if that is Azriel, then to deal with it. Capture is *my* only option, and since I'm sick of this 'him not dying' thing, I'll deliver him straight to Caleb and Morgan and watch with my own fucking eyes while he burns.

Luckily, Colt seems to have worked enough aggression out of his system. He'll be working with Locke and I to try to track this son of a bitch down. I can't tell if he regrets volunteering to help find Azriel now, but this is all for Fallon, so hopefully he just swallows down any bitching he might have.

I got what I wanted out in the open, so I'm past it. There's no use in dwelling on shit. That's just like injecting myself with poison. Fucking stupid and pointless.

I find him waiting in my office along with Locke. I'd like to say he doesn't look uncomfortable, but I'd be lying. Last night, I let Fallon know everything that happened with Colt and about my intentions for working with him. She seemed happy enough and didn't object, so I'm storming ahead. I'd much rather keep her out of it completely, but that isn't my way. I'll protect her until my last breath, but I won't lie to her.

Not about any of it.

"Morning," I say as I move around my desk to sit down. Locke murmurs a 'good morning' while Colt nods. "Has Locke brought you up to speed?"

"For the most part. Where do we start?" Colt asks, and I lean back in my chair.

"First, we start by identifying who the bodies are, at least the ones we don't already know. We want to see if there are any patterns to the deaths. We also need to see if we can track where they're coming from."

"I spoke to Suzie this morning. She's been looking

over the remains, and she's found evidence that the bodies are coming from the Outliers." Locke gulps as he delivers the news, and I feel myself visibly pale.

Colt goes on alert straight away, and I take a deep breath. He glances back and forth between me and Locke before asking, "What the fuck are the Outliers?"

"It's the part of the Realm where we grew up. My Father ran the Outliers. It's a dark place, and that's saying something for the Realm. It's a part of level eight but is its own entity at the same time. It makes sense that someone would be pushing the boundaries since my parents are so very obviously dead. That technically leaves me in charge of the place, but no one has reached out to stake their claim for power. So them sending this shit to my door makes little sense," I tell them, trying to wrap my head around it all.

"We should see if we can get word from whoever's running level eight these days and see if they have any information," I say, and Locke nods, jumping to his feet.

"I'm on it. Anything else?"

"That's it for now," I tell him, shaking my head.

"Why aren't we just going straight to the source? If the bodies are coming from the Outliers, why don't we just go there?" Colt asks, and I feel my wolf come to the surface. I know my eyes are red.

"The Outliers aren't a place you go to willingly. And

I'll be fucking damned if I'm going back there without confirmation of what's actually happening. Going to a place like that without a full idea of what's happening is a death sentence."

"He's not wrong. You're new to all of this, so it's understandable that you don't know. But some places are better left alone," Locke tells him before disappearing from the room.

"So what do we do now?" Colt asks, and I pinch the bridge of my nose.

"Now… now we make this estate a fucking fortress."

SIXTEEN

FALLON

"You sure you're ready for this?" Killian asks, and I grin.

"More than ready. I'm tired of being caught on the back foot, and since no one knows where Azriel is and dead, mutilated bodies keep arriving at our door, I'd rather start learning how to use the power I have access to down here. I've been the girl who needs saving before, I don't want to be her ever again."

"That's what I like to hear." He smirks and then laughs when my eyes go wide. I don't know that I've ever seen him smile like that before. To be fair, when he volunteered to train me, I was pretty shocked. I'd be an idiot to turn down training from any of the Horsemen. Morgan seemed pretty amused by my reaction at the time, and I think I'm going to learn why now. "Morgan did a quick scan, but I'm going to do another one just to see what kind of levels we're working with."

I nod, and he moves closer to me. He puts one hand over my heart and the other on my temple. Apparently, his scan is a little different from Morgan's, and I try to not startle at the contact. I've only heard stories of what the legendary Famine can do to a person by touch alone, and I'm glad he's on my side. I feel a cold rush through my body, and I pull away on instinct.

"Sorry," I say, bashful, but he just smiles at me again and shakes his head.

"No, it's me. I should've warned you beforehand." He waves me back toward him, so I take a deep breath, and he takes the position again. He's far gentler than I would've thought he'd be; then again, I haven't pissed him off, so he has no reason not to be. His power floods my system again, and I suck in a breath at the cold but stay in place. It doesn't last long, but I'm shivering by the time he pulls back.

"Tell me about the power you felt from Azriel before and about your natural powers," he says, watching me closely. I can't read him, but then I doubt anyone could. His white-blond hair and somewhat pale complexion makes him look a little like a statue even with his pointed ears and teeth. I guess him not smiling could be because he's a little self-conscious about the teeth, but I mean, he's going to be feared whether people see those or not.

I think about his words and try to find the right words to describe it. "My natural power came from the earth. I mostly did a lot of potions and poisons, but obviously I could heal too. I could call on the earth for manifestation, and because of my blood line, I could manifest more than most, though some things take more energy than others. I also had empathic abilities once I got my emergence. Mama thought they might be able to be expanded to telepathy because reading emotions isn't such a giant stretch to that apparently.

"After the whole Azriel thing, I'm not sure what exactly was him and what was Gabe channeling through me, but I had this golden light that was almost overpowering when it was mixed with my earth magic. I could have killed someone with a thought, the light burned bodies to a crisp, and I could've stripped a Witch's power without thought."

"But you haven't had those abilities since Morgan stripped his soul from yours?" He looks at me intently, like he's seeing into my soul. For all I know, he actually might be.

"I haven't tried if I'm being honest. The thought of it is more than a little overwhelming. After his soul was shredded from mine, there was the Gabe thing, and then the Colt thing, and then the whole deep pit of depression and losing my heirship thing. I haven't really had a lot of opportunity to use my power on an extreme level. But…" I trail off trying to work out how to explain it to him.

"But what?" He crosses his arms, the lean muscles rippling, and I gulp. He could probably tear me to pieces without even breaking a sweat.

"But I've noticed in the last year or so I have these… echoes, I guess is the best way to describe them. Echoes of Azriel, or his memories anyway. At least, I think that's what they are."

"Hmmm," he squints a little, as if weighing my words before speaking again. "I guess that makes sense. Have you tried to use your powers at all since being down here? Using the gifts from your bond with Deacon?"

"No, like I said, I haven't really had the need to. When I'm here, I'm swarmed by Demons either at the estate or at the palace. It's not like I'm wandering off alone." I probably should have tried to use it, should have at least been curious about it, but after everything that happened, being here and knowing I didn't *have* to use my power was a little freeing.

"Okay, let's try something," he says, walking backward to the other side of the empty room. "That should be enough. I want you to focus on your energy and try to build a shield."

"A shield?"

"Yes, like a forcefield of energy around you." I think back to the black bubbles that Remy encased everyone in back at the manor and shrug. My power has never been anything like hers, but if he wants me to try, I guess it can't hurt to give it a go. So I picture the shield in my mind, thinking about the black bubble, but nothing happens.

At least not until blades of ice start flying through the air at me. I cross my arms in front of my face and close my eyes, hoping Killian isn't about to shish kebab me, when I feel a blast of heat come from my core.

It's gone almost as fast as it appeared, and I open my eyes, finding Killian gone from the room. A few seconds later, he reappears with a deep frown tugging his lips down. "What happened?"

"Shadow Fire. A weak form of it, but it was Shadow Fire nonetheless," he says, and I swear to the Goddess my heart damn near stops.

"Shadow Fire? How is that even possible?"

"It must be from Azriel fusing your soul with a Demon. But also its likely a crossover from the power Azriel gifted to you that was never taken away, and the Angel fucking around with your power the way he did likely is a factor too. The bond with Deacon will have made it stronger, and in turn, you will have made him stronger as well. I doubt he would have ever guessed this was possible. If I was to take a shot in the dark, I'd say you're a Shadow Weaver."

"What the actual fuck is a Shadow Weaver?" I ask, trying not to freak out. I'm pretty damn sure I'm failing.

"A Shadow Weaver is someone who is able to access all elements of the shadows of the realm without actually being a Demon. It is rare, mostly because it is rare for Demons to bond with humans and give them any sort of power, but it also means that when Morgan stripped Azriel from your soul, she must have left his power behind. It may be why you have the echoes, as you called them. I will need to speak with her. But we need to see if you can access other elements of the shadows first."

"Holy fucking shit."

"Something like that. Now let's get to work, shall we?"

Only four days have passed since I first started working with Killian. And it's been four days of pushing myself to the absolute brink of exhaustion while Deacon and Colt have been chasing dead bodies. Almost literally. I've tried to stay out of it because I don't want to pry when they're obviously trying to keep the worst of it all from me. After the last bodies I saw, the ones that I still see when I close my eyes at night, I don't think I really want to know the gruesome details anyway.

Plus, by the end of each day spent training with Killian, I've been fucking wiped. Fortunately, he thinks I'm finally ready to test myself with another Demon. One I don't know. One who I can't trust to pull their punches and not squish me like the bug I am compared to these guys.

I'm kind of excited. I haven't pushed too hard because I'm aware of how lethal something like Shadow Fire can be. We've been working on me using the shadows to hide myself, and using them for transport, or as they so kindly call it here… whispering.

I make my way to the empty room in the underbelly of the Shadow Palace again and find it much fuller than I expected. Morgan is here, along with all four of the Horsemen. Deacon and Colt are here too, along with Locke and a giant hulk of a man I don't recognize. Killian grins at me when he sees me and strolls over. He's much warmer than I realized in the past. I think the cool appearance, matched with his super pale aesthetic, makes him come off as very cold, but he might just be my favorite Horseman.

Or at least he was until I saw the juggernaut over there.

Fuck my life.

"Time to sink or swim, my friend," he says once he reaches me, and I can't help but laugh.

"Nothing like an audience to add pressure," I sass, and he barks out a laugh in return.

"Pressure is the key to success, Fallon. You'll see. Now, DeVante over here is a nice guy, but he really hates to lose. Especially to a mortal. So this will be interesting." He rubs his hands together like a little kid, and I can't help but laugh with him.

"Okay, well I guess we'll see just how good of a teacher you are really," I tease as he leads me to the middle of the room where DeVante is watching me intently, as if trying to weigh me up.

Good luck, buddy.

"Fair fight, ladies and gents," Killian says and heads over to where the others are standing. Colt is wedged between Caleb and Bryce, while Deacon stands with Malik. I guess the Horsemen are here more to keep those guys locked down if anything goes wrong.

Makes sense, I guess, but it doesn't exactly fill me with hope.

"I'm going to crush you, little Witch." DeVante grins at me, his yellow and blackening teeth churning my stomach, but I keep my face void.

"You wish, meathead."

I hear a laugh from the edges, and I don't have to look to know it's Colt, so I keep my focus on my opponent. One thing Killian drove into me was to keep my cards close to the chest. He taught me to use the smaller parts of my power unless it's a life or death moment. Shadow Fire is a brutal end, and it means a complete ending for a Demon.

There's no coming back from it. Which is why they usually don't use it to kill Demons, opting to lock their souls away with Korrín to serve a punishment instead.

I drag my thoughts back to the Demon in front of me, and a dome of shadow forms around us. I glance toward Killian who tilts his head to Morgan. I mean, good idea... Because if I go full catastrophe, it'd be good to not wipe out all the people I love.

I feel DeVante drawing his power, and I reach out for the shadows, trying to prepare myself. Nothing could have ever prepared me for the assault coming my way. He runs at me, and I ground myself, ready to wrap the shadows around me and move, when he stops and pushes his hands forwards.

Lightning moves toward me so quickly I barely even see it before pain racks my entire fucking body. I fly back into the dome of shadow and clatter to the floor. My ears ring, and my face feels wet. I lift my hand, my body hurting with the motion, and realize my nose is bleeding.

Well shit. He really didn't hold back.

Fuck that.

I groan as I climb to my feet, and I reach for the shadows that naturally cling to the Demon, just like Killian taught me. I grin, even with blood still streaming over my lips from my nose. He looks smug as fuck, and that makes me want to teach him a lesson even more. I block out the shouting from outside of the dome, the ringing in my ears helps to dull the roars, and then I tug on the shadows, dropping DeVante to his knees with a roar as he freezes in place. Once he's down, I try to manipulate the shadows into a blade the way I've been practicing with Killian.

DeVante's eyes go wide as he sees the blade forming, and I grin wider. I did tell Killian I was sick of being the girl who needed saving. In just a few days, he's pushed me on a path toward not being that girl anymore.

Hands pounding on the shadow dome steals my attention, and my hold on the shadows drops. It takes less than a heartbeat for DeVante to launch his attack in response. I fall to the ground, screams shredding my throat as my bones break and crunch. "I told you, little Witch, you will never win against me."

He grins as he stands over me, and I scream again, my throat hoarse as the pain rips through me. I try to pull on the shadows to move myself out of the range of his power, but the pain is too much.

The shadow dome comes down, and DeVante's head rolls from his body. A darkness envelops the room, but I can feel Deacon through our bond. He's afraid and so, so fucking angry. In a second, he's at my side. The darkness is all encompassing, leaving me thankful for our bond.

"Colt!" I hear Caleb call. It sounds so quiet among the

darkness, but his tone sounds almost as if he's shouting. The darkness begins receding, and I see Colt, crouched in front of me. Except it's not Colt. Or at least, not the Colt I know. He is the all-encompassing darkness. It pours from him. His eyes, his claws, even his hair is jet fucking black as he growls at the others, standing between them and me. I see DeVante's body, and my stomach churns at the sight. Decapitation is not something I'll ever get used to.

"Colt, fucking rein it in," Caleb demands, and the Demon that is Colt just growls at him. "Stupid motherfucking powerful Demon of my own fucking creation." The grumble is enough to make me smile, but I realize in that moment that he's like this because of me. I get a feeling I'm the only one who can pull him back from the brink he's so obviously teetering on.

I move from Deacon's arms, my body having mostly healed, and crawl toward the Demon who is the man I love.

"Colt," I say, my voice scratchy. "Colt, I'm okay. It's okay. You don't need to protect me now."

I glance at Caleb who nods at me, and I know it's working as the cloud of darkness that ripples from Colt starts to recede. "Come back to me, Colt. I'm safe now."

Once the rippling darkness is gone, Colt still has most of his Demon features. I find that I love this side of him too. Even if it should be terrifying, it isn't to me. Maybe I really am just broken.

"Colt, shut it the fuck down," Caleb commands, and Colt's body shudders before the Demon pulls back completely, and he falls face first to the floor.

Caleb walks forward, checking Colt over. "He's knocked the fuck out. Drained, I imagine. Thank the hells for that."

"Is he going to be okay?" I ask, and Caleb looks at me with a grim smile.

"He will, eventually, after I beat his ass. I think his Demon and mine need to have a little one-on-one to remind him who his master truly is. Until Colt can control himself better, he needs that leash. When it comes to your safety, he apparently manages to ignore the usual barriers that should be in place."

I frown, and he crouches down to me. "Don't worry, Fallon. He'll be okay. Now then, let's get you fixed up properly, shall we?"

SEVENTEEN

COLT

I've been in lockdown since I hulked out in Fallon's training session, and it fucking sucks. I'm a grown-ass man, grounded like a fucking kid. On one hand, I get it. I apparently don't have full control over my Demon yet. Since he seems to have claimed Fallon as ours, I really need to get my shit in check. Caleb was pissed when I finally woke back up. I've never been that drained in my life, and then he bounced my ass around the training room like I was a goddamn rag doll, trying to teach my Demon exactly who's boss.

Apparently, I shouldn't be powerful enough to not follow his orders, and yet that's exactly what happened when Fallon was hurt.

So I haven't been allowed to leave the palace in a week. My monster requires a lesson, and that means I'm back to where I was months ago, pulling my fucking hair out. I don't see why I can't see Fallon, my monster responded to her just fine.

I hit the punching bag again, trying to get some of the roiling anger inside of me out, and the bag bursts, sand spilling all over the floor. I hear a slow clap and turn and find Caleb shaking his head, trying not to laugh. "Frustrated, are we?"

Without meaning to, my Demon growls. I beat my chest to stop that shit, but Caleb just laughs some more.

"Our kind of monsters rarely like being shut down. They rage against the restraints we put in place. I'm lucky mine doesn't need that anymore, but you aren't there yet. You need to work out what your limits are, what your trigger points are, and learn how to control them properly."

"Well, obviously Fallon is a big trigger point, but I imagine anyone I love being hurt would be the same. As for my limits, I thought we were going to go to the pits to test those out properly?"

"We will," he says nodding. "But since your Demon seems to be under control well enough for now, I think it's safe enough for you to roam the Realm. I'm still hesitant about you leaving here, even if your Demon isn't as strong on Earth. The last thing we want is accidental collateral damage."

"Okay, I guess I can live with that for now. I'm going to keep working to get my shit sorted out, though, because I refuse to miss out on my nephews' childhoods."

"I understand that. We'll get you to a point where you're ready. I just underestimated how strong you would be. I've never made a Demon other than Mireya or Ares, and that process is a little different.. Still, I'll be here to help you every step of the way."

"Thank you for loosening my leash," I say with a sarcastic smirk, and he rolls his eyes. "Deacon and Fallon invited me to move into the estate. I think I'm going to do it."

"Oh really?" He looks genuinely shocked, which means I've been a bigger prick than I thought. "You sure that's a good idea?"

"Deacon and I are working through our shit, and I'd rather be close to Fallon. No offense, you guys are awesome…"

"But we're not your girl. I get it. Just know you'll always have a home here if you need it."

"Thanks, man," I say, clapping a hand down on his shoulder. "But I think if this thing with Fallon and me is going to work, I need to at least be close to her."

"What about the whole ménage thing?" he asks, and I

know he's trying to push my buttons, but fuck it.

"I'm still not on board with it all, but I can be civil, and Deacon wasn't wrong about one thing. If I want her, and I love her, I need to put my ego aside."

"Look at you, growing up and all that shit," he laughs, and I shake my head, throwing my towel at him. "But honestly, I think it's a good step. Keep an open mind, like I said to you before. If you love her, you'll make it work. And if you need to rage out, the gym is always here for you."

"Thanks."

"Now then, we need to sort out when we're heading to the pits. Killian wants to take Fallon there too, so I figure we probably shouldn't go at the same time after last time."

"Yeah, probably not. But we'll work it out. I'm still trying to help hunt down the asshole who's sending bodies to the estate, so maybe once I know Fallon is safe, it'll be easier for me to go?"

"Makes sense. And if you guys need any help with the bodies…"

"We know where to come."

"You really want to do this?" Fallon asks again, despite the fact that I'm standing in the entry hall of the estate with my bags at my feet. Deacon stands beside her, completely unreadable, but I know he probably isn't completely ecstatic that I decided to take him up on the offer.

"Fallon, he's here. That should be proof enough that he wants to do this," Deacon chuckles, his hands squeezing her shoulders before moving toward me with a smile, shocking the shit out of me. "Let's get you settled in."

He picks up one of the bags, and my gaze bounces from him to Fallon, who looks amused as fuck at my shock. I pick up my other bag and smile back. "Let's do this."

Fake it till you make it, right?

I lift the strap of the bag onto my shoulder and follow Deacon up the giant fucking staircase in the room, realizing quickly this place is a fucking maze. I'm definitely going to get lost here more than once.

Fallon trails behind us, and I slow down a little to let her catch up to me. "You sure you're okay with me moving in here?"

"Of course. I mean, it was Deacon's idea, but I'm happy you're here. I just don't want you guys clashing or whatever since we're all in one spot."

"I'm working on my issues. I just want you, and I want you to be happy. If that means stuffing my ego in a fucking box, I'm going to try. But my monster has claimed you as ours, Fal, so you're not getting rid of me that easily," I tell her as I take her hand.

"Okay, good." She smiles and squeezes my hand. We walk in a comfortable silence for a few minutes, following Deacon through the maze. "Oh, he's put you near us."

"Yeah?"

"Yes. Our room's the one at the end," she says, pointing to the unassuming double doors on the opposite end of the hall.

"This is you," Deacon announces, stopping at a door on the other end of the hall from theirs, but I guess that makes sense. He opens the door and motions for me to enter.

The room is much bigger than I expected, with a far wall that is almost entirely glass. It looks out over the back of the estate and the lush, well-tended gardens. The black iron framing is beautiful, and I find myself hoping it isn't salted iron. The ceilings are high, and mixed with the windows, the room looks fucking massive.

There's a four-poster bed on one side of the monochrome room, with a navy sofa at the end of it. There's a TV, plus a black dresser almost in the middle of the room, dividing the space. On the other side of the room are two doors, and in the corner hanging from the ceiling by a chain is a punching bag. "I had it put together for you once I made the offer. If anything isn't to your liking just let Locke or I know, and we'll get it sorted for you."

"Thanks, man," I say, still kind of in awe of the room.

"No worries, I'll let you get acquainted with everything. I need to go sort some stuff out with Tex. I'm sure Fallon will help show you around," he says with a wink before moving over to her, dropping a kiss on her cheek and leaving the room.

"He's really something, huh," I say to Fallon. It sounds way more sarcastic than I meant it to, and she frowns. "I didn't mean it like that, I just mean… I don't know. I'm going to shut up before I put my foot in my mouth."

"He's a good man. I'm sure you'll come to see that eventually. Is this all okay for you? It feels weird this being your room and that being our room, but since you guys aren't seeing eye to eye, we figured this might be the best idea for now..." she rambles, standing almost awkwardly in the space. I move to her and wrap my arms around her waist. She plants her hands on my chest as she looks up at me, and I can't help but smile.

"This is more than okay. I'm here with you, and that is literally all that matters. I could be in a cupboard, but as long as you were there with me, I'd be fine."

"Such a sweet talker," she says, and my grin widens.

"You know it, baby." She laughs at me, swatting my chest. "Now, let's check out more of this room, and then you can show me around this maze so I don't get lost trying to find food, yeah?"

"Sounds good to me. I got lost here plenty when I

was here before… with Azriel." My monster stirs at the mention of her time here back then, but he doesn't seem like he's going to beast out, so I leave him half-aware.

"This is the same place?"

"Yeah, but Deacon's done a lot of work to the place since then. It doesn't really look the same anymore. And the floor where I was held is completely different now. You'd never even know it was the same place from the inside."

"And you're okay being here?" I watch her closely. Because if she's not, I'll have us all out of here in a fucking heartbeat.

"I'm good. I've dealt with my time here and everything that happened. I'm stronger for it, and I wouldn't be who I am now without it. None of us would be. So I can't regret the experience. I embrace who I am, even the darker, twistier parts. I just hope you can do the same. Not just for me, but for you… and for Deacon."

I let out a deep breath and consider her words. She's not wrong. None of us would be where we are now if everything hadn't happened the way it did. While I'd prefer some of it be different, I wouldn't change the fact that I'm here with the ability to protect her like I never would've possessed otherwise, and we're together.

I guess everything really does happen for a reason, even if the fates are a little fucked up in the way they got us here.

"I promise to try," I say before leaning down to kiss her chastely. "Now let's explore."

"Let's do it!"

It's been a week, and the jury's still out on whether moving to the estate was the best or worst decision I've ever made. At least Fallon's here in arm's reach, all day every day. I'm looking forward to getting reacquainted with her. We've had some bad moments recently, and we haven't reconnected since I moved here, so I want to show her just how much I love her, how much I've missed her, without words. My words always seem to get me in fucking trouble anyway.

Now that I'm settled in and I've finally taken the steps to get this thing between us off the ground, I want to show her I'm here for this. All of it. Well, the me and her part of it anyway. I'm not quite ready for the rest.

I just need to find her, without getting lost in this maze of a place. I finish dressing, and I'm just pulling my black tee over my head when there's a knock at the door.

I open it to find my girl staring back at me. I guess she found me instead. I take her hand and pull her into the room. She squeaks out a laugh, and I slam the door, pushing her up against it. "Hey, beautiful."

"Hey, yourself," she says, almost breathless. I hear her heart rate pick up and grin down at her. She might've been afraid of me when I hulked out, but she's definitely not afraid now.

Mine, my Demon says in my head, and I couldn't agree more. The urge to show her just how much she's mine is overwhelming. I want to mark her, and I feel my teeth elongate a little, like they did when I hulked out.

Not right now, we don't want to scare her off, I tell the Demon, and he withdraws a little. I feel my teeth retracting back to normal, and I focus back on my wide-eyed girl.

"Your eyes," she gasps, reaching up to touch my face. I close my eyes, realizing she means I've gone all Demon on her. "No, don't hide from me. I want to see all of you."

When I open my eyes again, my Demon roars in my head. Glancing down at her, I only last a second before I pull her against me, kissing her hard enough to bruise her lips. Need for her swells inside of me. I missed this too much, and I need to show her just how much she is mine.

With both hands on her cheeks, I let my tongue invade every inch of her mouth. I scorch her with my presence, making sure she can feel me all around her.

"My monster… He wants you too, Fallon. And I don't want to stop him." The gasp that travels from her mouth to mine isn't filled with fear. I can sense her desire emanating from each of her pores.

She wants this. I can feel it, even if she doesn't know it yet.

Inside my head, my Demon purrs with satisfaction knowing his day will come.

My body vibrates with pent-up need. I'm making a mental checklist of all the filthy things I have planned for her, but she blows my mind by handing me her wrists, offering me her complete submission.

I have no idea how the fuck I manage to not come in my fucking pants on the spot. With her fists closed, wrists facing each other, she looks up at me, silently telling me she's mine. Her eyes are amber pools of trust that make my black heart beat faster for her. Her mouth parts slightly with trepidation and need. Her cheeks are rosy with the flush of her desire. I'm a fucking goner for this woman, and I always have been.

I think my monster might just be a goner too.

I don't need to ask her to know that my eyes are as black as coal, because I can feel my teeth slowly elongating again as my monster pays closer attention.

Control. I need control over myself so I don't scare the living fuck out of her. Though, she has to get used to the idea of loving who I am now.

My gaze falls to her wrists just as my hands cradle her offering, bringing them to my lips where I gently kiss each of her knuckles. I linger on the last one, and then, with my lips barely ghosting her skin, I whisper, "Thank you for the gift of your trust. I will protect it, but make no mistake, Fallon, I will fuck you to within an inch of your life. Are you ready for that?"

The half a second it takes for her to respond is the longest of my life.

"Yes. I'm yours for the taking. Both of you."

I can't help the faint bite mark I leave on her last knuckle, as if it's a contract and I've just signed my love and my life away to this incredible woman.

"So it shall be."

Without giving her a second to backpedal on her words, I bend at the knees just enough to clasp her thighs in my hands, lifting her against the wall. My mouth crashes down on hers, and we kiss each other with an intensity that makes my Demon rattle the bars on the cage of my control. Fallon moans into my kiss as our tongues tangle, fueling my need for her. Her little body tries to hurry me along by rubbing against my steel-hard dick.

Fuck, the things this woman does to me.

I push harder into her, letting her feel my dick while silently reminding her of all the things I plan on doing to her.

Our mouths never parting, I turn her around and carry her to the bed. We both fall on it with me landing on top of her, bracing myself on my elbows so I don't crush her under my weight. I can't get enough of her taste, of her kisses. She pulls on my hair, tightening her fingers painfully with every passing second.

I'd let her rip that shit all out if it meant I got to kiss her like this forever.

"Strip."

Complete sentences aren't possible right now. If I try to use up any of my mental power on speaking, I might just lose the battle against my Demon and scare the fuck out of Fallon. She may have given herself to me and my Demon, but she doesn't really know what that means—my beast is different to Deacon's. The consequences of her promises could prove to be too much for her. Even if she did see what we were, though I know he wouldn't hurt her, I don't want to scare her at this moment.

Kneeling on my haunches, I watch with rapt attention as she slips off every article of her clothing, one by one, her gaze never wavering from my own.

The intensity of the moment is almost suffocating, though in a good way. Like I'm waiting for the next breath, and it's one that only she can give me.

"You're fucking beautiful, you know that, right?"

"So you keep telling me—"

I cut her off just as she bites her bottom lip. That one little action breaks a piece of my control, making it almost impossible for me to keep from biting it for her.

With one hand at the nape of her neck, my fingers digging into her skin, I let my own teeth sink into that delicious flesh, reveling in the taste of her blood. The pure and unique essence of her life.

Fuck. Knowing her life is on the tip of my tongue is such a heady feeling.

When she's finally naked and completely bared to me, I pull her close, placing her legs on my shoulders so I can bring her pussy to my mouth and feast on her.

My tongue explores, licking at her soaked walls, biting on her clit, and sucking up every inch of her flesh until her moans are like music filling the room.

With each lick, I can feel my Demon trying to break through my control.

My teeth are longer, scraping more easily at her. My nails are sharper, digging into the flesh of her ass and undoubtedly leaving my mark for later. My eyes, I know, are black as night as I devour her every drop.

"Oh, Colt, oh Goddess, I can't..."

"Don't hold back, Fallon. Come on my face, do it right now!"

And the beauty in her submission is her capacity to let herself go completely at the sound of my command.

Like a dam being released by the power of my words, she comes as beautifully as she breathes.

My tongue laps up her orgasm as though it's the only reason for my heartbeat. So strong is my need for her that I push up against her, her legs folding between us as I drink up her orgasm, lapping at her until she can no longer handle it.

Fallon's hands fall to her side, her chest heaving with the effort of breathing. Her nostrils flare with her heavy pants, and she's never looked more beautiful.

Sated is a great look on her.

Undoing the button and the zipper of my jeans, I let my dick out. Before she recovers fully from the aftershocks of her orgasm, I'm inside her right down to the hilt. Her entire torso arches at the intrusion, giving me the opportunity to slide my hands around her and let her legs fall to the side of my thighs. I pull her into a sitting position, delving even deeper inside of her. We both exhale roughly at the feel of our union. It's been far too long.

Hell, an hour of not being inside her is too fucking long for me.

I have one hand in her hair, and the other pushes down on her shoulder as I look deep into her eyes, trying to read her soul.

"Ride me, Fallon. Fuck me like your life depends on it."

I don't know where she pulls her strength from, but she doesn't hesitate. Sitting up on her knees, she bobs up and down on my shaft, her hands on my chest, our eyes transfixed in one another's gazes.

"Feels so good," she whispers the words across my lips, and my Demon purrs at the sensation.

"My Demon wants you, Fal," I tell her honestly, expecting a flinch at the revelation.

It never comes, which fuels my hope that this could actually work.

"Colt?"

"Yeah, baby?"

"I want your Demon. I want him to fuck me like I'm his."

All.

Fucking.

Hell.

Breaks.

Loose.

The last barrier separating me from the Demon explodes into a million pieces, and I find myself completely naked. My jeans are gone, and I have no idea how they came off. Fallon is no longer riding my cock, she's lying on her back, legs spread and pussy in perfect view of my black eyes.

She doesn't look scared. She looks excited, like this is the thrill of a lifetime.

Fucking hell, I may not survive this.

With my cock in my hand, I see the black tips of my

fingers and the long claws that lightly scrape my skin with every hard pull I take.

My teeth are elongated, making it harder to speak, but it doesn't matter.

"Give me your ass."

With a sly smile curving her beautiful lips, Fal rolls to her side before climbing on all fours and pushing out her ass to present her pink hole to me.

Careful not to hurt her, I grab onto her ass cheeks and squeeze just enough to leave a red imprint of my fingers.

Leaving a mark on her satisfies my Demon, though not entirely. It's not enough, and he wants more. But it will have to be enough for now.

Grabbing the lube from the bedside table, I open the cap and let a long string coat the rim of her asshole.

I'm fucking panting, the need to take her everywhere fucking possible is like a fucking mantra beating over and over in my head. I want to be everywhere, touch everything, feel all of her completely.

Once she's properly lubricated, I slowly push in one finger, then two. I fuck her carefully, knowing that my claws could hurt her.

"Fuck me, Colt. Please stop teasing me."

I'm done.

Just fucking done.

Coating lube all over my dick, I push in the head,

retreat once, and then slam into her like the fucking beast that I am.

Fallon's cry is like music to my fucking ears. It's pain-laced pleasure and a dash of 'fucking finally'.

I place both hands on her tits, fucking her with abandon. In and out, I pound her ass like it's the last fuck I'll ever have.

She scrambles for leverage, her head so damn close to the headboard I'm afraid I'll hurt her.

Still, I can't stop. I can't keep my Demon from giving her everything we have. The sound of my skin slapping against hers is like gasoline on the fire of my lust. Part of me expects Fallon to beg me to stop, but she doesn't.

She calls out for more, over and over again, and I can't wrap my fucking mind around how goddamn perfect she is.

One hand leaves her tit and travels down to her pussy, where I push in three fingers and fuck her like my own personal toy. In tandem, my dick in her ass and my fingers slamming against the trigger deep inside her, I fuck her until her breath catches and her orgasm lets loose from every pore in her body.

When both her ass and pussy squeeze my dick and fingers, I let myself go as well.

Leaning in, I allow my Demon to do what it's been begging to do for weeks.

Right at the nook between her nape and her shoulder, I sink my teeth into her flesh and come harder than I ever have all the while marking her like the fucking animal I have become.

My cock inside her ass, my fingers pressing her g-spot as my thumb presses against her clit, and my teeth leaving my mark on her skin, I own Fallon.

We both own her.

We are hers, and she is ours.

EIGHTEEN

FALLON

The last few weeks have been somewhat uneventful, which has been so fucking nice. No dead bodies have shown up on our lawn. There hasn't been any fighting between Deacon and Colt. We haven't had anyone trying to blow up our lives. I've been training with Killian almost daily, and while it almost feels like it isn't needed, I'm not going to stop. I'm not foolish enough to think that we might finally have found some semblance of normal, for fear of fucking it up, but it's definitely been easy to appreciate life for a minute.

"Is there cheesecake?" I ask Ellis as we start putting the finishing touches on the main course dishes. Remy and

Creek are coming to the estate for dinner, and since it's their first time here, I might be a touch nervous.

Deacon is off with Locke for the night chasing down another lead. I know he's beyond frustrated that they've had very little luck figuring out who the fuck is messing with us, and even more frustrated there's still no sign of Az, but I don't really want him to go to the Outliers. Even if that's where all of the bodies are coming from, I feel his fear through our bond every time the place is mentioned. We haven't really spoken about his past much, and I get it. He's old as dirt, which I enjoy teasing him about, and there's a lot of time to cover. A lot of horrors from growing up in this place. But sometimes I wish I could just help him deal with it.

"Yes, I made chocolate brownie cheesecake," Ellis says with a smile, pulling me from my thoughts, and I do a small fist pump.

"If there's one way to swing Remy's mood, it's cheesecake." I laugh, and Ellis shakes his head.

"I'll have to remember that. Everyone is a little freaked out about having a Shadow Walker come here," he admits, and I gulp.

This is exactly why I've not really spoken to anyone except Deacon and Colt yet about the whole Shadow Weaver thing. I don't want to be feared, and Deacon doesn't want an even bigger target on my back. It makes sense to keep it as need-to-know info. Morgan, the Horsemen, and Colt are on that list, and no one else needs to know. Not yet. I especially don't want to scare the people in our home. While I understand their fear, I don't have to like it. And it does make me a little sad that Remy is instantly feared, though I'm sure she'd likely get a kick from it. "Remy is a softie. You'll see."

"It's just her and her Demon coming, right? The Archangel isn't coming?" he asks, his hands shaking a little.

"No, Leviathan is staying home with Raze," I reassure him. and he lets out a deep breath. Now that fear is one I totally get. Levi can be fucking terrifying.

"Oh, thank hells."

I chuckle softly and head back to the dining room to make sure everything is all set out. It looks a little fancy, but my mama taught me that hosting is never a small task. And since this is their first time here, I feel a weird sense of pride at presenting the place properly. Deacon let me help redecorate the estate over the last few years, so it really does feel like home and not at all like the place that was once my prison.

"They're here!" Colt yells from the main entrance hall, and I startle before rushing out. He takes me by the shoulders and squeezes me. "Chill, Fal. It's just Remy and Creek. We've known them forever. They're not going to care what the place looks like."

"You don't know that," I hiss, very aware that I'm being more than a little extra right now.

"Yes I do," he chuckles and kisses my forehead before the front door bursts open and Remy crosses the threshold.

"Honey, I'm home!" she calls out, and I start laughing before darting over to her and hugging her tightly. I notice Colt and Creek saying hi while she hugs me so tight I can barely breathe. I take it though because I've missed her massively.

She pulls back and takes in the giant entry hall, her eyes going wide. "I should put in a complaint to Levi. How come we don't have a giant sweeping staircase?"

Creek laughs and shakes his head, "Hey, Fal. How are you doing?" He hugs me tightly too while Colt says hello to his sister.

"We all know if you even hinted to Levi that you wanted a staircase like this, he'd tear the manor apart to make it happen," Colt teases, and Remy scoffs but then grins.

"You're right, he totally would. Maybe after this one is a little older. The house is in enough chaos right now as it is."

"How are you doing with the pregnancy this time?" I ask as we move through the hall toward the dining room, while Colt and Creek walk and talk behind us.

"It's okay, though I swear, every day with this one makes me feel like I'm a bottomless pit of hunger. The boys gave me heartburn, but she just makes me want to eat everything in sight."

"I'm sure you and Nonnie are real sad about that," I tease, and she laughs.

"Yeah, it's not exactly a hardship on any of us. Though Nonnie is in full-blown grandma mode with the boys, and now with a baby Dracul on the way... Let's just say she's beyond excited."

"I still can't get over the fact that you can just birth any species."

"What can I say, I have a magical vajay," she laughs, shaking her head. "But honestly, I think it's possible for everyone, it's just that interspecies stuff hasn't ever really been a thing before. All of my kids seem to be whatever their father is, with a sprinkle of just a little bit extra from me. I'm not complaining. As long as they're healthy and happy, I'm good. How are you guys doing since Colt moved in?"

"It's been… good. A working peace. He's still not in the whole 'let's all be one big happy family' mindset, but he's here for me, and he's being civil with Deacon. I can't ask for much more, right?" I say with a shrug as we move into the dining room.

"Girl, damn. Look at this fancy pants set up for little

old me. It's beautiful." I blush a little as she fusses, and we both take a seat. I notice Colt lead Creek past the door, winking at me as he does, and I realize he's giving me some time with my friend. That right there is just another reason I love him.

"So come on, spill, give me all the details," Remy says in the moment before her stomach growls so loudly it almost startles me.

"Maybe after dinner?" I say, trying not to laugh.

"I heard that from down the hall!" Colt yells a few seconds before Creek and he walks back through the door. "Ellis is on the way, so I guess grub's up."

Remy rubs her stomach, and Creek kisses the top of her head before taking the seat next to her. Colt sits beside me, naturally. Remy picks up her cutlery and grins like a kid. "Thank the Fates for that."

After eating more than any one person should, I groan and push my plate away. "I can't eat another bite."

"Amateur," Remy snorts and adds another serving of the stroganoff to her plate. "Ellis is a fucking culinary wonder."

"He's no Nonnie," Creek chuckles, "but considering your love for food right now, we won't tell her how much you enjoyed it here."

"Good plan, Batman." She grins at him before groaning around another mouthful of the beef dish.

Deacon pops his head around the corner and smiles once his gaze finds mine. "Hey, just wanted to let you know I'm back. Hey, everyone."

"Hey, Deac, how are you doing?" Remy asks between mouthfuls, and he chuckles at her softly.

"I'm good, just a long day."

"Did you find anything?" Colt asks, and all the focus in the room shifts to Deacon.

"We did, and we'll need to follow up tomorrow if you're game."

"You know I am," Colt affirms.

"Anything I can help with?" Creek asks, wiping his mouth with the cloth and focusing on Colt and Deacon.

"Maybe," Colt says standing. "You girls good if we leave you to it? I'll get Ellis to have the cheesecake on standby?"

"There's cheesecake?" Remy groans happily. "Hell yes, go away so we can talk girl shit, please."

"You sure?" Deacon asks, looking between Remy and I.

"Of course we're sure. We can't discuss the penis parade if you're all in here, can we?"

"Please don't talk about my dick," Colt groans before

dropping a kiss on the top of my head. He moves over to Deacon, and Creek follows.

"No worries there," Remy says, waving as they leave. I feel a pang through the bond from Deacon and smile. At least I know he actually is okay, even if he is a little tired. "So now, back to where we were before dinner. How are things going here, really?"

So I tell her all about the discovery of me being a Shadow Weaver and my training with Killian, the fight with DeVante, and seeing Colt's Demon for the first time. I fill her in on the bodies, Azriel, and the echoes I'm left with from his time attached to my soul. I tell her all of it, and she barely says a word until I'm done. Even then, she just sits next to me, looking kind of stunned.

"Shit, that's… well first off, hello my badass friend, welcome to the shadow club. Second, it's weird to think of my brother as a Demon, but I totally want to push his buttons now and see if he hulks out. I'm sure that makes me a terrible person, but I'm his little sister, pushing his buttons is what I do."

"Maybe wait until you're not pregnant?" I suggest, laughing. She tilts her head as if pondering the idea.

"Yeah, maybe. I don't want Colt to end up dead or anything, I guess. But I definitely want to see which of us would win. It's been a while since I fought Caleb, and that was pretty even, so I'm pretty sure I'd still take Colt."

"You guys are way too competitive," I tease, and she nods.

"Yes, yes we are, but it's so much fun squashing his ego." She grins as Ellis walks in with the cheesecake. "Holy shit, what is that?"

Ellis almost drops the cake at the sound of her voice but manages to get a grip on it before the worst happens. "This is a chocolate brownie cheesecake. Fallon said cheesecake was your favorite, followed by brownies, so I figured we'd put the two together."

"You are my hero, Ellis." She grins, and his hands tremble as he puts the dessert on the table.

"You can take the rest of the night off," I tell him, and his eyes go wide.

"But the clean-up—"

"I've got it," I tell him, though he almost looks nervous. "It's fine, I promise."

"As long as you're sure."

"I swear I am." He nods quickly before scooting out of the room like his ass is on fire.

"You seem to have settled into your place here nicely," Remy says softly.

"It's a little weird. I have no job, no real responsibilities, and everything gets done around me. I don't even have to clean. It's a long way from how I grew up, but it's been fun spending my time doing things because I want to, rather than because I have to. I do miss Mama and Rebel like crazy, but I also check in with them pretty regularly thanks to the note system I discovered a few years ago. They're both super busy with all things coven, so I don't have to feel too guilty about enjoying my time here."

"Do you think you're going to make the move permanently?" she asks, and I bite my lip.

"Maybe. My bond to Deacon means I'm essentially immortal too. The thought of seeing the people I love grow old and die while I stay the same hurts me a lot. Even though the Hunters don't age like they used to, my Mama and Rebel are still mortal."

"I get that, I do. You should talk to Kain about it, maybe? He's really good at this stuff, whereas my words aren't so great." She grins. "Give me a sword, however, and I can literally set the world straight."

"Oh I know," I laugh. "And yeah, I might talk to Kain. I guess all of your guys have been around for forever and have gone through this stuff before. I hadn't even thought about talking to them."

"Of course, what else are friends for? I'd say talk to Emrys for a woman's point of view, but I'm pretty sure she's more twisted than I am."

"Yeah, I kind of got that from your birthday night. Girl has some interesting views on the world. I guess spending her entire life as a Reaper would do that to a girl."

"Yeah," Remy says, eyeing the cheesecake.

"You just want a fork to attack it don't you?" I laugh, and she nods, not looking even a little bashful about her love for the dessert. So I hand her a fork from the end of the table, and she grins back at me. "Have at it."

Once Remy and Creek leave, I go to my room and find Deacon passed out in our bed. I don't want to disturb him since he's been working so hard dealing with everything and making sure that none of it affects me, so I creep back out of the room and close the door softly.

I hear soft music coming from the far end of the hall and find myself standing outside of Colt's room, debating whether or not I should knock. The door opens, and I let out a squeak when Colt appears in the doorway, putting a hand over my mouth so I don't scream too loudly. His eyes flash to black as he keeps his hand over my mouth and uses his other to pull me in the room. "Fancy finding you here."

"I was er… not tired?" I say, trying to explain being weird and creeping outside of his door rather than just knocking.

"Same. It was fun seeing Remy and Creek. I miss him way more than I thought I would."

"I'm not that surprised, you two were kind of

inseparable for a good while. Life's just sort of pulled you in different directions. You know you can have him here whenever though, right? This is your home now too."

"I know, I'm still adjusting to that. I'm sure I'll get there, though. But thank you." He smiles at me, and despite the fact that he has me pinned against the door, he seems softer than usual.

"Are you okay? For real?" I ask, looking up at him. He still looks like my Colt, the same guy I grew up crushing on, but the light behind his eyes is a little dimmer, and some of his cheekiness has disappeared. I can't help but be sad about that.

"I'm good," he says softly, caging his arms around me. "So what are you doing here really?"

"Deacon's passed out, and I didn't want to disturb him. I'm really not even close to tired."

"You want to just chill? It's been a while since we just hung out," he says, and I smile.

"That sounds amazing."

"How the fuck did you guys get Watchbox here, by the way? I keep meaning to ask. It's fucking awesome though."

"Honestly, I have no idea, I just never complain. Remy got me hooked on your Chicago shows, and I might've had a tantrum if I didn't get to keep up with it."

"Right! She got me hooked too. Are you up to date?

Wanna Watchbox and chill?" He wags his eyebrows, and I push against his chest with a laugh.

"You're such a nerd."

"I'm a hot nerd, and you love it."

"Yes, yes I do. Let me go get some popcorn, and we can binge properly."

"Oh, sweetheart, you know I already got popcorn in here." He tilts his head over to the left, and I realize he's had a little kitchenette set up in here.

Because of course he has.

"Well, that saves me some time then. You make the popcorn, and I'll set up the TV." I grin and slip out of the cage of his arms, practically skipping across the room and jumping onto his bed. The navy sheets envelop me like a hug, and I make myself comfortable after grabbing the remote from his bedside table.

It doesn't take him long to get the popcorn made, and despite eating more than I should've earlier, my mouth still drools at the smell of the buttery goodness. Come to momma!

He slides onto the bed beside me and tucks me in under his arm, and it's almost like the last two and a bit years never happened as I snuggle in against him and hit play on the remote.

Like nothing has changed at all.

NINETEEN

DEACON

Waking up without Fallon beside me a few times has been strange to adjust to, but I'm not mad about it. She needs time with Colt as well as with me, and since she's still in our bed more than his, I can't complain.

I really wish his very human mindset wasn't so rigid, though. I'd happily just knock out a few walls and make this room bigger, with a substantially larger bed so we could both be near her every night. But I swore I'd be patient, and so patient I will be. I imagine it'll take Fallon a minute to be okay with that, too, but I'm quietly hoping it won't take them too long to come around to it.

But today I have bigger things to worry about. Locke

finally returned with news about the Outliers. He met with the current higher Demon on level eight, and he just got back late last night. Usually, I'd have asked for the information straight away, but he looked dead on his feet. That being said, I slept like shit, tossing and turning, unable to turn my mind off. I hate how long this is taking.

My reluctance to go to the Outliers is a big part of the reason it's taking so long, and that pisses me off too. I really need to just Demon up and face the darkness that waits for me there. But I have more to live for now than I've had before. The last thing I want is to go there without all of the information in my arsenal that I can get and end up dead.

Yeah, that would fuck up my plans majorly.

I'd also rather not traumatize Fallon like that. She's dealt with enough death and loss for several lifetimes.

I climb out of bed and dress in a crisp white shirt and a pair of black suit pants. If I'm going to have to be any type of an authority figure today, I need to look the part to get my head in the game. I might just throw back a few gallons of coffee too. Maybe that would help.

I head out of the door and find Colt and Fallon leaving his room at the same time. Fallon looks somewhat awkward as she spots me, so I just smile. I know she'll feel through the bond that I'm chill. Having the bond while we navigate all of this is amazing because it means she'll actually believe me when I tell her that I'm good with everything going on between the two of us and the two of them. You can't lie via the bond. I feel a pang of relief from her as she smiles back, and Colt takes her hand.

"I'm going to meet Locke this morning. He has news from level eight if you want to join me," I say to Colt as we meet in the middle of the hall.

"Sounds good. Hopefully it's good news, and we can finally take some action," he says, and I nod.

"I couldn't agree more. This shit has taken too long."

"Woah," Fallon exclaims. "Did you guys actually agree on something? Stop the freaking press!"

I bark out a laugh at her, but I mean, she's not wrong. It's been happening more and more as Colt and I work together, but she hasn't been around to see it. He's slowly coming around to the fact that I'm not just a giant asshole.

I hope so, anyway.

"The sass on this one," Colt jokes, swatting her ass lightly, and she squeaks.

"I know, right. It's almost a shame she likes a good spanking," I counter, and his eyes go wide before he smirks.

"I'm sure we could still spank the sass right out of her."

"Y'all can stop ganging up on me anytime now," she says, but I can feel just how excited she is by that prospect.

"We'll behave," I say with a wink. "Let's go eat, and then we can find Locke."

We head down to the nook where Ellis has breakfast set up for me. When he sees Fallon and Colt with me, he scurries away with a quick garble about coming back with food for them. We settle in, talking about nothing of importance, until Ellis brings their breakfast too, then we fall into a comfortable silence. It's something I wouldn't have thought possible a few months ago.

Tex arrives about halfway through breakfast, clasping that damn hat of his in his hands, looking like he's about to piss himself.

"What's up, Tex?" I ask, and his gaze flits between the three of us.

"It's Locke, sir… I mean, Deacon. I went to check on him this morning… and it seems, well… he can't be woken up."

"He's dead?" I ask, horror filling my heart.

"No, sir. He's very much alive. He's just, er, unwakeable," Tex stammers, and I can't help but frown.

"Could it be a spell?" Fallon asks, and I mull it over.

"It's not out of the realm of possibility, but I have no idea who would've managed it between me speaking to him last night and now."

"It could've been cast before he even got here," she says, before pausing to think. "It could've been cast so that it was untraceable until he fell asleep, and then it would go into effect. It wouldn't be too hard to achieve. I can have a look if you like?"

I weigh up her offer but shake my head. "It's not that I doubt your skill, but until I know the cause of it, I'd rather not lose you to whatever has him knocked the fuck out. Tex, has anyone else come under the same spell?"

"I don't know, but I can try to find out. It's still early, not everyone's awake."

"Please. Then we'll know if it's just a Locke thing or if it's a bigger problem."

"Yes, sir," he says before scurrying away.

"Well, I guess that puts a damper in our plans for the day," Colt says, looking as frustrated as I feel. "Maybe I'll head to the pits with Caleb for some training if you don't need my help. I need to burn off some of this excess energy."

"Sounds good, I'll come find you if we find anything out." He nods and stands, moving to kiss Fallon chastely before leaving the room.

"I guess that means we can spend the day together?" Fallon says cheerily, and it occurs to me that I've been more than a little absent lately.

"It absolutely does. You finish eating, all of it, and then when I call you through the bond, come and find me in our room."

Colt being at the estate has made things a little tense at times, but we're slowly settling into our new version of normal. However, I am craving some time with Fallon, just the two of us. I understand that I only have half of her attention anymore, and my wolf isn't exactly the happiest about it. But I always told her I'd happily share her, as long as I still got a part of her. Thanks to the bond, I know just how happy she is, so I'm just hoping that Colt and I are starting to turn a corner.

Since the week in the ring we've been a lot better, other than when he went full beast mode of course.

But I need to not think about him right now. I have big plans for my girl since I have her to myself for the day. It's been too long since I've had her kneel for me, and my beast is growing restless beneath the surface. Too much has been outside of our control recently, and I need this to keep me sane.

I'm such a lucky son of a bitch that she seems to need and enjoy the power play as much as I do. I call her through the bond, and I know she won't be long, so I roll up the sleeves of my shirt and wait for her. It's hard not to notice how she pants over my forearms. I've already laid out both my silk ropes and the blindfold on the bed.

I can't wait to heighten her senses by taking away her sight. She'll fucking love it. I already know that much.

Though I know by the time I bury myself in her the blindfold will be gone, because I love seeing her amber eyes flash as she comes. It's just fucking beautiful.

I readjust my dick in my pants because it's already straining at the thought of her coming unglued from my attention. Just as I get myself sorted out, she walks into the nook, and I feel my beast rise up to greet her. I already know my eyes are red.

"Good girl, you came. Now kneel," I command, and she drops to her knees without question, leaving the door open. Colt is out with Caleb, so I want to push her a little and keep it open. See if that adds to the thrill for her.

Her hair lands loosely down her back, cascading in a waterfall of dark strands that I can't wait to wrap around my hand. She's perfect, waiting in position and ready for inspection. She has her head and eyes down with her shoulders back and hands on her lap, one folded over the other. I taught her that. I gave her the option and safe space to submit, and it's a heady feeling.

I walk around her, taking in the sight of her. I tell her how gorgeous she is. I tell her how happy she makes me before taking the blindfold and running the silky fabric between my hands.

"We're going to change it up a little, tonight. Do you trust me?" I already know the answer but hearing her say it makes me fucking hard as steel.

"Yes, I trust you."

"Good girl. Now, lift your head and close your eyes."

It only takes her a second to do as I ask, and she doesn't even flinch as I place the soft fabric across her eyes.

Such a good girl.

"With your vision gone, your other senses will be heightened."

I tie the knot behind her head, taking advantage of the moment to run my fingers through her silky hair. When I do, a shudder runs through her body, and I know through our bond that it's a shudder of pleasure.

"Now, use only our bond to do as I say."

A slight smile etches over her plump lips, and I know it's because she loves the addition to our game. My beastly heart swells at the thought and so does my cock.

"Undress me, baby girl."

With a deep intake of breath, she reaches out tentatively, hesitating in which direction she should go. At first she's far from her mark, but then she freezes, reassesses her position, and redirects her hand, landing right on my crotch.

I have to bite the inside of my cheek to keep my self-control in check. There's nothing I want more than to say fuck it all to hell and fuck the breath right out of her right now. But I need this, and so does she. Plus, the build up is so fucking sweet.

Slowly, she pops the button of my slacks and slides the

zipper down so slowly it feels like she's making me wait on purpose. Through our bond, however, I can feel that she's being careful not to hurt me.

As soon as she reaches the bottom of the zipper, my dick pops out, hard and ready to play.

I grunt with my need to be in her mouth and just when I'm about to give her the command, something in the corner of my eye catches my attention. I glance up to see Colt standing at the entrance of our room, his gaze fixed on the beauty that is Fallon submitting to me. When he notices that I've seen him, he subtly shakes his head, telling me with that one quick movement that he doesn't want Fallon to know he's there. I'm shocked, but I keep my mouth closed because I don't want her to know yet either. Besides, her attention needs to be on me and me alone.

That doesn't mean he can't watch and maybe even learn something about her.

Fallon, the sublime submissive.

Lifting my chin, I tell him without a single word to stay. To watch. To learn.

It's up to him if he chooses to stay, but I'm happy either way. Maybe this will be enough to push him in the direction we've all been moving toward.

Pushing his hands deep into his pockets, Colt makes himself comfortable against the doorjamb and redirects his attention to Fallon, who opens her mouth without me having to say a word.

I want Colt to see this so I move us just enough for him to have an unhindered view of my cock as I tap the throbbing head against her tongue, sliding it up and around her lips. I grab the back of her head and glide right inside her until I feel the back of her throat.

Through the years, Fallon has improved her gag reflex and can now take me deep in her throat, without hesitation. I give her a little push at the end as I begin to fuck her mouth, a little rougher than usual. Colt's presence is, surprisingly, making me hornier than I thought it would. Knowing he's in love with the love of my life and watching her pleasure me is fucking heady.

Empowering.

Maybe a little good for the ego too, but I push that back. Because if this thing between us is going to work, there's no room for ego.

My cock swells, and as I push once more to the back of Fallon's throat, I get the satisfaction of seeing her tears wet the silk of the blindfold.

Fuck, her tears always fuel my passion.

Running my thumb over her cheek, I pull out completely before ramming my dick back into her mouth and accelerating my thrusts.

"That's it, suck on my dick like a good girl. Make me

come, nice and hard. I want you to drink up every last drop of my cum."

My fingers tighten on her hair, my thrusts getting a little messier, and my control slips just a little bit before I reach the point of no return.

Fallon hollows out her cheeks and sucks my cock like a fucking hoover, and I lose it all, right down her throat.

I'm too consumed by my orgasm to see Colt, but I can tell he's shifting at the door. Is he disgusted? Or is dying to rub one out as the woman he loves makes another man explode in her mouth? He might even wish he could join us.

Gritting my teeth, I hold in my curses as she not only swallows down every drop, but she cleans off my cock with her tongue as though it were a goddamn popsicle too.

Fuck, she's going to make me hard all over again.

Not that that's a bad thing. I have plans, and although they are not the same ones from before Colt's arrival, I'm still going to make sure she's as satisfied as I am before we're done here.

Taking Fallon's hand, I help her to her feet. As she rises to her full height, I palm her chin and brand her lips with a searing kiss.

Mine.

All fucking mine. For now at least.

Our lips are hungry for one another, and her tongue

searches out for mine, giving as good as she gets.

It takes everything in me to back up and separate from her long enough to guide her to the bed. I strip off her shirt and bra, enjoying the view before giving my next command.

"Lean down, baby girl."

Grabbing the silk ties, I wrap her wrists nice and tight before tying her to one of the posters, low enough that she has to bend down with her ass out.

She's a fucking sight. And I might have just chosen the poster that offers Colt the best view.

She's still partially dressed, offering me a little bit of satisfaction as I remove the last articles of her clothing. Exposing her little by little to myself and the voyeur watching our every move.

Unbeknownst to her, of course. Which makes it even hotter, though I know she'd definitely be on board if she did know. I wouldn't do it if I thought otherwise.

By the time Fallon is completely, deliciously naked, her ass and pussy are in full view for Colt. Her pussy teases me, begging to be licked and fucked. I know he can see her wetness running down her thighs, showing how turned on she truly is.

But before she gets any pleasure, she's going to give us her pain. She's going to give us the beauty of her ass streaked red.

Bending down to whisper words that are only for us, I tell her, "You're the most beautiful woman on this planet. I can't wait to taste your tears. Will you give them to me?"

Rubbing her thighs together, she tries to be discreet, but I see the tiny movement and decide there's no better time than the present to begin playing.

My palm lands on one cheek, and the pink flares immediately on her ass. The contrast with her tan legs makes my mouth water.

"Yes."

She answers my earlier question, and for that, I reward her with a caress over the spot that feels a little warm to the touch. Just as I get her nice and comfortable with loving touches, I slap her again on the other cheek. Fallon grunts but takes it like the brave girl she is.

This time, I don't just caress her, I kneel behind her and lick up the juices from her pussy. The pain is there, no doubt, but the pleasure she feels cannot be hidden. It's right there, dripping from between her lips, and I'm here to claim it all.

I stand back to my full height, licking a path up the slit of her pussy, between the cheeks of her ass and over her puckered hole before raining kisses along her spine.

Her moans give me life.

And just when she's feeling relaxed again, I bring my palm down five times in rapid succession.

My actions are controlled, and the rush from watching my handprint bloom on her skin is fucking intoxicating. Fuck, I won't be able to last much longer. Even though I came like a fucking water hose down her throat, I'm hard all over again. In fact, I didn't even bother to tuck my cock back in my pants, because I knew I wouldn't be able to last very long without burying myself inside of her.

A quick glance at Colt tells me he's as hard as I am, but he's not touching himself the way I am at this very second. My hand runs up and down my cock leisurely as I walk behind Fallon and position myself at her pussy.

Until now, Colt had a prime view of Fallon's ass, but this moment belongs to just the two of us. All he can see is me as I thrust inside of her for the first time.

"You're so fucking tight, Fallon. You feel so good when you squeeze my cock with your pussy." My words are meted with the rhythm of my thrusts, which have turned into the cues for Fallon's cries of pleasure.

With both of my hands on her breasts, I pinch her nipples every time I bottom out deep inside of her. Everything about her feels perfect, but I don't want to come like this—behind her with her eyes hidden from me. I want to see the lust in her amber irises when I empty my load inside of her.

One of my hands travels up her torso, across her neck, and over her chin, and on her next cry, I push two fingers inside her mouth. "Suck them," I command.

And she does. She works my fingers as her pussy clamps down on my dick with every deep, measured push.

Just when I think I won't last much longer, I stop everything and pull out. Her gasp of indignation almost makes me feel sorry for her. If I'm being honest, not being inside her is the hardest thing for me to do, but it's not time yet.

I slap her ass to remind her who's in charge.

"Don't make me take out the paddle." This doesn't scare her. In fact, it has quite the opposite effect judging by her groan.

Looking over my shoulder, I see Colt with his hands closed into tight fists at his sides, and he looks like he's in pain with his jaw working overtime. If he doesn't do something soon to alleviate the pressure he's feeling, he's going to break his jaw.

Walking around to the poster, I carefully untie Fallon and lead her to the bed. I position her on the bed in such a way that she can't see Colt, but I make sure he sure as fuck can see her. All of her.

Once she's on her back, with her legs spread wide for my perusal, I kiss her pussy. Her clit. Her belly button. Then both of her nipples, making sure to suck hard on them so she can feel the pull of pleasure straight to her clit.

Once I've had my fill of her tits, I kiss her mouth, licking and biting at the soft flesh of her tender lips. Slowly, I pull back the blindfold and kiss both of her eyelids, letting her know she's beautiful, and perfect, and everything I've ever wanted.

As she opens her amber eyes, looking at me with all the love that she feels for me reflecting in her eyes, I bury my dick to the hilt and drag in a breath through my teeth. Ecstasy floods my entire being as her pussy closes tightly around me.

With her wrists still bound by the silk ties, I hold her down with one hand above her head and my other at her clit, my thumb circling the hard, wet nub.

"Let yourself go. Show me how good you feel with me inside of you. Show me your pleasure, Fallon."

With her chest arching up off the bed, searching out the pleasure, she looks wild and animalistic. I continue fucking her in earnest, keeping her gaze on me as my cock hits that sweet spot inside of her with every thrust inside.

I keep on pushing in and out with more and more force, chest tightening every time I bottom out.

Pulling her knees up and then pushing them down on her chest, I get the sweet angle that drives her crazy. Her ass is halfway off the bed, and her cries echo all around the room. I know, without having to look, that our lovemaking is driving Colt out of his goddamn mind.

I know because I would be losing my mind if I were in

his position.

When I know she can't hold on any longer, I give her the gift of release.

"Come for me, pretty girl."

The dam breaks, and her entire body tightens and convulses as her screams travel throughout the entire estate.

It fills my soul with pride knowing I do this to her. I drown her in intense pleasure and then bring her back to life.

And just when she can no longer take it, I give in to my need and explode like a fucking volcano. I throw my head back, and the veins in my neck are tight with my tension. My fingers dig deep into her flesh as I empty myself inside of her.

We take a second to come back down to Earth as we share kisses and sweet words of gratitude.

As I'm about to stand, I see movement in my peripheral vision. Although my wolf might want to rip open Colt's chest and eat his heart for disturbing us in this moment, I know better. I rein it in and watch his every move.

It takes Fallon a second to understand what's happening, but by the time she does, Colt grabs her by the nape and crashes his mouth on hers, not giving either one of us the chance to protest.

I see his tongue spear inside her mouth, kissing her

senseless with abandon. And just as quickly as he came in, he's gone, leaving her gaping up at me like her entire world just changed.

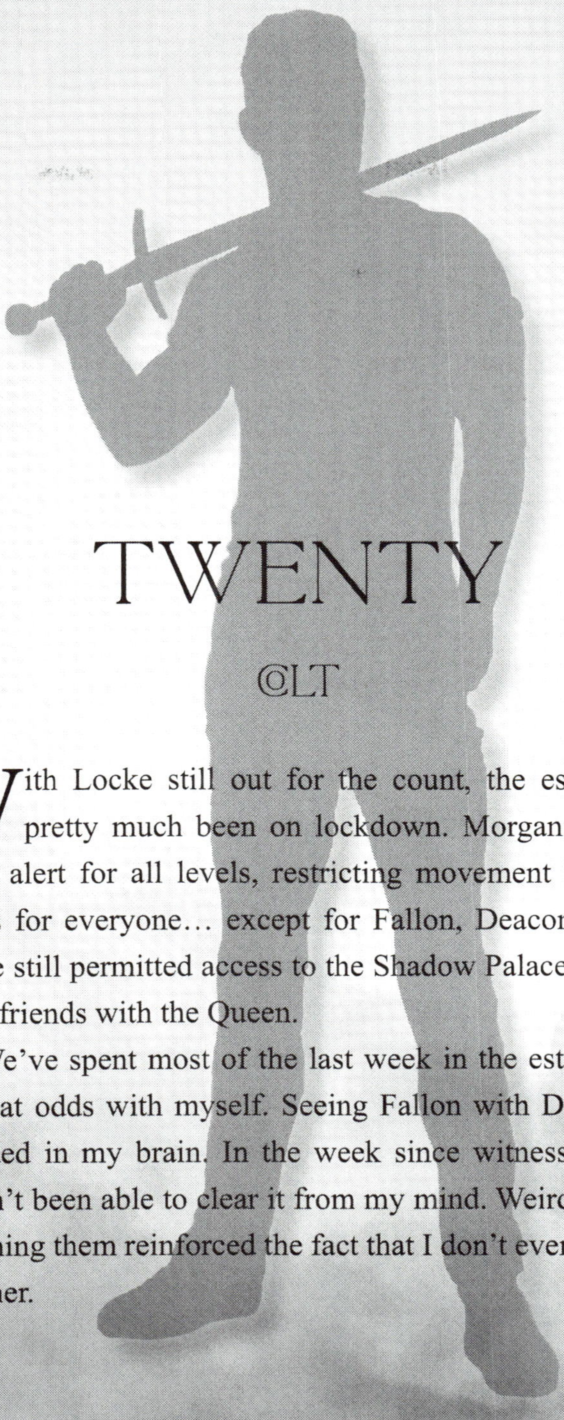

TWENTY

COLT

With Locke still out for the count, the estate has pretty much been on lockdown. Morgan put out a red alert for all levels, restricting movement between levels for everyone… except for Fallon, Deacon, and I. We're still permitted access to the Shadow Palace. It pays to be friends with the Queen.

We've spent most of the last week in the estate. I've been at odds with myself. Seeing Fallon with Deacon is branded in my brain. In the week since witnessing it, I haven't been able to clear it from my mind. Weird as it is, watching them reinforced the fact that I don't ever want to lose her.

Which is why I feel so fucking antsy right now. Not only have I been trying to wrap my mind around having the sort of relationship my sister and Morgan have between the three of us, but I've also been bouncing around the idea of asking Fallon to bond with me.

I'm not sure how any of it works, but I've seen how Morgan, Caleb, and the others interact without even having to speak. The closeness it seems to bring Fallon and Deacon makes my soul ache with something that I can't quite name, though it's a little less than outright jealousy. I'm not sure if it's even possible to bond with her since she already bonded with Deacon, and you know, she's not the Shadow Queen. But I want the Demon bond between us too.

I want everything with her.

I feel like a nervous schoolboy trying to build up the nerve to ask out my first crush. It's fucking stupid. We've been through so much together, but this feels like a big step. Or well, a major fucking behemoth of a leap.

But I don't want her to think that she doesn't mean literally *everything* to me. I know I've been a giant jackass about shit lately, and I put my foot in my mouth more often than not, but I'm trying. I want to be everything she needs me to be and more.

I wander through the estate looking for her, hoping Ellis managed to get the picnic I set up outside. I was hoping for something nice and low-key. A picnic is good for this sort of shit, right?

Fuck me, I don't even remember the last time I was this nervous. Maybe I should've talked to Caleb first or something to see if this was even possible. To find out how it's actually done. But I didn't want to tell anyone about it before I had the chance to ask her. Call me selfish, but I'd like to keep this between us and maybe Deacon. Maybe.

I don't think she'll say no, but if she does, it'll be enough of a punch in the junk all on its own without other people knowing about it. And considering how much of a jackass I've been recently, anything is possible.

Fates, I need to get a grip of myself and stop acting like such a ball sack. I am Colt motherfucking Bennett. Hunter. Demon. Asshole. All around go-getter. I am not this nervous, pansy-ass whining bitch.

I find Fallon in the nook watching TV, and I stand back and watch her for a few minutes. She doesn't even realize I'm standing here. I'm not sure that's such a great thing considering the fact we're literally surrounded by beings that could kill her in a heartbeat, but I'm glad she feels so safe here that she can lose herself like this.

"Hey," I say softly as I enter the room, and she jumps a little before she realizes it's me.

"Hey, you okay?" she asks, pausing the TV before turning to focus on me.

"Yeah, I'm good. I was wondering if you wanted to hang out with me for a bit?"

"Sure, what did you have in mind?" she asks, looking up at me with that smile of hers that's like a hit of pure sunshine, and a small glimmer of hope that she might actually say yes slices through me.

"Maybe we could go for a walk around the estate? It's beautiful outside, and despite looking out at it all from my bedroom, I actually haven't spent any time out there."

"That sounds perfect," she says with a wide smile and jumps up off of the couch. "It feels like forever since I went outside, which I probably shouldn't admit too loudly."

"Hey, no judgment here. I can't say that I've been out that much either. Which is funny, because back on Earth, I was outside all the fucking time."

"I mean, same. The sun just doesn't feel quite as warm here."

"Yeah, I know exactly what you mean," I say, and she giggles before taking my hand.

"Lead the way!"

We head outside and stroll around the grounds, talking about everything and nothing at all, until I lead her around the back to the blossoming cherry tree I asked Ellis to arrange the picnic under.

"Oh, Colt! Did you do this?" she exclaims when she sees it, and I internally fist pump.

“I had some help, but yes. I wanted to do something fun, just the two of us. We haven’t done something like this in forever.” I smile, and she squeezes my hand, her excitement palpable. She practically skips over to the blanket and drops down onto it, opening the basket once I settle beside her. There’s all sorts of food in the basket: mini baguettes, chocolate covered strawberries, a bottle of champagne, macaroons, little cupcakes and other tiny cakes. Ellis really went all out.

We eat and reminisce about old times, laughing at stupid shit from when we were younger before everything got so crazy when I turned twenty-one. We steer clear of any heavy topics.

“Thank you for this,” she gushes as I pour her another glass of champagne. “This is exactly what I needed. It feels like it’s been a while since I laughed this hard.”

“Anything to make you happy, Fallon. And uh, speaking of...” I run a hand through my hair, trying to think of the right words.

“You look like you’re about to tell me you peed your pants. What’s going on?” she asks with a laugh, and I gulp a little.

Ready or not, here we go, I guess.

“I’ve been thinking a lot about our situation—about everything we’ve been through up to this point. Fallon, I already know I want all of eternity with you. I want to be with you, to be yours and for you to be mine. I know this isn't the life we originally saw for ourselves, but I think we're navigating it pretty well, all things considered..."

"I agree, and I want all those things too." She smiles and squeezes my hand, so I take a deep breath and prepare myself for the big question.

"Okay, uh yeah... Good. Fates, I sound like a bumbling idiot. I hoped I would have the right words, the flowery kinds that would make you swoon, but that isn't who I am. I'm not a flowery kind of guy. Regardless, I want you to be mine forever, and I wondered if you'd consider bonding with me and my Demon." I swear to fuck I hold my breath once the word vomit is finished spilling from my mouth. It feels as if time stands still as she processes what I said.

She opens her mouth to speak but stops, and I can't tell if that's good or bad. I swear to the Fates if she doesn't say something, *anything*, soon, I'm going to burst.

A wild grin breaks out over her face, and she leaps into my lap, showering my face with kisses. "Colt, you had me so worried! Of course I will, you big, crazy asshole. I already consider you and your monster mine, especially with your bite permanently marking my skin."

"So is that a yes?" I ask, needing to hear the word specifically, because my monster is pacing back and forth in my mind. He wants the simple clarification as much as I do.

"Of course it's a yes!"

TWENTY ONE

FALLON

"So, we need to talk." I wring out my hands as I fidget, waiting for Deacon's reaction.

"That doesn't sound good." He frowns but puts his pen down and gives me all of his attention regardless. "What's wrong?"

"Nothing, really." I bite my lip and try to get a handle on my nerves. Why the fuck am I so nervous? This will be fine. I'm sure.

"Okay, so why do we need to talk?" he asks, and the warmth of relief I feel due to his patience and calm spilling through our bond calms me a little. My stomach jolts when I realize I can also feel that he's a little worried, which is probably because I'm so freaking worked up.

"Colt asked me to bond with him." The words fall from my mouth in a nervous rush, but Deacon just smiles at me.

"So why are you so worried?" he asks, chuckling softly before standing and moving across his office to stand in front of me. He tucks my hair behind my ear and cups my cheeks. "This is good news."

"It is?"

"Well, I assume you said yes?" I nod, and he grins.

"Then of course it's good news. It means he's in this for the long haul, and it likely means things will be easier for us all around here."

"You're not mad?" I ask, biting my bottom lip. His eyes zero in on the action and flash red before going back to normal.

"Why would I be mad? I keep telling you I'm good with all of this. Demons don't view relationships in the same way that humans do. Monogamy isn't the be-all and end-all to us. You've probably noticed that Morgan isn't the only person with more than one lover down here. I love you, you love me, *and* you love Colt. I've said more than once that I'm open to whatever else might happen. That's all that matters to me. That and your happiness."

"You're way too good to me." I sigh, feeling much calmer. I was so excited when I said yes to Colt yesterday, and it didn't immediately register to me that Deacon might have a problem with it. Until I fell asleep, and to say my nightmares were chaos is an understatement.

"No, I'm really not. This isn't something you ever needed to be worried about."

"Can I even bond with him? Since I'm bonded to you?" I ask, relieved that he's happy. Warmth radiates through my body, starting in my heart and spilling to the very tips of my fingers, knowing that Deacon will support me and that he'll answer almost anything I ask of him.

"As far as I'm aware, yes. The only issue might be that you're human, but since you're not *just* human, it shouldn't be a problem."

"Okay," I say, nodding, like obviously that was what I thought already, even though it definitely wasn't. *Should I have been considering that?*

He pauses, looking deep in thought. "Has Colt spoken to Caleb or anyone about it yet?"

"I don't think so." I shake my head, and he pulls me into his arms, hugging me tight.

"Okay, well I'm going to talk to him. I want to make sure he does it right. If he doesn't want my help, though, I'll make sure he speaks to Caleb."

"I'm sure he'll be fine with your offer to help. The bond between Colt and I is solid, so he has no reason not to." I smile up at him, and he kisses my forehead.

"We'll see," he says, and I know he's thinking back to

the other day when Colt watched us together. I don't know if they've even spoken since then. Colt hasn't mentioned it to me, so I can't imagine they have. To be a fly on the wall if they did, though…

I'm still not really over the fact that Colt was there. Deacon told me after that he'd been there the whole time. I won't lie and say that didn't make me even hotter. Sweet Goddess, the two of them might be more than I can take, but you can bet your ass I'm willing to sacrifice myself to try.

I'm not going to lie, the thought of submitting to them both makes me way more excited than it should. And maybe having a bond with them both will bring them closer together naturally. The possibilities seem endless… and delicious.

I'm pretty sure I could get used to being shared.

"When did you plan on bonding?" he asks, pulling me from my fantasies.

"Hadn't really thought that far ahead yet," I tell him softly as he lifts me and moves us to sit on the sofa in his office.

"Okay, well I'll talk to Colt to make sure he knows what he's doing, and then I'll keep my nose out of it." He grins down at me, and I boop his nose.

I can't help but laugh when he almost growls at me, and I grin widely in response. "But it's such a pretty nose."

I can't believe in the space of four days we've gone from Colt asking me to bond with him to us actually doing it. When it was Deacon and I, it was just a small ceremony. It was just the two of us and Morgan for the part she needed to play, but she was literally in and out.

I figured it would be the same this time.

But apparently with Colt, it's a bigger deal because Colt told Creek, who told Remy, who demanded to be here. Then since Remy was coming, Caleb decided he should also show up as he's responsible for Colt even being alive. So now all four Horsemen are coming, along with Morgan, and it's this whole big-ass thing.

I went from being only kind of nervous, to being like... want-to-vomit nervous.

I really wanted Mama and Rebel to be here, but Mama is still against coming to the Realm of Darkness as she calls it, so neither of them will be here. I try not to be too sad about it and just focus on the positives of the day instead.

Which is how I find myself in a small room down the hall from the throne room, wearing a beautiful lace black dress and hoping to the Goddess that I don't trip and fall as I walk through the throne room. A bonding ceremony between lovers or mates is similar to a human wedding, though it leaves out the religious stuff and adds in some eternal life mumbo jumbo. Plus the whole, you know, actual magical bond, which is more like a pagan handfasting ceremony if the ribbons were shadows. Goddess, my mind is a hot mess.

I know Colt's talked to Caleb about everything that could happen. The strangest thing to come from all of this was Caleb mentioning to me that since I'm bonded to them both, they might both be able to feel one another, though that doesn't always happen. It also means we might all get a power boost again too.

Each extra person added to a bond makes the bond stronger apparently, making the people it's connected to stronger by proxy.

It all just kind of makes my head hurt if I'm being real.

"Are you ready?"

I jump at the sound of Remy's voice, and she grins when I turn to face her. "Fallon, you look stunning."

"Thanks." I try not to blush at the compliment. There are bigger things to think about than my dress. Like the two Demons I'm in love with and how this affects all of us. "Is everyone here?"

"They are. We're just waiting on you." She grins and moves toward me. She takes my hands and squeezes them. "I always figured you and Colt would get married, though this isn't exactly what I pictured at the time. Just remember to beat his ass when he gets too cocky and that your wants and needs are just as important as his. I am so excited for you guys to start this new part of your lives."

"It's definitely a leap," I say, letting out a deep breath. "But we're ready. All three of us. I think… at least I hope we are." I laugh nervously, and she hugs me tightly.

"You've got this, and if all else fails, I'll kick both their asses on your behalf. Let's get this show on the road, shall we?"

I nod, and she kisses my cheek. "Okay, let's do this."

She turns, crooking her arm for me, and I place my arm through hers. "Let's do it."

We walk toward the throne room, and I don't remember having ever felt so nervous in my entire life. It's not even like I'm bad at talking in front of a room full of people—being the coven's heir for as long as I was meant I had that shit down. These nerves are some next level shit, though.

But as soon as we cross the threshold and I see Colt and Deacon standing up by the dais together, all of my nerves melt away.

We walk down the black carpet to where the others are standing waiting for us, and Remy kisses my cheek before leaving me to stand in-between Colt and Deacon.

Deacon kisses my cheek before moving away, stepping to where he is still just behind me, leaving Colt and I as the main focus of the room. Morgan stands before us, a sparkle in her eyes.

She clears her throat and smiles down at me before speaking. "Know now before you go further, that your bonding is eternal. As the bond is made, so are your lives now bound. Do you still seek to enter this ceremony?"

"I do," we both say at the same time, and Remy snorts a laugh. Of course she does. Morgan smiles before bringing her focus back to the two of us.

"Woven into the shadow of creation are all the hopes of your friends and family, and of yourselves, for your new life together. With the fasting of your bond, all of the desires, dreams, love, and happiness wished here in this place for as long as your souls exist they shall be tied together. In the joining of souls so are your lives now bound, one to the other."

Morgan finishes speaking, and as I look back at Colt, he gulps, preparing to speak his part as the shadows around our joined hands grow tighter.

"Fallon… Love is a word that is much too soft and used far too often to ever describe the fierce, infinite, and blazing passion that I have in my heart for you. Everything in me recognizes your heart as my home and your arms as my shelter. You are my better half and my very best friend. I will love you, honor you, respect and cherish you in sickness and health, through sorrows and success, for all the days of my existence. I am forever yours." I swoon hard, but I know that I still have my vows to go, so I mouth a 'thank you' to him, and he grins.

"Colt, I want so badly to be able to fully explain the love I have for you. Not a simple kind of love made up of butterflies and stomach knots—but more the blurring of self and the entanglement with another soul kind of love. You are the million dreams and wishes of a little girl come true. You are kind. You are silly. You are intelligent. You acknowledge my strengths and accept my faults. You make me want to be a better person every day. I take you as you are now, tomorrow, and for eternity to come, to be my bonded. I promise to always pursue you, to fight for you, and to love you unconditionally and wholeheartedly for the rest of my life. You are my best friend, and I'm the luckiest person within the realms to call you mine and to have you join my family."

"So it is decreed, it is done," Morgan murmurs, and the shadows sink beneath our skin. Despite having been through this before, I'm still not prepared for the feeling of it. It only takes a few seconds before heat blooms in my chest. It's hot enough to leave me breathless, but Colt squeezes my hand and keeps me present while Deacon steadies me with a hand at the small of my back. The sensation fades, and then I feel it.

His happiness.

We are officially bonded.

TWENTY TWO

FALLON

It's hard to wrap my head around the fact that I've been bonded to Colt for three weeks now. It's still been a little tense here and there with him and Deacon, but I think they're finally getting there. My relationship with each of them continues to grow stronger and deeper, and I couldn't be happier about it.

Beyond bonded bliss, what I'm excited about is that Killian and Bryce are finally taking me down to the pits. I've never been, but if this is where I get to truly find out what my powers are, what I'm actually capable of, then I'm all for it.

No more damsel in distress bullshit for me.

Give me my cape, Batman. I'm ready to do some superhero shit.

I mean not actual superhero stuff. I'll leave that to the super powerful crazies, but I'm feeling good, and I'm ready to kick some ass. I pull on a sports bra and a pair of leggings before zipping up a hoodie to keep me warm. Slipping my feet into a pair of sneakers feels weird since I'm not usually a sneakers kind of girl, but I have no idea what I'm walking into today, and sneakers feel practical.

"You ready?" Deacon asks as he exits the bathroom, and I grin.

"So freaking ready."

"You look hot, like, too hot. Damn, I'm a lucky man. You sure you don't just want to wrestle with me instead?" he jokes, and I laugh as he walks over to me. His hands slide under the hoodie and around my bare waist. He groans before kissing me with so much heat and need that I think my lips will bruise under his demands.

"While that sounds tempting, I'll have to take a raincheck. I'm already too geared up to do this today."

"Okay, I can live with that. Has Killian prepared you for today? Has he told you what the pits actually are?" he asks with a slight frown on his lips, so I peck them chastely.

"He said it's a prison of sorts," I tell him with a shrug.

"That's mostly it. It is a prison, but it's also like… a

Colosseum I think is what the humans called them once upon a time."

"It's a fighting arena?" I'm pretty sure I sound as shocked as I feel because I didn't expect that.

"Yeah, we allow people to earn their way out of the pits—once they've been there long enough that Bryce feels they deserve the chance anyway. He runs the pits, and well, we're Demons. We thrive on violence. Trust me, everyone who fights at the pits asks to be in that arena."

"Okay, that's cool. I just wasn't expecting it. Honestly, I'm not sure what I was expecting. Where are the pits?"

"They're within a space between level eight and the center ring of the Realm. It's more of an extension of the center ring, but it's separated for safety reasons, I guess. You don't have anything to worry about other than yourself and your powers. I have faith in you, and I know that Killian or Bryce will step in if shit gets out of hand." He runs his hands up and down my arms before hugging me again. I sink against the hard planes of his chest and take the moment of comfort before psyching myself up again.

I've totally got this.

"Holy shit," I gasp as we whisper into the pits. I know Deacon tried to prepare me for this place but hearing about it and seeing it are two very, very different things.

"Thanks," Bryce smiles before taking a deep breath. "This place is kind of my baby."

I look out over the sandy ground and then up at the seven story high arena. The stone structure is awe-inspiring. It's so fucking big, so I totally get why he takes such pride in it. I can also see the appeal here for the other Demons. Though fuck knows how many people this place would actually fit.

"The cells sit below this. They go down a fair way, so don't wander off anywhere on your own," Bryce warns, and I nod.

"I don't intend on getting myself killed or captured, so you're good."

"Let me know if you need anything. I'm going down to make sure all is in order," Bryce says to Killian, who nods and smiles before Bryce whispers away.

"Take a deep breath," he says softly, watching me closely. "You've totally got this. I wouldn't have brought you here if you weren't ready."

"It's just… so big," I say with a nervous laugh. "Where do we even start?"

"We'll do some warm-ups here to get you used to the arena. Then once you're ready, we'll bring out your first opponent."

"First?" I gulp, and he laughs.

"Yeah, you got this. I kept the crowd away for you since I figured that was extra pressure you didn't need for your first go. If you like it, we can always bring you back."

"Somehow, I don't see myself as the bloodthirsty type, but who knows."

"Power can be intoxicating. Just keep a firm grasp on who you are, and you'll be fine. You ready to do this?" he asks, and I shake out my arms, mentally putting on my badass panties before I grin back at him.

"Hell yes I am, let's do this."

He leads me around the arena, showing me all of the traps contained under the sand and giving me a chance to build a mental map of which areas are safest. He then shows me a few tricks to escape some of the hairier areas of the arena. Once I think I've got it, we spar, both physically and with my power. It takes more strength than I expected to contain some parts of my power, especially since I've worked with magic my entire life. However, the power I have here is very different from the power I grew up with. It even feels different. I didn't notice it at the beginning, but since I've been working with it more, I notice it's heavier and darker. I guess power born of shadows will always feel different from power born of earth and light.

We spar until sweat runs down my spine, and I start to drag. "How was this just the warm-up?" I pant as I take off my hoodie and put my hair up in a ponytail.

Killian just grins at me and throws me a water bottle. “You think any of your opponents are going to take it easy on you just because of who you are? They’re fighting to escape this place. They won’t quit just because.”

“Way to make me feel better.” I roll my eyes before chugging the icy cold water. It tastes a little off, but I feel rejuvenated almost instantly once I finish the bottle. “Okay, actually that did make me feel better. What was that?”

“Just a little trick that my grandmother taught me a long time ago,” he says with a wink. “You think you’re ready for your first opponent?”

“I think so?” I don’t sound as confident as I’d like to, but it’s about as confident as I feel. It’ll be good to work on my power with someone who I know isn’t actually pulling their punches, but it’s also a little scary. I’m not like Remy. The rush of a fight has never held much appeal to me, but ready or not here we go, right?

“You’ve got this. I’ll let Bryce know we’re ready to go.” He hands me another bottle of water before whispering away, leaving me standing in the middle of the giant amphitheater. I feel so small right now, and I know that thinking isn’t going to work in my favor, so I push it down and find a new mantra.

What would Remy do? What would Remy do? What would Remy do?

It repeats over and over again in my head.

She's a badass, so I need to channel my friend right now. Maybe if I think like Remy, I can learn to be an actual badass all of my own.

"Okay, Bryce is bringing up the first guy. Power-wise, he's weaker than you. Don't be put off by how he looks," Killian says once he pops back over to me, and I gulp. He's not exactly filling me with hope.

I follow him to the place he's set out for me to start when Bryce whispers back into the arena with a guy who looks about four times the size of me.

"Remember, don't let his looks scare you. A fight is rarely fair, but you've got this. I believe in you," Killian coaches me quietly while Bryce removes the chains from his prisoner. I don't hear what he says to the guy, but the beast of a man sets his gray gaze on me, and I swear my blood turns to ice.

You've got this, Fallon. You've been practicing. You have your new power. And your badass panties are on.

Bryce and Killian whisper out of the arena, and I see them reappear on a platform about four floors up. I guess that's the royal viewing platform based on the throne I can just make out. I don't have time to pay it much attention because the beast of a guy roars and runs at me, the ground shaking as his feet pound into the sand

Right, don't panic. Easier said than done, Killian!

I move into position to meet the beast head on and let

him get close enough that I know I'm within range. When he's finally close enough, I lash out with my shadows and pull him off his feet. He lands face down in the sand with a thud, and as much as I want to celebrate the small win, the roar that comes from him tells me that I probably don't have time. He knows a little of what I can do now, and that could be good, but it might be bad too.

I move further back, staying away from where the ground disappears under an illusion, and ready myself for the next onslaught as the gray-eyed beast climbs back to his feet. "I'm going to destroy you and dance on your bones, little girl."

"Do your worst," I shout, sounding and feeling far more confident than I thought I would. He runs at me again, and I wait until he's within arm's reach, and then whisper so I'm sitting on his shoulders. I draw my power to my hands and put them on his temples before pushing it forward, stunning him on the spot. He falls to his knees before face-planting again, giving me just enough time to whisper away from him before he hits the ground.

I do a little dance on the spot until the guy disappears from sight and Killian whispers in front of me.

"Well done, not bad for your first go. You ready for round two?"

"Hell yes!" I cheer, giving myself a little pat on the back for not completely fucking up, and he grins at me.

"Well then, let the games begin!"

"Ouch," I groan as I walk into the kitchen. While yesterday was awesome, and I totally kicked some Demon ass, I got my own ass kicked too. To say I'm sore today is an understatement, but I wear my bruises like badges that I won… or at least I won a bit. Killian taught me how to use the shadows to help me heal, but I'm still getting the hang of that. It's not as easy as it was to heal with light.

And saying that Colt and Deacon were okay with the state I arrived back home in might be the oversell of the freaking century. The new hole in the nook wall is testament to that, but after each of them took a turn fussing over me, checking me over for themselves to see I wasn't broken, I was rewarded with plenty of praise for slaying in the pits.

And slay I fucking did.

Though it was a ton of fun, I'm not in any rush to go back to the pits or get in any other fights. The day did make me feel much more confident in what I am capable of with my new powers, and I feel more comfortable with the shadows now too. It's positive all round.

I slide onto a chair at the kitchen table and let out a sigh of relief as Ellis puts a mug of coffee in front of me. "Thank you."

He smiles and scurries back to the stove. I vow that one day he won't be so afraid of me, or anyone… including his own shadow. He's so skittish, and I know this place does not favor many, but he's so kind and so very good at what he does. He deserves to feel happiness and safety too.

"Miss, this came for you." I turn to see Kevin hurrying toward me with a box in his hands. He drops it on the table and rushes away before I even get a chance to open my mouth.

"What the…" I start, just as Deacon and Colt walk into the kitchen. I try to keep the surprise off of my face at seeing them together like this so I don't freak them out or scare them into realizing that they're actually getting along. I think Colt being here, becoming part of everything, is really helping them both. The better they are with each other, the more likely it is we'll become one unit, which is all I can hope for.

I turn my focus back to the box, leaving them to whatever they're talking about, and use the knife at my place setting to cut through the ties. I open the box to find a smaller one inside, so I open it too. Inside, I find a dagger, except it's not quite like any dagger I've ever seen before. Pieces of the blade are cut out, and the hilt looks like bone.

"Fallon," Deacon starts just as I lift the dagger from the box, but then I don't hear anything else as I fall into a pit of darkness.

"Stop! Please, just stop!"

The screams make my head hurt, and the pain is like a thousand cuts across my body. I blink, trying to work out what's going on, when I see a dark-haired girl chained down. A man holding the knife I just picked up in the kitchen is leaning over her on one side while Azriel stands on her other.

"What the actual fuck!" I shout, but no one notices me. I storm over and try to push Azriel to get his attention, but my hands go through him, like I'm not really here. Or he's not real.

What is going on?

"You know how much I love your screams, Scout. Give them to me, give me them all," the man I don't recognize says, grinning down at the girl.

I try to move, but I'm frozen in place while the man and Azriel taunt and torture the girl, getting off on her screams.

"Isn't it funny how the children always pay for the sins of the father?" Azriel laughs, but it's as if the girl can't see him either.

None of this makes any sense.

The man laughs, and lifts the strange blade again, running it from her throat down to the 'v' between her legs. I swear to fuck I can't breathe as his sinister smile widens.

"You're going to enjoy this. Just like you always do. You might scream, but I know you like it really."

I struggle within the hold on my body, and after a few minutes of her screams, I close my eyes to the horrors before me, and I'm finally able to move again.

I move to see if I can interact with her but freeze.

She looks just like… Holy shit.

I'm hurtled back to my body and open my eyes to find myself lying on the floor with Colt and Deacon looking down at me. I groan as I sit up, noticing the destruction in the room around me.

"Fallon, are you okay?" Colt asks, his voice more growl than anything else.

"I'm fine," I tell him once I'm finally sitting upright, but the memory of what I just saw hits me, nearly bowling me right back over.

"What happened?" Deacon asks, and I just blink at him, almost seeing double.

"Deacon… do you have a sister?"

TWENTY THREE

DEACON

I rock back on my haunches at her question. Why the fuck would she ask that the minute she opens her eyes?

"You know I do… She was my twin, but she's been dead for far longer than I want to mention. Why?" I help her to her feet while Colt stands the chair she was sitting on back up, and I usher her onto it.

"I didn't know… I don't think. But that's not important. What is though, is that I'm pretty sure I just saw her," she says, and I swear to hell the room spins.

"That's not possible, Fallon. She died about three hundred years ago." I drop into a chair beside her, trying to steady myself. "What do you mean you saw her?"

"I think I had an echo when I touched the dagger. Sometimes they're of the past, but sometimes it feels like they're in real time. This one felt like the past, but Azriel didn't look any different to how I knew him." She shrugs, and I can tell how drained she is from it all.

The echoes are a fucking curse. I wish I could get my hands on Azriel and wipe him from existence. Just as soon as we find him, I intend on doing exactly that. I didn't want to think he could be mixed up in all of this, but I don't understand why she'd have the echo from the dagger otherwise. He must have handled it at some point, and if he is the one behind all of this shit, I still don't know what his reasoning is.

"Maybe you should explain where the dagger came from, and what actually happened when you touched it so we can go from there?" Colt says, standing across from me with arms crossed as he glares. His concern for Fallon is obvious; and while I'm concerned myself, I'm also trying to make sense of how Fallon could have possibly seen Scout.

Ellis appears with a glass of water and hands it to Fallon who thanks him before he disappears again. Fallon gulps the water, finishing nearly the entire glass, before telling us about what she saw. About a girl named Scout, the man, and Azriel. I almost don't want to hear it because it can't be possible. Azriel didn't know Scout. He was The

Carver's apprentice, and it sounds like he was the one in Fallon's vision. I'm just confused because Scout never suffered at the hands of The Carver.

"None of this makes sense," I say, dropping my head into my hands. "Do we know where the box came from?" I ask, looking at Fallon.

"Kevin brought it in." Colt storms from the room at her words, and a few moments later reappears with a terrified Kevin, who shakes even harder when he notices my red eyes.

"Speak," Colt growls, his eyes fully black as his anger allows his Demon through.

"Erm," the kid squeaks, and I frown. He's fucking terrified.

"Will the two of you dial back on the crazy Demon thing, please? Kevin, it's fine. Can you tell us where you got the box from?" Fallon says softly, standing and bringing him over to the table. She encourages him to sit in the seat opposite me, next to her. Colt stands behind her, with his arms crossed and looking as menacing as ever. He doesn't pay any attention to her request. "Just ignore these two for now. I won't let them hurt you because you didn't do anything wrong. Right?"

"Right. I just collected the packages from the gate like always. I gave you the box because it was addressed to you and then took everything else to Deacon's office. I didn't think anything of it. It's not like you haven't got stuff here before," he says, and Fallon nods.

"He's not wrong. I've had all sorts of things appear for me here over the years, so there was no reason for him to suspect anything," she tells us both, and I frown at the same time as Colt.

"Fine, Kevin is off the hook. But that doesn't explain who sent it to you, or why you went fucking catatonic when you touched it," I snarl, and Kevin scampers from the room faster than I can say boo.

She moves and picks up the dagger from the table before I have the chance to stop her. I feel the shift come over me and snarl at my loss of control. She's never seen me in this form before, but my anger, impatience, and worry are winning. She looks at me, half-wolf, half-man as I stare intently at the dagger in her hand. I swear to fuck she needs to put the fucking dagger back down.

"Put the dagger down," I snarl, and Colt grunts his agreement. She just passed out after touching it, and now she's picking it up like it was nothing at all. Hells give me strength.

"I'm okay," she tells me, before looking back at Colt and noticing that he's also struggling to keep his Demon under wraps. Through our bond I feel her, showing me that she's okay, and my wolf calms in my mind until the shift goes back. She must be doing the same for Colt because he turns back into the human version of himself, and even his dark eyes disappear. "So I think what I saw was an echo, like the others I've had in the past. Echoes from Azriel's memory."

"That can't be possible. He never met Scout, and neither did The Carver. I'd have known if my twin was tortured," I choke out. It would break me if I found out she'd ever been one of his playthings. I saw with my own eyes, witnessed with my own body, just what that monster was capable of. "But I still don't understand why you passed out when you touched the dagger."

"Power rush?" she offers with a shrug. It pisses me off how nonchalant she is about this all. It's like she has no sense of self-preservation.

"I still want to know where the fuck it came from, and why you got an echo from it."

"Azriel must have touched it at some point," she says, shrugging again. "Maybe whoever is doing this knows about my little quirks," she offers, and I mull it over. Not that many people know about the echoes, but the walls in this place have fucking ears. I really need Locke to get back so we can get this shit sorted out.

Tex rushes into the room, stopping the conversation in its tracks, his eyes wide.

"What's wrong?" I ask him, and he shakes his head.

"Nothing… Locke's awake. He's weak, but he asked

for you."

We all rush to the hospital wing where Locke has been comatose. We found no answers about what was wrong with him, or even where he'd actually been on his travels to find out what the fuck has been going on.

We reach the medical wing to find Locke sitting up in bed with his bonded, Laura, sitting by his side, in the same place she's been since we discovered we couldn't wake him. Except now she's smiling and holding his hand, and the relief on her face matches my own.

"You sure know how to fuck people up, don't you, man?" I joke as I reach him. He laughs, coughing. Laura passes him a glass of water which he sips from before looking back to me.

"I had no idea, but I should've known. I should have just spoken to you as soon as I got back." The air grows tense at his words.

"What happened?"

"I came across someone on level eight who said they had information. I met them for a drink, and then they showed me something that I thought was a fake until they proved it to be true. We went to the Outliers, and I didn't believe it until I saw it with my own eyes." He takes a deep breath and frowns. "I don't even know how it's possible, but it's Scout. She's alive. And I think she's with The Carver."

"What do you mean, she's dead?" The words tumble from my lips as my knees give way, and I fall onto the chair beside me. This can't be happening.

"You heard me, boy. We've searched for her for weeks. Today we found what was left of her." My father tells me the news like he's describing the weather. It feels like he just tore my heart from my chest.

She can't be dead. Surely, I'd know if my twin was dead.

"She can't be dead," I utter, and he backhands me across the jaw. I fall from my seat from the force of it, crashing to the floor.

"I just told you she was! Are you calling me a liar?" His eyes flash black, and I wince from instinct.

"No, of course not, she just… I can still feel her." I climb back up to my seat at the table and try to steady my breath, glad my jaw isn't broken this time.

"That twin crap is exactly that. It's bullshit. You're not bonded, so there's no way for you to feel her, dead or alive. Grow up, boy," he sneers down at me, his dark hair falling across his face as he practically spits at me.

"I want to see her," I stutter, trying to find some sort of strength to face off with my father. I won't believe it until

I see it for myself.

"Of course you fucking do," he mutters as he pours himself a drink. "Worthless sack of skin that you are. Of course you couldn't just trust my word. Fine, I'll have the remains brought here, shall I?"

I feel the pulse of his power fill the room and assume he's signaled for his captain. My father might answer to the Demon King, but because he runs the Outliers, he has more power than he should. But then again, this place is as dark as it is because of him. No one else would want the responsibility. The Outliers are the birthplace of his kind, the Shadowed. What my mother ever saw in him, I'll never know. He's always been a savage, worse than cruel, but I tried to shield Scout from as much of it as I could.

She was the very light in the darkness of our home.

I thought I'd managed to protect her from all of the horrors of our world.

Until I got home from one of my father's disgusting hunts four weeks ago, and she was gone.

At first, I'd hoped she'd run far from here, but then I noticed nothing of hers was gone. Not even the necklace I got for her for our last birthday, and I know she wouldn't have gone anywhere without that. She only ever took it off to shower. Once I found the necklace, my panic set in properly. I spent the last four weeks combing the Outliers for any word, any sighting, even a whisper of what had happened to her, but it was like she disappeared without a trace.

Father didn't bother to help until I got the guard on board, when he couldn't ignore me anymore. He's spent the last week out searching for her with me and the guard, and then beating my ass every night. Last night he beat me so badly, I was still broken this morning. It's the only reason I wasn't out today, so of course today is the day they find a trace of her.

But I won't believe it until I see it for myself.

Olivié, the captain of the guard, enters the room with a sack, which he drops on the table before me. He shoots me a sad look before leaving the room.

I smell it before I see it, the blood... the scent that is so very much Scout.

I can't believe it.

This can't be her. Maybe she really did get away. She just made this a trap and left her blood behind enough to convince everyone.

My father lifts the sack and empties the contents onto the table. I vomit on the floor as her head rolls across the table. Her face is cut and swollen beyond recognition, but her dark hair is matted with blood. The smell is so very much her. The eyes are even the icy blue of her eyes. Just dead, with no joy or sparkle that always adorned her face.

"Are you satisfied now?" My father laughs as I lose the

contents of my stomach on the floor. I nod my head, not wanting to look at the rest of the pieces of my twin on the kitchen table.

"Good, now dispose of her. I have people coming over this evening, and we'll be hosting dinner. I expect this room to be fucking spotless. Do you understand?"

"Yes, father," I say quietly, wishing to be anywhere but here.

"This is your own fault. If you'd looked after your sister like you were meant to, she'd still be alive. You're a disgrace to this family and a dishonor to our name. I'll think up a fitting punishment later." He storms from the room, slamming the door as he leaves, and only then do I let a tear fall.

My stomach heaves as I lift the body parts and place them back in the sack.

I'll bury her by the water on the edge of the Outliers. It was one of her favorite places in the entire Realm. Not that we've been all that many places, but the water brought her more happiness than almost anything else in our lives.

I'm glad my mother isn't here to see any of this. My father's darkness definitely grew once she retreated from us all, but I think she was still checked into this reality. This would have been enough to send her further down the bottle she lives inside of.

If Regan were here, this would never have happened.

But my big brother paid the price for my father's mistakes a few years ago. That was when Mother retreated. He was the light of her life. Closely followed by Scout—I've always been the disappointment. After Regan died, I was the one left to protect Scout from this world… and I failed.

Once I've pulled myself together and put her remains back in the sack, I clear the rest of the room before heading to my bedroom. I take her with me, not knowing what else to do with her.

The door to my room slams open, and my father staggers in. Apparently he's already had too much of the shadow flower tonight.

"You are such a fucking disappointment." His words slur from the intoxication, but I stay quiet. When he's like this, he's even more unpredictable than normal. "So I thought of the best way to be rid of you and to punish you all at once."

He staggers forward and punches me in the face, and I rock back. The blow isn't quite hard enough to knock me from my feet, but still it's hard enough to really fucking hurt. He laughs when he sees me still on my feet.

"I don't want to have to see your fucking face ever again. So your punishment will be enslavement."

I feel the blood rush from my face, and he laughs harder. I've seen what happens to his slaves.

"But Father," I start, and he hits me again, this time

with enough force to throw me across the room.

"Don't you, but father, me. You'll be sent to the Demon King. Maybe time with him will show you how to be a real fucking man." He spits on me before turning and leaving the room, taking Scout's remains with him.

A hopelessness I've never felt before swallows me whole, and I wonder if I shouldn't have died right along with Scout.

TWENTY FOUR

FALLON

To say the news of Scout being alive rocked Deacon is like saying an earthquake clocking in at eight on the Richter Scale is merely a slight quiver. A serious understatement.

I swear he went almost catatonic when Locke explained more about what he'd discovered. Especially with the news about The Carver too. Morgan and Caleb already confirmed he was dead, so none of it makes any sense, but Locke was adamant that Scout was alive. That he'd seen her in the Outliers.

After confirmation from Locke that she looked alive and happy, I managed to convince Deacon that we needed to make a plan. That we couldn't just rush to the Outliers to get her, because one, we don't know how she's still alive, and two, she hasn't reached out to Deacon.

That, coupled with her being with The Carver and their parents' body parts delivered to our front door, leaves me with a bad feeling in my gut. It's like we can only see a very small part of the picture, and not knowing the whole of it is going to bite us in the ass.

Thankfully, he listened to me. I could feel his worry through the bond—his desperate need to rush to his twin—but logic managed to win out. I had the nurse sort out a tonic to help him sleep, and he's been out for the last twelve hours while I've been sitting at his bedside.

Colt's been with Locke trying to get more information to make any of the pieces fit together. Like me, he agrees that none of this quite adds up the way it should.

I have an insistent feeling inside of me that I can't quite decipher, but I just know that if we rush in, guns blazing, it'll bite us on the ass.

"Fallon…" Deacon mumbles as he stirs, and I squeeze his hand. "Was it a dream?"

"I'm afraid not," I tell him softly, wishing I could take the pain from him that I feel spear through our bond.

"My entire life has been a lie. Everything that happened was because of her death. My father… He told me she was dead. There was a body. It was her, I was sure of it. I would've never given up otherwise."

"I know you wouldn't have. But you were only a child. You couldn't have known."

"Why would he do this?" he moans as he pulls me into his arms.

"I don't know, but we'll work it all out; and when we have more of the picture, we'll go to your sister. Locke says she's okay, and I really don't want you to risk yourself going after her until we know more," I plead with him, and his arms tighten around me.

"I won't. I won't do anything to risk this, and you're right. Even though Locke says she's okay, I'm going to send a few trusted scouts out to the Outliers to try and get some more information. If all of that fails, then we'll go. But we'll go together."

"Okay," I whisper, praying that he doesn't go and get himself killed, just when everything is starting to settle back down for us. I should have known something would come and shatter the peace we'd found, but I never saw this coming.

How could I?

"Is there anything I can do?" I ask as I feel his sadness rip through our bond once more.

"Just exactly what you're doing," he murmurs into my hair, his grip on me not loosening. I sigh against his chest and relax into his hold. If this is what will help him,

I'll stay here for as long he needs. I feel fucking useless, though.

"She can't be with The Carver so who could she possibly be with?" I ask, not really expecting an answer.

"I don't know, but whoever it is has taken up his mantle. I lost track of my father's interactions with The Carver and his apprentices once I was enslaved to the Demon King. I only ever saw them when their games were forced upon me."

"It still doesn't make sense why she would work with this person, and why they would send bodies and parts here," I think aloud, and he grunts.

"I have no fucking idea, but I'm tired of not understanding what the fuck is going on." He sighs before sitting up, pulling me with him. "Let's get up. I've been in bed long enough. I want to get the ball rolling on all of this. The sooner we work out if this really is Scout, the sooner we can get on with the rest of our lives."

"You don't think it's her?" I ask, shocked.

"Locke knew my sister, but he didn't know her like I did. I saw her body. I saw the pieces of her quite literally dumped on a table inches from my face. Anyone could be wearing her face to fuck with us. She's been dead long enough that most people would have forgotten her. If someone is trying to fuck with me, this is one hell of a way to do it."

"I think you might be right. How best to throw you off from what's really happening than to send you down some rabbit hole of desperation at the possibility of your family not being dead?" As I say the words, the truer it feels to me, and I feel the same instinct from him.

"If someone thinks they can get to me this easily, they're severely fucking wrong. And if it does turn out to be her, well... then I have no fucking answers for that." He lets out a deep breath and pulls me further onto his lap. "But we'll deal with it all together."

He kisses me softly at first but deepens it, pulling on my hair as his other hand grips my hip. He growls, and I know he'll enjoy this distraction as much as I will.

I left Deacon sleeping this morning when I woke. He's been working like crazy these last few days with Locke and Colt, and I've barely seen them. He's tried to keep me out of it as much as possible, which I get since he doesn't want me to get hurt, but I can look after myself. I want to be there for him in this, and I can't do that if he keeps pushing me aside.

I find Colt half-asleep, cradling a cup of coffee in the nook, and I smile at him before crawling next to him on the sofa and tucking myself under his arm.

"You look tired," I say, hoping he'll let me in on what's

been going on.

"I feel it too. I didn't even know it was possible to feel this tired as an immortal." He smirks, but he lacks the sparkle in his eyes, and I feel through the bond just how tired he really is.

"What have you guys been doing?" I ask, prying even though I know Deacon wants me out of it. But fuck that. Colt knows I'm not a delicate petal, so I'm hoping he'll let me in the circle of trust.

"We've been organizing scouts to go to the Outliers, but it's not as simple as it sounds. We're trying to find Demons we can trust who aren't recognizable to people in the Outliers as friends of Deacon's, but who will still be trusted enough by people there to gain useful information." He sighs, pinching the bridge of his nose. "The problem is the Outliers is almost outside of Morgan's domain. It's not, but it's like its own entity. It's weird as fuck, and the people there are about as trusting as Leviathan."

I chuckle at the comparison because it seems pretty fair considering Levi doesn't trust anymore he's not shed blood with.

"So are you getting anywhere with it all?" I ask softly.

"We are. We spent yesterday securing entry with Locke's brother. He's risking a lot by getting people in that aren't family, but luckily, he was willing to help us."

"Well that's good." I smile, but I feel kind of like a

spare part. I just want to help. I hate being left on the sidelines, but I also don't want to sound like a petulant child who feels left out.

Rock, meet hard place.

"Is there anything I can do to help?"

"I don't think so, just being here for him and letting him know you're safe is probably the best thing you can do." I groan at his words because that's so freaking typical. I don't want to just sit here on my ass. "There is something else I've been thinking about though that I think that could help."

"Oh?" I ask, willing to give him my full attention. Because if there is anything I can do, I am so there.

"I don't want to be another problem for us. Any of us," he says, and I hold my breath, having no idea where this is going but hoping it's going to go where I want it to.

"Oh?" I ask, trying to remain calm.

"Yeah," he answers simply, chuckling. "You can try to shut down your smile all you like, Fal, but we're bonded. I can feel what you're feeling."

"Pssh, stop changing the subject and continue… please." I grin up at him, and he shakes his head.

"Okay, since you asked so nicely." He chuckles before taking a deep breath. "I want to try. This thing with you. Us. All three of us as a unit. It turns out you were right, and Deacon isn't the giant asshole I thought he was. Plus, we have so much going on outside of our dynamic right now, I don't want me being an asshole to be another stressor. So if this is still what you want, I'm willing to try."

Colt saying the words I've been so desperate to hear floods my body with relief.

"You'll really try?" I ask, wanting to make sure I heard what he said, not just what I wanted him to say.

"I'm in this, Fallon. You and me. You and him. However this ends up going. I'm here. I can't say I won't fuck up sometimes, but I'm going to try." His words are like music to my ears. I swear I could almost cry. "Just be patient with me. I might not be the best at this, but I love you. I don't want to lose you."

"I love you too," I gasp, jumping into his arms and kissing him. He grabs my ass and lifts me, and I wrap my legs around his waist to stay in place, not that he'd ever let me fall.

I rain kisses all over his face, his cheeks, his chin, his mouth, down his neck where I land a harmless bite that has its desired effect, if that steel mast in his pants is any indication.

It's not until I hear Deacon's deep baritone that I realize Colt's brought me to the room I share with Deacon as he gently places me on the end of the bed.

I'm shocked, considering everything else that's going on, that they chose now to try this now, but I am not going to object. I think we could all use something to feel a little better right now.

It's surreal, both of my men standing in front of me, looking at me like they each want to devour every inch of me and then start all over again.

"Are you happy, baby girl?" Deacon asks softly.

Bringing my legs up to the bed, I sit cross-legged and grin like a toddler.

"Ecstatic."

"Good." Deacon turns his attention to Colt, and for a second, it's like they're having their own conversation with just eye contact. I'm just enjoying the view. Two total hotties, and they're both all mine. I can't even imagine the conversation they must have had that got us to this point, but I'm looking forward to being thoroughly fucked. Literally.

When Deacon's gaze circles back around to me, I feel like I'm caught in his web; his Dominant web. The one that summons my entire control and syphons it all until I'm his perfect little submissive.

"Take his clothes off, baby girl. Make him feel like a king."

Licking my lips, I jump from the bed and take the two steps that lead me to Colt, whose chest is heaving with pent-up hunger. His eyes are fixed on my lips, and I lick them once for effect.

"Quit teasing, Fallon. No topping from the bottom or else it's the flogger that comes out tonight."

I shiver at the thought, but it isn't fear that elicited the reaction. No, it's complete and utter need. For a second, I consider disobeying, craving the feel of the soft leather kissing my skin in pain. Colt's hunger and my desire to have them both inside me at once is the only reason I behave. We can save the flogger for another time.

Placing my hands on the hem of Colt's t-shirt, I skim his skin with my nails and the electric jolt that I receive pulls a gasp from my mouth.

Our eyes meet, and one side of Colt's mouth rises slightly in a smirk. His elongated teeth peek out, telling me he's already skirting the edge of control.

He lets me do my job unhindered. I undress him as slowly as I can without teasing the beast inside him too much and enjoy myself thoroughly the entire time. I savor taking my time unwrapping him until Colt is standing proudly in front of me, his tattoos a colorful masterpiece decorating the perfect canvas of his body. I chance a look at his cock just to be met with the sight of it, long and hard with the head resting at his belly button. The piercings are scintillating against the lighting of the room.

"Nice metal, it'll add to her pleasure."

Deacon's approval of Colt makes me smile internally, I didn't think we'd get here, but I'm getting exactly what

I want, and I'm going to savor it in case it's the only time I get it.

"It definitely doesn't hurt." Colt smirks, and I curl my toes merely at the thought of it.

I don't say a thing, but I almost want to scream that his Jacob's ladder is the epitome of pleasure. If I didn't know that Deacon would shoot the idea down in a heartbeat, I'd suggest he do the same.

"Lie down on the bed, Colt, on your back."

Of course, Deacon would be the one to take charge of this, again, I have no idea if they discussed this or not, but I'm not going to object to one goddamn thing. I guess Deacon running the show is one way to ease Colt into this thing between us. I cross my fingers and hope the alpha within each of them reacts well to the other, especially with me being a submissive doe, at their total mercy. Colt growls a little, and they have a momentary standoff while I hold my breath, hoping like fuck this isn't about to blow up.

It takes a moment longer, but Colt seems to sort out whatever made his hackles rise before climbing onto the bed. Once he's on his back, he folds his arms behind his head and proudly shows off his body, his smirk as cocky as I've ever seen it.

My mouth waters... Like actual saliva pools on my tongue at the sight of him all hard and colorful.

Deacon is behind me suddenly with his lips at my neck while his hands rip away every single article of clothing from my body. His tongue leads a path up to my ear before he whispers, “Get into position, straddling his face.” He pulls a small groan from me when he bites my lobe, hard.

Colt growls again at the order, so I send a wave of love through our bond, letting him know that I’m good and that all of this is okay. The rumble in his chest stops, and he looks at me, nodding, telling me he’s okay before I do as Deacon asked.

Scrambling, I crawl to Colt’s head and fold my thighs on either side of his face, resting my ass on his chest and placing my hands, neatly, right above my knees. My head is down, my hair falling over my breasts, but my eyes are on Colt. Our gazes are heated, the black Demon pools have pushed aside his green depths, and it seems as if the thought of having me here, with my pussy so close to his mouth, is making his control falter, which causes my body buzz with anticipation.

“Good girl.” Deacon is now on the side of the bed, assessing my posture.

“See how well she’s been trained, Colt?”

Licking his lips, Colt nods, but I can feel a jolt of unease from him at the word “trained”. Through our bond I can feel that he doesn’t exactly love the idea, but I get it, considering everything I’ve been through. That just means I need to explain all of this better to him. Make him understand that this is exactly what I want. What I need. Maybe not always, but it's definitely something I couldn't imagine living without now, and I send as much of that emotion through our bond in the hopes he gets it until I can properly use my words.

"Rise up, my beautiful angel, and let Colt taste your pussy," Deacon commands, and when Colt doesn't object, I smirk. Of course he doesn't object to that.

I do as I'm told, riding the line between following the order and making sure Colt's comfortable with everything. When Colt's wet tongue glides through my pussy lips, I close my eyes and lose myself in the sensation of how good it feels. I feel Deacon's hands on my wrists, tying them with the silk ropes before binding me to the headboard. In this position with my head down between my arms, my view of Colt eating my pussy is clear as day, and it's hot as fuck.

I can't stop the moan that escapes my mouth. The visual coupled with the feel of his skilled, pierced tongue does me in.

"That's it, baby girl. Ride his face. Show him how much you love the feel of him on you."

My hips move as though I'm riding a horse.

I suppose I am riding a Colt. I smirk at the stupid pun until he applies more pressure to my clit with his tongue, bringing my attention right the fuck back on him and his mouth.

Unfolding his arms, Colt brings his hands to my thighs and guides my rhythm as he fucks my pussy with his tongue, lapping up my juices and sucking on my clit. I grind on his face, lost completely to the sensation of his oral talents.

Throwing my head back with abandon, something catches my eye. And there, to my right, I see Deacon pulling his cock out and giving himself a couple of strokes before leaving it out for me to salivate over. One quick glance at his face shows me a devilish smirk firmly planted on his mouth, and his eyes bore into mine with a clear message. I want you. He sends the same emotion through our bond.

But he doesn't move. He doesn't demand I suck his cock. He just stands there, hard and filled with need, watching as another man brings me pleasure.

This is why I love him.

His love for me is so great that he's willing to share just because he knows it'll make me happy.

I'm one lucky bitch.

I gasp when I feel a pinch of pain and realize Colt bit my clit just hard enough to pull my attention back on him.

Through our bond, I can feel that he's calling for my undivided attention, so I give it to him while keeping my peripheral on Deacon until he disappears behind me.

With my hands holding on to the headboard like my life depends on it, I try not to suffocate Colt as he feasts on my pussy like a beast deprived of a hundred meals. I startle at the feel of a wet finger tracing a path down the line of my spine, slowly and meticulously. As Deacon reaches the small of my back, I feel his other hand on my head, pushing me forward.

That's when I feel his finger slide across my puckered hole. I'm so wet from my cum and Colt's saliva that I'm sure I'm lubricated all the way back there, but I know for a fact that no matter the circumstances, Deacon will always use lube when playing with my ass.

This is no different. His finger slides easily inside me, and the double sensation of Colt's mouth and Deacon's finger rockets me to the very edge of orgasm. I hold back, not wanting to come until he gives me the order, and the restraint feels so fucking good.

"Do you see her almost losing control, Colt? She wants to come, her entire body is shaking with the need, but she won't. Because I haven't given her permission."

Colt just moans against me, the vibration travelling across the walls of my pussy and making me shake with my need to let go.

It's when I clench my thighs, my entire core clamping down on Colt's tongue and my ass squeezing Deacon's finger that I hear the words I need the most.

"Come for us, pretty girl."

And I do.

The cry that escapes my lungs is feral, an animal in need of release. Below me, Colt drinks me up, takes everything I have to give while Deacon fucks the orgasm right through me by curling his finger and exacerbating the already too intense sensations.

When I feel the climax recede, I almost fall forward but Deacon catches me.

"Easy there, baby girl. We're not done yet."

"Not by a long shot." I open my eyes and see black Demon eyes and the elongated teeth of Colt's Demon, but my Colt's smirk is still there, his personality shining through as bright as the sun.

"Feels so good. You. Both." I can't even use complete sentences with my mind filled with complete mush.

As Deacon retreats from my ass, I see him grab the wipes and clean himself off while Colt sexily drags the back of his hand across his mouth and blinds me with a satisfied grin.

"Sit back against the headboard, Colt. It's time to give our girl everything she's ever wanted."

When Colt pushes himself up, backing toward the headboard and sitting up, he's right there, his mouth a mere breath from mine. When we crash together, I can taste myself on his lips. I swear his kiss has the power to bring me back to life, filling me with the energy I need until I'm ready to be fucked like the good girl I am.

I can't touch him since my hands are still bound to the headboard, with his head between my forearms, but I can feel his dick sliding between the lips of my pussy, slowly, leisurely, like he's preparing me for what's to come. The best part is when he slides all the way back to my ass and then back through my slick folds again.

I'm so wet, I can hear as he moves below me and I barely manage to keep my whimper in. When I see Deacon come back with the bottle of lube, I sink my teeth into my bottom lip, stopping myself from moaning in excitement.

What I really want is to scream a resounding, "YES," at the idea of having two big, beautiful dicks inside me at the same time.

"This is going to hurt a little, but it's no different than when I fuck you with a dildo. Understand?"

I nod. Yes, yes, I understand. Let's get on with it.

Of course, I don't say any of this, but Deacon knows me too well. Our bond is too strong for him to miss the impatience buzzing around my body.

Feeling the dip of the bed behind me, I know Deacon is there, the heat of his body crashing against my back.

"Sink inside that pretty little pussy. Is she wet?" he says to Colt, who looks me straight in the eye and grins. He lifts me up just enough for me to hover above the tip of his cock before he winks, slamming me down on top of him.

"She's fucking drenched," he groans as I cry out. I can't help it. The fullness, the thickness of him… His presence inside of me is overwhelming.

We both freeze, taking a second to appreciate the feeling of being joined together. Colt crashes his mouth to mine and kisses me thoroughly, licking, biting, and sucking on my tongue.

Meanwhile, behind me, Deacon is preparing my ass for the monster that is his cock. One and then two fingers pump inside my channel before he adds a third and scissors them just enough to spread the lube. I can't help but wonder if his cock will even fit, and if it does, how I'll even be able to breathe.

"Does he feel good in your pussy, pretty girl?" Deacon fucks my ass with his fingers, his mouth at my ear. I imagine he's watching Colt's cock slowly slide out of me and then push right back inside.

The visual in my mind is h-o-t, HOT. So fucking hot that it makes my pussy involuntarily clench on Colt's dick, causing him to suck in a breath through his teeth.

"Are you ready for this?" I'm not sure if he's asking me or Colt. Maybe he's asking us both, but it doesn't really matter. All I know is that in the seconds that follow, I feel the pressure of Deacon's cock at my ass and have to remember to breathe in through my nose and out through my mouth, to relax fully in order to allow him entrance.

He's right, the mechanics are the same as when he uses a dildo, but none of our toys are as big as either of them which makes me anticipate a bite of pain.

I'm not disappointed. As Deacon breaches my tightness, no amount of lube could prepare me for the sting that follows. He pushes through slowly, not stopping until I find myself pinned by the two of them. They're embedded deep inside the most intimate parts of me.

"How do you feel, baby?" This comes from Colt, who's mere inches in front of me.

"It feels…" I can't find the words, so I settle for the most telling, "perfect."

Colt's gaze shifts behind me and when he looks back at me, I feel them shifting. Deacon retreats while Colt stays planted, then Deacon pushes back in as Colt slides me up his shaft. In tandem, they fuck me slowly, tentatively, getting me used to the feel of their penetrating cocks.

I pant, my fingers aching from the tight hold on the headboard, but I don't want it to stop. I don't ever want this feeling of fullness, of belonging, of completion, to ever stop. I want this for the rest of my life.

Colt sinks his fingers into my thighs, his elongated nails breaking the skin and giving me that extra bite of pain I crave, while Deacon reaches my front and engulfs my tits with his big hands. His calloused fingers roll and pinch my nipples, sending a bolt of lightning between my legs. As if I haven't already reached the culmination of all that is pleasure and pain, as if they'd practiced the move endless times in private, Deacon pinches my nipples so hard I see stars just as Colt brings his mouth to mine and kisses me senseless.

"Come for us, beautiful," Deacon murmurs, and I lose myself.

I fall over the edge with Deacon's mouth on my shoulder, his teeth sinking into my flesh on the opposite side of my mark from Colt. All while Colt, on my other side, sinks his Demon teeth into my neck where he did before and comes with me. Deacon follows a moment later, and it drives my own orgasm to a level I didn't know existed.

My cry is otherworldly, a sound I've never heard.

I sag against Colt's chest and thank the Goddess for blessing me with so much love in my life.

TWENTY FIVE

FALLON

"None of this is working," the dark-haired woman says, stomping her feet like a toddler in the thrums of a tantrum.

"Patience, my love. It takes time. We're working through all those who deserved this ending. The best revenge takes time," Azriel soothes the woman, who I'm still not convinced is Scout, despite her face. "All things will end just as you want."

"He has to pay for what he did to me!" she complains, and he pulls her in for a hug.

"And he will. I would never lie to you, or hurt you the way they all did. I just need you to trust me."

"I do." She sags in his arms and rests her head on his shoulder. "You saved me."

"And I'd do it all over again, a thousand times."

I watch them, trying to work out if this is the past, despite the fact that it feels like I'm watching in real time. I've seen this softer side of Az, and for me, it was all a lie. Is that what this is? Or was this before he became so broken?

It's all so fucking confusing.

"Just be patient, we have them exactly where we want them. He won't be able to resist the pull to his birthplace much longer. We both know that his hero complex will win out. Then we'll have him exactly where we want him. I just need a little more time to make sure he won't be able to call for help, that he'll be truly helpless once we get him here, and then... then you get your revenge."

She squeals with happiness, and my stomach flips before the falling sensation starts again.

I wake up in a fit, feeling like I'm falling from the bed. It takes a second to get myself reorientated, and I realize I'm fine. It was just a dream.

But it didn't feel like a dream.

I look around and notice I'm alone in bed, which I'm half glad for because otherwise Deacon would know something isn't quite right. The emotion I can just attribute to a bad dream… But there's something inside of me telling me this isn't all just a coincidence.

It can't be, and I won't let Deacon walk into a trap. That didn't feel like a dream. It felt like I was spying on Azriel, and if I still have a connection to him because of his time leaching my soul, then I'm not about to let go of the only advantage we have.

My biggest issue is that if I say something to Colt or Deacon, they're going to rush in there guns blazing, leaving me behind. But if this is all Azriel, I have to find out for myself. I can't lose anyone else, and if what I saw was real, they intend to take something huge from me... again.

I want to work this out for myself before I call in the big guns. I can't explain why, but I feel like this is what *I* have to do if we're ever going to get our chance at happiness together. I've always trusted my intuition, and it screams at me that if I let the boys handle this, and they go in guns blazing, then I'll lose one or both of them.

And I know I won't survive that.

Any of it.

Now I just need to figure out how I'm going to make this work without running to either of them for help. I've been working with Killian to make sure I can survive and thrive in these exact sort of situations. So I know I can do it, I just need help with the logistics.

Which is kind of a problem, but dammit, I am a strong,

independent woman. I can work this shit out.

I think.

I spend the morning puttering around the estate, trying to glean as much information about what's going on as I can while remaining seemingly oblivious and unaware at the same time. The time spent is worth it. With the snippets of information I overhear, along with the information from the echo, I think I have it just about pieced together.

From what I can tell, the hardest part will be getting to the Outliers. It's not like the other levels, which are entirely inaccessible without the help of a higher demon. What I'm gathering is that the Outliers are like their own closed community and getting in without permission or knowing someone from there is not simple.

So that tells me I need to either stealth my way in, or I need to find an accomplice. I'm not sure which will be easier, but that's food for thought for the rest of the day.

As I seem to have an abundance of spare time with both Colt and Deacon gone, I guess I have time to think about it without them figuring me out.

I mean, I get that they're out looking into the dagger that was delivered to me—which was totally creepy, but still...

Maybe once life settles down, I should like, get a job or something here, if that's even a thing. Having this much time to myself would usually drive me nuts. Maybe I can apprentice with one of the Horsemen or something.

The day passes by quickly enough, and it's not until I climb into bed that I realize I already know what I have to do.

I guess tomorrow I put my plan into place.

"Are you sure this is a good idea?" Killian asks once I explain my plan to him.

"I mean, yes and no. I don't want Deacon to get hurt. And they're so busy trying to keep me safe that they're not giving any thought to keeping themselves safe. I'm also kind of sick of being saved. Ultimately, like I told you, I don't think any of this is really about me."

"And you're sure this is Azriel fucking with you guys again?"

"I'm not sure of anything, but that's what I saw. And I'm the one with the power to end this once and for all. I deserve my own closure when it comes to him. I'm not saying I'm going to run in there and blow shit up—that's Remy's style not mine—but I want our lives back."

"I understand that. Hells, they're going to kill me if they find out I helped you." He sighs, and my stomach clenches and my heart beats an erratic cadence in my chest at the realization that he said he'll help me. He walks over to the dresser in the corner of the training room before coming back toward me, shaking his head.

"Take this," he says, handing me a bracelet. I look at it questioningly, and he chuckles. "Look, I trust that you can handle yourself. I trained you, so I know exactly what you're capable of even if the others don't. I have faith that you can either get in and out without being noticed or that you can handle yourself if you do run into trouble. Either way, it would be remiss of me not to have a fail-safe. So this bracelet works two ways. It's a tracker, so I'll know where you are at all times, but it's also a touch sensor."

He takes the bracelet and ties it to my wrist before tying a matching one around his. "Tap once to check in. Push and hold if you're stuck and need an extraction. Tap three times if I need to bring the cavalry in."

I examine the bracelet as he places a finger over the black bead where the buckle is and my wrist gets zapped gently. I squeak in shock even though I knew something was coming.

"See, simple but effective," he says with a devilish grin, and I can't help but laugh.

"Okay, this is kind of perfect. Thank you."

"You're more than welcome, I believe in you. Just try not to get yourself killed because I've only fought with Mara once, and I really don't want to do it again. I'd also kinda miss you. So yeah, be a badass bitch."

"I'll try to bear that in mind if shit gets hairy." I laugh, shaking my head. "So how am I getting into the Outliers exactly?"

He grins at me, and I get a thrill of excitement from the devious look on his face. "There's intelligence in the simplest plans, Fallon. You'll be my guest."

I look like a freaking Scottish widow or some shit. Killian gave me this get-up, and I feel like a Hunter or something equally as badass… Which leaves me with total imposter syndrome right now. Also? I never realized just how uncomfortable leather pants are. I'm definitely going to ask Remy what her fascination with them is because all they've done so far is annoy me by riding up my ass.

The pants paired with impractical, thick-heeled boots, a corset, and a full-length freaking hooded cape finish the look, and I feel ridiculous.

"Is this really necessary?" I ask Killian for the eleventy billionth time, and he just laughs at me yet again.

"Yes, if you want to get in here reasonably undetected, and manage not to stick out like a sore thumb, then you need to blend in. This outfit will help you blend. I told you before, this place is a bit weird. It hasn't really moved on with the times, so this is how you keep yourself unnoticed."

I roll my eyes, and he chuckles once again. I don't see him in a stupid-ass get-up. "Once I get you through the gates, it's on you. It might be uncomfortable and weird, but this was your plan. Stealth remember?"

"Yeah, yeah, I remember. I also remember why I'm not the one who usually makes the plans. I'm used to cleaning up the mess after." I blow out a deep breath, pushing the hair from my face, and he shakes his head at me again.

"Yeah, but you're doing the whole growing as a person thing. Now you're not the clean-up crew, you get to be the mess maker… Maybe… Just, again, please do not get yourself smushed."

"Yeah, I know, angry Angel best friend."

"Exactly." He grins as we approach the black gate at what seems to be the end of the dusty track. It feels like we've been walking down it for forever.

"Just remember, if Colt and Deacon turn up looking for me…"

"Then I'll send them if you haven't checked in," he says sternly, and I let out a huff.

"I thought we agreed you'd only send the cavalry if I called for them."

"In theory, yes, but if your two bonded Demons end up tearing the palace apart, Morgan will be pissed…"

"And you don't want to deal with that. Got it." I sign him an okay then look at my fingers like they're not even my own. What the fuck was that?

"You've got this. Badass bitch, remember?"

"I know." I nod, wishing I could do the Superwoman pose just for a minute to make me feel better. But I'd look fucking ridiculous, and I'm pretty sure that won't help with the whole stealth thing.

"Wait here for a minute, and keep your hood up."

I wait out of earshot while he moves and talks to the guy at the gate. It doesn't take long, but he waves me over.

"Thanks, I owe you one," I hear him murmur quietly once I reach them. He turns his attention back to me. "Just please, *please*, keep your head down and remember to check in every few hours. If you miss a check-in, I'll give you an hour before I come storming in."

"Thank you," I say and pull him in for a quick hug. He's rigid at first, shocked I think by the action, but he hugs me back after a second before pulling away. "I promise to try to not get into any trouble."

"Let's hope you're not too much like Mara after all," he says softly. "Cause those are some famous last words."

It takes me an embarrassingly long time to work out where the fuck I am on Killian's map, and I will literally never admit that fact to another fucking soul.

Once I finally work out where the fuck I am, and plan out my route, I start making the trek. I lose track of time, but thankfully, at the first check-in point, Killian buzzes me, so I tap the bracelet to let him know I'm ok.

Over three fucking hours.

It takes me more than three fucking hours to work out where I am and to cross the Outliers to Deacon's family estate. Thankfully, Killian wasn't lying when he said my outfit would help me blend in. Every person I've come across is dressed in a similar sort of get-up, and it blows my mind that they're okay with all of these ass-eating pants. It blows my fucking mind.

I'm aware I should probably be more focused on what I'm doing, where I'm going, and on my surroundings, but you walk for over three hours in leather pants, with them riding up your ass crack, and see if you can focus. Throw the heels in and this has been nothing short of a fucking shitshow.

The upside? The estate is in view… except everyone forgot to mention that it looks like a house of fucking horrors. The Shadow Palace is daunting, but at least it's beautiful. This place genuinely has heads on spikes around the fucking wall that surrounds it like some Vlad the Impaler shit.

Did I puke when I saw them? Yes, yes I fucking did.

Am I still heading toward the house of horrors? Yes,

yes I am. Because there is no way I got dressed like this, and went through all of this, to turn back at the sight of a severed head. Or more like a couple dozen heads. I guess this is where the heads from the bodies ended up, because if I had to take a bet, I'd definitely put my life savings on the fact that this is one hundred percent where the bodies that ended up at our house came from.

It's so fucking skeevy.

The house of horrors seems like a fortress, but thanks to Killian, I know about the staff's entrance at the back of the estate. I head in that direction across the black sandy ground, grateful that the hooded cape both shields me from the elements and helps me blend in.

This place might be called the Outliers, but it's definitely more suited to the name of the Shadow Realm than anywhere else I've been. Everything here exists in shades of black, white, and gray. It's like there's no life here at all. Only death.

As I get closer, the smell of rotting flesh envelops me, and my stomach rolls.

This is so fucking gross.

But I refuse to leave here without some sort of fucking information.

Once I'm closer, I notice the sentry guards dotted around the wall. Of course this couldn't be easy, why would it be? I couldn't get just one break in this Goddess forsaken place. I keep moving, trying to remain as out of sight as I can until I can see the back staff entrance Killian mentioned.

"Thank fuck," I whisper to myself, realizing there's only one Demon at the gate. I can handle one Demon.

Right?

I try to think about the best way to do this, but I come up blank. So I do what Killian told me to do. Fake it till I make it. Badass panties are firmly on, even if they are riding straight up my ass crack thanks to the leather pants.

I've totally got this.

I walk up to the gate like I have every right to be here. My shoulders back, head high, even though he can't see my face with this hood up. I'm starting to see the advantages of the ridiculous get-up after all.

"What the fuck do you want? This entryway is closed," the Demon sneers, and I smile to myself even though he can't see it. I could have been nice, but manners don't cost a goddamn thing. So now I won't be so nice.

I call on the shadows and dart forward, placing a hand on his heart before he realizes what I'm doing. I push the power directly into his heart, feeling the second it slows. It won't kill him, but it'll sure as shit put him on his ass.

I groan as his weight slumps against me, and my legs tremble as I try to keep us standing.

"Giant lump of a shitty Demon," I grumble as I push

him backward until he slides down the wall, looking like he's sleeping on the job. I put two fingers to his temple and push shadows into his mind. That will at least keep him asleep, even if his heart restarts.

One down, Goddess only knows how many more to go.

Making it through the gate was apparently the easy part. There's a part of me that thinks that maybe I should've left this to the others because I'm shitting myself knowing I probably should've asked for help. Apparently being a spontaneous badass isn't actually my thing. But there's a much louder part of me that keeps yelling at me that I can do this. Killian's vote of confidence definitely helps, but I have to say, having years of people telling me that something isn't my place, or it's something I shouldn't be doing, apparently has given me more of a complex than I realized.

Once I make my way into the house of horrors, I tap the bracelet letting Killian know I'm still alive and kicking—especially because I have no idea of how long I've actually been here—and then try to figure out where to go from here.

If I was a batshit crazy, evil mastermind, where would

I be?

I move as quietly as I can through the halls on the ground floor. What is with this fucking Realm and the houses all being fucking giant? Doesn't anyone understand the value of a cozy freaking cottage?

I mean, seriously.

I realize I haven't come across one other living soul as I work my way through the eerily quiet house, and it's enough to make my blood run cold.

What if there's no one here? What if it *was* just a dream? I'll have pissed Deacon and Colt both off and all for nothing.

I close my eyes and take a deep breath. This can't have been for nothing. I did not wear these stupid pants and go through all of this for nothing. Surely there wouldn't have been guards here if there's no one inside the house.

Right?

Unless they're just here from before Deacon's family died, and they're merely waiting for orders on what to do next.

Fuck.

Shit.

Goddammit.

I continue making my way through the house. I'm halfway through examining the third floor when a scream pierces through the silence. I nearly jump a foot in the air at the desperate sound, but it didn't sound close.

Maybe I should've gone down instead of up. The crazy shit always happens in the basement in the movies.

I make my way toward the screams as quickly and quietly as I can. In another lifetime, I'd be screaming at myself for running toward the danger, but that was a different time and a different me. If Azriel is here, and he's torturing someone the way he tortured me… I don't even want to think about it.

I reach the door where the screams seem to be coming from and open it as softly as I can.

Stairs that go down, of course. I freaking knew it.

I start down the stairs, and the screams start again, so I move faster than I have up until now. I reach the last step, and my stomach bottoms out when I find Azriel grinning at me with the woman I've been seeing in the echoes laughing at his side.

She moves forward so quickly that she disappears from sight, and then I feel her hand tug my hair as she places a knife to my throat.

I swear my whole body shudders as she holds me still as he smiles at me. I feel instantly dirty, thrown down a path of memory I really don't want to take.

The smile on Azriel's face makes me want to scream. "Oh look, pet, you found my favorite toy."

TWENTY SIX

FALLON

"I fucking knew it," I huff, trying to call on my shadows and failing. I glance back at the woman holding me and stare in shock. It's weird how much she looks like Deacon. "What even are you?"

"My pretty little pet is a Void, aren't you, love?" Azriel coos, and I think I vomit in my mouth a little.

"I never knew it before, but Azriel saved me. He made me realize exactly what I was capable of. Now no one can hurt me ever again. I can take their power from them. They can't hurt me if they don't have their power." Scout swoons over him, and I swear I see the inside of my head from rolling my eyes just a little too damn hard.

"You know he's just using you, right?" She yanks on my hair and shoves me to my knees. I wince at the bite of the pain, but these god- awful leather pants cushion the blow a bit. But when I feel panic flooding through me via my bond with Colt and Deacon, I realize that they know that not only am I a bit hurt, but I'm not at home either.

Shit.

I send back as much of an "I'm okay," as I can muster, and try to discreetly tap my bracelet too. I'm not in any real danger yet. Scout might be a Void, but she can't keep me contained at all times. I'm not willing to call for help just yet. Killian trained me well; I can handle this. And if I can't? Well, *then* I'll call in the cavalry.

"He's not using me," she hisses. "He loves me."

"Yeah, he tried that one on me too." She lets go of my hair, and I feel the rush of power fill me before she slaps me around the face so hard I see stars. She grabs my hair again and drags me across the room, all while Azriel stands there, watching and smiling.

The upside to being hit, is getting the knowledge that apparently the Void thing really does only work when she's touching me. Good to know.

"I'm glad to see you didn't forget me, pet. Though I am interested as to how you knew I was here," Azriel questions as Scout slams me back to the floor.

"It seems we're still connected," I grit out, trying to

breathe through the pain. I'm only willing to take this so far, but I want some answers, and pretending I'm still weak seems like the best way to get him talking.

"We'll always be connected, pet."

"But he'll never love you, he's mine," Scout snarls, yanking on my hair again. Goddammit, did no one tell this bitch that hair pulling isn't actually a requirement of a cat fight? Fuck me.

"You can have him," I utter, and Azriel frowns.

"Of course, you fell in love with the wannabe me. He took you from me, and then you fell into his trap. He took *everything* from me, and now I'm going to take everything back."

"Is that why the bodies kept showing up?" I ask, hoping that he'll be stupid enough to answer.

"Oh no, that was all for my Scout. So many people had tortured her, used her, and this was my way of showing her just how much I love her. She was kept down here because of Deacon, so it was only right that he got the end result of my efforts." Scout swoons over him again, and I swear I want to die. These two are a match made in hell. Batshit fucking crazy, the pair of them. But at least now I'm under no illusions. She is who Locke thought she was.

"And the dagger?" I ask, curious.

"That was just to piss Deacon off. I figured he'd see it as a threat to you and come storming here to try to find out the truth. Then Scout could take her final revenge, and in turn, so would I. You ending up here is a nice little bonus. Now I can take everything from him, the same way he did to me, before he dies," Azriel gloats.

I just want him to keep talking all about his stupid plans, but I already know he's not that stupid. He's only said this much because he thinks I'm going to die. His eyes narrow as he assesses me. "For now, we'll lock you down here, keeping a few guards with you, and then, when we're ready, we'll send Deacon your head too. I can't wait to see how badly he loses it."

I try not to smile, if they're leaving me alone, then Scout can't keep my power from me.

"Remember this?" Azriel asks, pulling a syringe filled with black liquid from his pocket. "It made you so compliant before. I can't wait to see its effects on you properly this time." He struts over to me and crouches before me, waving the needle in front of my face.

My eyes go wide at the sight of it. How he got that with Gabriel and Nevin being dead I don't know, but fuck. I take a deep breath and calm my heart rate as best I can. I know that Deacon and Colt must be losing it already. I have no way of knowing if they're trying to find me, or if they've even thought about talking to Morgan and the others. I tap my bracelet once anyway, because the last thing I want is them getting hurt.

I wince at the prick of the needle in my neck and ignore their callous laughter. I can handle this. I just need to deal with the effects of the poison, and once it wears off, I'll have access to my power. I'm stronger than I was the last time I went through this. I've trained, and I've learned how far I can go.

They have no idea what I'm capable of, and I can't wait to show them just how badly they're fucking up.

I wake up, my hands bound behind my back. My throat is so dry it feels like I swallowed the fucking Sahara.

I fucking hate nightshade.

I open my eyes slowly, they feel stuck together, and it occurs to me that one is likely swollen from where Scout hit me earlier. I groan as the aches and pains hit me fully. Apparently someone whaled on me while I was out. Nothing like a few cracked ribs to really make a girl's day.

I take in the rest of my surroundings, and notice there are nearly a dozen Demons in here with me. Fuck my life. Maybe they do know a little something about my new powers, though twelve seems like a bit of overkill.

I have no idea how much time has passed, but luckily I can still feel Killian's bracelet on my wrist.

Unfortunately I can also feel the anger and panic

coming through the bond from both of my Demons. I'm going to be in so much trouble if they turn up here and they find me like this. But also, hell to the fucking no.

I don't need to be saved.

I just need to pull myself together.

I take a deep breath and call on the shadows to try and help heal myself the way I would've called on the light before. It doesn't work as well, but I feel like I can breathe without feeling like there's glass in my lungs.

I use the shadows to burn away the ropes around my wrist, but try not to give away what I'm doing to the Demons dotted around the room. To be fair, they look bored as fuck, and I guess all of them guarding one woman seems like overkill to them too.

Now I just need to work out how I'm going to disable them all so I can find and destroy Azriel once and for all. As crazy as Scout seems, I'm hoping she's just under his spell. I don't want Deacon to have to lose her twice. After what they told me earlier, I'm under no illusions. She's definitely Deacon's sister.

I figure I have two options. Unleash my Shadow Fire and hope I can keep it quiet enough that Azriel and Scout don't work out what I can do, or try to knock them all out. I'm not sure mass murder is something I want on my conscience, but I also really don't want to die.

I do not want to be the stupid girl who thought she

could when she really couldn't.

I straight up *refuse* to be that girl.

I notice one of the Demons watching me intently. I don't recognize him, but he barely blinks as he stares at me. Did he notice me using the shadows?

Shit.

If I'm going to move, I need to do it quickly, and I should probably start with him. I gather as much power as I can. He must realize what I'm doing because he storms toward me, a snarl on his face. This is not going how I wanted it to go. Not at all.

He pulls to a stop just in front of me, and I can feel the anger rolling off of him in waves.

"Everything okay?" I ask, wincing at the sting in my lip. Apparently that's cut up too. He just growls and takes another step toward me. He looks pissed and hesitant all at the same time, so I launch myself forward and push the shadows into him. His consciousness slips away, and he drops to the ground.

Which is awesome. It totally worked… except now the other eleven are looking at me, realizing that not only am I no longer bound, but I'm not quite as hopeless as they thought.

Oops?

They all just watch me as I scramble to my feet. I'm not sure if they're stunned, stupid, or just being careful. "Hi, guys, I mean, uh… well… let's just forget I was here, yeah?"

My attempt at funny just sounds awkward, even to my own ears, but it's like my words make them realize this wasn't all just an illusion. That I actually just did that.

"Please don't make me kill you," I half-plead, half-whisper, and just like that, they all rush toward me. So I do exactly what I didn't want to do.

I call on the Shadow Fire and push the flames out from me in a semicircle, with the wall at my back.

Their deaths are quiet. The flames swallow them so quickly they don't even have time to scream. Even the guy who was passed out is wiped from existence.

Suddenly, I understand why the Demons here fear Remy as much as they do . As much as I didn't want to die, and eleven-on-one wasn't exactly odds in my favor, I didn't want to have to kill them. They were just following orders, and they never stood a chance.

My heart hurts from the needless loss. They likely had families who will miss them, but I push my indignation toward Azriel. Once again, this is all his fucking fault.

I grab my hooded cape from the ground and tie it back around my shoulders, determined to end Azriel once and for fucking all. I take a minute to clear the last grogginess from the nightshade. Apparently all of the changes I've been through have made it so it doesn't fuck me up as badly as it once did. That, or he didn't give me as much as Nevin did.

I climb out of the basement as quietly as I can and start my journey through this fucking ridiculous place once again. I pretend to not see the giant puddles of blood, the blood spatter, and stains that are practically fucking everywhere.

It doesn't take long to find them.

They eat in the front room as if they didn't just have me tied up in the basement. As if there isn't a dead body on the table between them.

This is so fucking gross.

I hope they're not actually eating the body.

Nope. Gag. I'm just glad they haven't realized I'm here yet.

"See, love, my plan is coming together, just as I said. Now that we have the girl, it won't be long until Deacon rushes here, half out of his mind to save her."

"He never saved me," she pouts, and I can't help but want to yell at her that he thought she was dead.

"He never wanted to," Azriel says to her with a frown. "But I did. I saved you, and now you'll be my queen. Just like I promised. I'll get my power back, and then we'll rule this place."

He doesn't have his power? Well that explains a lot. It also explains why he let her do the heavy lifting earlier.

I reach out with my shadows and disable them both before they even spot me in the room, and I sag with relief as they both slump down in their chairs, the shadows taking their consciousness.

I pull back the shadows and lean back against the wall before taking a deep breath. I maneuver them both into the main entry hall, lying them down, and create a ring of Shadow Fire around them both. At least I know this way if they wake, they're not getting anywhere.

The bracelet on my wrist buzzes three times, and I cuss out loud. I'd forgotten about checking in. Three times means help is on the way. I'm in so much trouble.

Just as I think it, the front door to the estate bursts open, and I squeak as Deacon and Colt burst into the hall, both in full Demon mode.

"Oh, hey," I say, waving super awkwardly at them both. "Fancy seeing you guys here."

Deacon growls at me and paces forward, but I put my arms out in front of me, motioning for him to keep back.

"I'm fine, shit is handled. Will you two stop hulking out, please?" I huff. It takes a minute, and they shift back into the men I know and love, but they still both look pissed.

"We came to save you," Colt says, taking in my cuts and bruises.

"Well, as you can both see, I saved myself," I huff, crossing my arms.

"It looks like we were too late," Deacon says, inspecting me all over.

"Oh please, I looked worse than this when I was training with Killian." I roll my eyes at them both. "Now do you want to know what happened or what?"

It doesn't take me long to bring them up to speed, though it would've been quicker without the growling and the grunting. But I get it. They don't agree with my decisions and what I did here, but they're learning that I'm just as fucking capable as they are.

"So what's the plan now?" Colt asks, smirking. Surprisingly, he's taking this better than Deacon is. Totally didn't expect that, but I'm not going to complain either.

"My plan was to get rid of Azriel once and for all," I say, just as the asshole in question stirs.

"Come on now, love, there's no need for that."

"Shut your fucking mouth," Deacon roars, and I touch his chest as he moves toward the ring of Shadow Fire.

"Don't, he's not worth it."

"Maybe not, but I'd probably feel a lot better if I beat his ass to dust," he grunts, and I nod. I mean, I get it.

"Your sister is alive, Deacon. Focus on that bit. She seems more than a little broken, but she's alive." He winces at the reminder. He took that information earlier about as well as I expected. Especially when I told him what they'd said to me about the torture and stuff. Lead freaking balloon moment there.

He glances over at Scout, who is still passed out inside the ring of fire, and tears gather in his eyes. "I didn't know," he croaks, and Colt claps a hand on his shoulder.

"Just explain that to her. I'm sure once you guys talk it out, this could be a fresh start," Colt encourages, but the longer Deacon looks at her, the more defeated he seems. I hate that I couldn't save him from this… I just hope that she can be saved.

"We could have a fresh start as well you know, love. Maybe I'm just misunderstood too," Azriel chirps up, and I grit my teeth. I send a wave of shadows in his direction and enjoy his scream as they tear at his mind. That's a fun little party favor I picked up from Killian.

"I'll take that as a no," Azriel chokes out.

I drop the ring of fire around Scout, and look over at Deacon. "There's a body in the room to your left, but if you go to the room on the right, you should be body free. Maybe take her and try to talk to her?"

He nods at me, before walking over to her and scooping her limp form into his arms.

"I'll go with him. You've got this, right?" Colt asks, and I grin at his confidence in me.

"Hell yes I do."

"That's my girl." He kisses me quickly, and I can feel just how proud he is of me through our bond before he follows Deacon out of the room, leaving me with the man who took so much joy from my torture.

"You know, love, we're more alike than you think. That rage in your heart, the delight in your mind at the thought of hurting me… that's what makes us so alike," he says, grinning, but his eyes show his fear.

"I am nothing like you," I tell him calmly. "I won't take joy in your pain, well, not too much anyway. I just want you gone. I don't want you to be able to hurt me or the people I love ever again. You're a waste of a soul, Azriel. All you do is tear things down. But I do have to thank you for one thing. You gave me Deacon. And really, you created your own downfall."

"I wasn't always a monster, you know," he says sadly. "I didn't even want anything to do with Nevin and his ridiculous schemes. But sometimes people hold things over you to get what they want."

"While I believe that might be true, I also know everything you've done since then. No one made you do any of it. You sealed your own fate."

He hangs his head, and I know my words hit their mark. I wasn't lying, I don't find joy in this. Not really. It's more relief than anything else. Relief that we won't have to be constantly looking over our shoulders. Relief that this chapter of our story is finally fucking closed, and we can put it in the past. Where it belongs.

It hurts me to end a life. Even one as rotten as Azriel's, but I'll always do what I must to ensure the safety of the ones I love. I take no real joy in ending his life. Not like I once thought I would. Honestly, as my Shadow Fire turns Azriel to ash, I almost feel sad for him.

I take a deep breath once he's gone, my throat thick with emotion. I didn't think it would be that hard, but with him being powerless, it just felt… wrong.

"Fal… I think we need you," Colt shouts, and I rush toward the room the three of them disappeared into. Colt stands just inside the door while Scout attacks Deacon. He isn't fighting back or defending himself at all.

"What the fuck?" I utter as I try to move past Colt, but he holds me still.

"He doesn't want to hurt her. He thinks she's been through enough already. So he's trying to let her work out some anger, but she looks like she's going to kill him. Talk to him."

"Deacon, she's a Void. If she takes your power, she can kill you. Please, please don't let her. You need to fight back," I plead with him, but I don't know if he hears me because he doesn't make a move to stop her.

"We need to do something," I stress to Colt, who holds me in place.

"I know, but what?"

"We stop her," I practically growl. "I'm not letting her kill him, Colt. If that means she dies, then that's what it means. I didn't want that for him, but look at her, she's fucking batshit crazy. I'm not even sure she's able to be saved at this point. Three hundred years of torture is more than a lot. I wouldn't survive it."

"You might be right, but how do we get him on board with that? Look at him." I do look, only to see ribbons of blood streaming down his arms and chest as he lets her attack him. She fights without finesse, like she really has lost control of herself, and it seems as if he's just going to let her take it out on him until she's done.

"Enough!" I shout, and Scout seems to be shocked from her frenzy.

"It will never be enough! Every single time he fucked up, I was hurt. Tortured. Raped. All because he wouldn't do what he was fucking asked! It was his fault I was taken—

his fault that everything happened to me."

"I thought you were dead," Deacon says, his voice breaking. "I searched for you, for weeks. Father showed me your remains…"

"Liar!!" she screams and tries to attack him again. I step forward to stop her but Colt stops me.

"He's going to need you. If he hates me for doing what needs to be done, it won't be the end of the world for me. Let me do this, for you and for him." I nod and stay in place as Colt whips forward, faster than I thought he could move, and wrenches Scout from Deacon. She attacks him, but Colt has been a fighter his entire existence. She goes for his throat, while Deacon watches, almost stunned to stillness.

Colt reacts, and before I can blink, her heart is in his bloodied hand, rather than in her chest.

A puff of air escapes her before she drops to the ground and Deacon falls to his knees with her, tears streaming down his face. "I failed her."

TWENTY SEVEN

COLT

It's been six weeks since that day in the Outliers, and to say things have been tense here is an understatement. Deacon didn't speak at all for the first few weeks, and then it took another few for him to talk to me.

I get it, and I don't hold it against him. He lost his sister all over again. I've felt that grief more times than I care to count, and I was the one who took her from him. We're pretty much back to where we were before that day, but it hasn't been easy.

Luckily, he knows I took no joy in it. That it wasn't something I wanted to do, and after a lot of talking with both Fallon and I, he agrees that it had to be done. There was no coming back for her. Killian came at Fallon's request and helped me sort out the fucked- up state the estate was in while she brought Deacon home.

There were more than a few bodies in that place, and if I think about it too hard, it makes me feel like I need to shower. I've seen a lot of loss, but that was just way too extreme. Rotted corpses are not exactly my idea of fun.

"How's it going?" Locke asks as he walks into the kitchen. I've been hiding in here most of the morning since I kind of feel like a spare part right now. When I came here, we had shit that needed to be done, and that's been the story of my existence for the last Fates only knows how long. But now I have nothing to do, and since I'm trying to not get under Deacon's feet while he grieves, I feel like I'm in the way.

"I'm good," I say, and I know the smile on my face looks as fake as my words feel coming out of my mouth.

"I'm starting the hunt for a new wave of guards today, and then we start training. Want in?" he asks, and despite the fact that I'm aware he's taking pity on my uselessness right now, I jump at the chance.

"Hell fucking yes."

"I thought you might." He laughs, shaking his head as he puts sugar in his coffee. "I know this is all new for you, but you'll find your feet. We've been in a weird period of transition for just over two years. It's slowly starting to settle, and with Azriel finally handled, I think this level is going to finally let out a deep breath."

"I have to say, the Demon way of life is awfully human." I grin at him, and he shakes his head again.

"Where do you think they learned it from?" I laugh at his question, realizing he's probably right. "I'm going to go and talk to Laura. Come find me in an hour, and we'll start the recruitment bullshit. I much prefer the training part."

"I will, thank you."

"Any time. You're part of the family now. Just remember that, and you'll be fine." He nods before leaving, and I feel a bit better. Not having a purpose really doesn't sit well with me.

"There you are," Fallon sings as she waltzes into the room. She moves into my arms and snuggles into my chest.

Mine the Demon inside of me purrs and I smile, planting a kiss on top of her head as I hug her back.

"I'm sorry I haven't been around much," she apologizes, but I only hold her tighter.

"Fallon, he lost his sister. Not just his sister, his twin. I've lost Remy enough times to know how much that hurts, but I knew each time I'd get to see her again. That isn't the case for Scout, even though I think we all know she deserves to finally be at peace."

"Thank you for being so amazing." She sighs and pops

up on the tips of her toes, kissing me gently. "Do you want to hang out with us today? I finally got him to agree to a bit of normalcy. We're just going to binge some TV and eat junk food, but I think he needs to do something that isn't staring at the ceiling."

"We all grieve differently. I know he looked after you while you grieved, but not everyone needs that. He'll get through this. As for joining you, I literally just agreed to help Locke with some stuff, but I can join you guys tonight?"

"That sounds perfect. And I'll try to remember to give him space. It's just hard, especially with the bond. I can feel every single iota of his pain. It's devastating."

"Just be you and be there for him. That's all you need to do."

"He doesn't hold it against you, you know. I know it's been hard. But I feel that too. He's just hurting."

"I get it, I really do." I smile down at the powerhouse of a woman who managed not only to bring us both to our knees, but managed to quite literally slay her own Demons. "Did I mention yet how proud I am of you for kicking ass? I mean, I'm a little pissed still that you went behind our backs to do it, and I'm sorry I made you feel like you needed to, but still super proud of how strong you've become. Especially after everything you've been through. I always knew you were a badass, and I'm glad you're starting to believe it, too."

"You might've mentioned it a few times," she says, her eyes scrunching at the sides when she smiles. "Also, don't forget that Remy is coming tomorrow."

"Pfft, like I'd forget. I finally get to meet my niece!" She laughs at my excitement and kisses me chastely before pulling away.

"I'm glad to hear it. I'm going to go back to Deacon, but you know where we are when you're done."

"Don't worry, I'll find you. I always do."

I hold the tiny bundle of happiness in my arms, and I swear my heart feels like it's going to burst. She's so freaking beautiful, I think I might die. I basically pounced on my sister the minute she arrived with Kain.

"What's her name?" I ask softly, not wanting to scare the babbling little cutie.

"Everly… but Evie for short," Remy says as she slides under Kain's arm on the sofa in the sitting room of the estate.

"I love it." I smile, unable to pull my eyes away from the little girl. I know how much Everly meant to Remy, and I love so much that she passed the name on.

Mine the Demon inside of me huffs, and I push him

back a little.

Not ours, buddy, but she is family.

Mine he huffs again, and I smile. He'll work it out.

"How's life been down here? It's been a minute since we saw you guys," Remy asks, and I look over to Fallon who is sitting next to Remy with Deacon beside her.

Fallon launches into the story about Azriel, Scout, and everything else that's been going on. I don't think I've ever seen my sister manage to look sad, happy, and disappointed all at once.

"Man, I missed out on all the fun being pregnant." She pouts, and Kain leans forward to kiss her cheek.

"You vowed to not get pregnant again for some time, my love, so I'm sure that you will be able to find some mischief to bury yourself in."

I snort a laugh at his words because he's not wrong.

"Plus, totally worth it," I say, aware I've become a big tub of goo around my niece, but she's the first one I've had the chance to meet this small, and it just makes me sad that I missed the others but also want some of my own. "Where are the other two?"

"Back home with the guys. It's been… an adjustment. Raze adapted fine to Maddox and again to Evie. But Maddox… well, he's not taking it as well. He'll be fine, I'm sure, but he seems to be upset that my attention is divided again." Remy sighs, frowning as she looks at the little girl in my arms.

"It will all be fine, *mon amour*. You'll see. Children are resilient."

"He's right," Deacon pipes up. "He'll come round. He's a pack animal. He's too young to understand what's going on, but once he realizes she's family, they'll be inseparable. You watch." He grins over at me, and I swear, I'll fight him if he tries to take the little beauty from my arms.

"Feeling broody, brother?" Remy smirks at me, and I laugh.

"She's just so little. I don't want to hurt her. Everything in me is screaming to protect," I tell her, and my Demon brings his attention up a little higher, scanning the parts of the room I can't see myself to make sure she's safe.

"It's the same for us all," Kain confesses. "I've been an anxious mess since she arrived in this world, and here I was thinking I would be equipped to deal with having a girl."

"We all thought you'd handle it best, buddy." Remy laughs, snuggling into him. "You'll get there. Just don't go crazy the first time she brings home a boy… or a girl. She has two brothers and four dads, Fates forbid anyone is brave enough to try and hurt her."

"She has two uncles too," I add, and she stirs in my arms, but I look up to see them all just smiling at me. "Shut up."

Evie wakes up and is so peaceful when her bright blue eyes open, it's like even this little, she can see straight into my soul. She grips my finger and brings it to her mouth.

"You shouldn't," Kain starts, but Remy hits him in the stomach. I have no idea what he was going to say until I feel a pinch on my finger.

"Well shit," I laugh, and Remy nearly dies from her laughter.

"She's a Dracul, you idiot. And apparently she's hungry."

"How was I meant to know? She's a baby!" I mutter. "But if she's hungry, she can have it all."

"He is officially the softest I've ever seen him," Deacon laughs, but I pay them no mind.

This little girl just lodged her place in my top five people, and I would literally destroy the world for her. So what's a little blood?

TWENTY EIGHT

DEACON

NINE MONTHS LATER

I look around the ballroom at the estate, amazed at just how far we've come. Last year, Fallon's birthday looked very different. It was a very small affair. This year we're in the freaking ballroom because so many people wanted to go to the party. Every person she comes into contact with here wants to be her friend. Everyone falls in love with her, just as quickly as I did.

The mix of faces and races is what puts such a big smile on her face, so I won't question it for the world. Technically, her birthday isn't until tomorrow, but Colt and I have plans for her, so we wanted to have her party tonight.

Tomorrow night, she's ours.

But for tonight, we'll share her with everyone we love.

"Little different from last year, huh?" Colt jokes as he comes to stand with me at the bar. A glass with ice and whiskey appears in front of him almost instantly, and he grins. "Man, I love the perks of being the boss… kinda."

"Kinda," I laugh and roll my eyes. He does more shit here these days than I do. For all his bitching about how much he never wanted to be an Elder with the Hunters, he took to helping run this place like a dragon to the skies. "But yeah, very different. Who would've thought back then that we'd be friends?"

"Hey, we're family now." He laughs before throwing back his drink. The minute it touches the bar, the girl reappears to refill it. "We've all come a long way, that's for sure."

He watches Fallon walk through the room with Remy and Morgan, the three of them thick as thieves these days. "How pissed is she that she can't drink tequila this year?"

"I think your sister was more pissed that the one year she can drink, Fallon can't." I chuckle, but I'm not even a little sorry. Fallon rubs the small bump of her stomach, and my grin widens. Yet another addition to our family, and I secretly think that Fallon is excited to have another girl in the house.

She’s going to be loved, that much is for sure. As long as she’s healthy, that’s all I really care about.

“I think you’re right, though I think Remy is secretly excited to have another baby around. Creek says she lifted the ban on pregnancy, so I don’t think it’ll be too long until she’s pregnant again too.”

“They’re going to have a whole fucking football team,” I laugh, shaking my head.

“Remy has always been all about family. I don’t think she ever let herself imagine having one of her own for so long, and now that she has the security and safety she does, she’s going to go a little crazy. Not that I’m complaining, being fun uncle Colt is the best.”

“You’ll be the fun dad too, I can already see it. I’m going to be the bad guy.” I look over at him, and he tries to look innocent but just ends up laughing out loud.

“Yeah, you’re probably right. I’m not going to lie.” Fallon spots us and heads in our direction, her smile widens, and I feel the love in her heart via our bond. My smile matches hers; and when she reaches me, I can’t help but pull her into my arms and kiss her until she’s breathless.

“My turn,” Colt quips as we pull apart, and he steals her from my embrace. If I didn’t love them both so much, I might get frustrated at the competitive streak he has. But I do, so I just smile and enjoy how happy she is.

"How are you feeling?" I ask once they separate, and she laughs.

"I am having the best time, thank you so much for tonight. Both of you. It was a lovely surprise having everyone here with us." She takes both of our hands and squeezes. "But I'm also looking forward to some sleep. The kids have so much energy, so I'm almost afraid of how tired I'm going to be once this one arrives."

"Good thing you'll have plenty of help then," Colt says and I nod, agreeing.

"We're all in this together," I say, and Colt agrees.

"Always."

Our girl has had a chill day with her friends, but tonight she's ours, and I very much intend on spoiling us all. I know Colt is on board. There's nothing quite like watching her while she's with us both. And having the spa installed in the estate was the best damn idea I think I've ever had. Having a hot tub available all day, every fucking day? Bliss.

So I know she'll come back to the bedroom in a bikini. Which makes what I have planned so much easier.

We're on the way back. Colt's voice filters into my mind. The bond between our Demons settled well and came with that small perk. We don't use it too often, but for times like this, it's perfect.

She still in the bikini? I ask.

No, she got dressed before the others left. But that's never stopped us before. I swear I can actually hear his demon grin.

She might be dressed, but she won't be for long.

I carry on tying the silk ropes to the four posters of the bed—second best upgrade we made. A bed big enough for us all, with plenty of space for play. All it meant was I needed longer rope. Not exactly a hardship.

The door opens as I finish securing the final rope, and Colt holds the door wide as Fallon walks in.

"Ready for your birthday treat, Princess?"

Her eyes do a quick sweep of the room, taking in everything I've prepared. Her beautiful face breaks into a luminous grin that shoots a ball of heat right to my heart.

And my dick. Fuck, I'm hard as a slab of concrete.

"Yes!" Her enthusiasm for us never wanes. In fact, it only seems to grow with every day that passes. Her appetite is out of this world, which is perfect since Colt and I both seem to have a deep-rooted need to be inside of her, especially when our Demons lust for her.

"Colt, I think our girl needs to be unwrapped."

"Hey! I thought it was my birthday. Shouldn't I be the one unwrap—" She doesn't get to finish her sentence because I'm on her in a fraction of a second with my hand in her hair, her face angled toward me. My mouth is a mere inch from her delicious lips.

"Careful, Fallon. Bad girls don't get to come." My teasing but firm words effectively shut down the rest of her objection. Since I'm so close to her, I take advantage of the moment and kiss her senseless while Colt stands behind her, and strips her down to nothing. Once she's naked and sandwiched between our big bodies, her indignation all but disappears.

"On your knees, baby girl." The way she fluidly goes down on her knees is a heady sight. I inspect her position, as I always do. This time, Colt does a round with me, shedding one piece of clothing at a time as he does until he's as naked as she is and ready for her.

"You look beautiful on your knees. Now, be a good girl and suck Colt's dick. Extra points if you can make him come." That earns me a bright smile from Fallon and a growl from Colt. I'd call that a win any day of the week.

Colt takes two steps toward her and buries his fingers in her hair, tightly enough to make her grunt. The wolf in me loves it when she sounds like an animal. My dick twitches at the sound, but it's not my turn yet. We're just whetting her appetite.

Crouching at her side, I reach out and pinch her nipple, making her moan while Colt curses. I know how he feels.

That vibration at the back of her throat is fucking heaven.

"Does he taste good in your mouth, baby girl? Do you want to taste his cum on your tongue?" My filthy words make her wetter. I know this because the scent of her arousal makes me impossibly hard.

"And what about the feel of his cum running down your throat?"

At this, I push two of my fingers inside her pussy and pump once, then again, earning another moan from her and a, "Fucking goddamn," from Colt.

When I put my wet fingers in my mouth and taste her, I have no idea how in the fuck I manage to restrain myself from picking her up and fucking the breath out of her.

"Want a taste?" I look up at Colt who's practically salivating at the thought of a hit of our girl, and then I look at Fallon who's working his cock like a beautiful muse.

"Dip your fingers in your pussy, baby girl. Let Colt taste you. I think he's forgotten how fucking delicious you are."

Like the perfect sub that she is, Fallon doesn't miss a beat as she keeps sucking him off. She dips two fingers in her pussy before bringing them to Colt's mouth as he bends down to suck on her fingers.

We all three moan at the moment. Me watching Colt suck her juices off her fingers. Colt because fuck, her taste is better than any Michelin five star meal. And Fallon because I can feel through our bond that she's so worked up right now that she may not be able to hold back her orgasm.

That could be fun too. A little climax deprivation.

No, we'd decided on something different, and we both need to see her lose her fucking mind on her birthday.

"That's enough." Colt pulls back, allowing his cock to fall from between Fallon's swollen lips.

"How's that hard on treating you?"

"Painfully well." Cheeky fucker.

"On the bed, baby girl. On your back, head hanging off the side." The way she obeys my command is like a drug for me.

As she settles into position, I open my jeans and let my cock spring out, keeping the pants on for the time being. Placing myself at the side of the bed, I watch as Colt crawls up the bed. Because the fucker cannot follow directions, he bends down and eats her pussy for a couple of minutes, like she's the fucking appetizer right before the whole- ass meal arrives.

"If you make her come, she'll pay the price."

That stops him, and he rights himself, licking his lips and winking at our girl. "Sorry, babe," he says to her, "I can't help myself when your pussy is open wide and just begging to be licked."

I roll my eyes as he makes her giggle, but then

concentrate back on the task at hand.

"Colt is going to fuck your pretty little pussy while you swallow my dick. I want to feel the inside of your throat, and we both know how much you love that." With a satisfied smile on her face, Fallon opens her mouth and breathes out through her nose while Colt gets into position. He kneels at her center, her knees bent at his shoulders, his dick just barely touching her fucking soaked opening.

Reaching over to the bedside, I take out the butt plug and throw it at him, making sure that Fallon can't see it. The lube is next, and Colt places them both right next to his leg.

"Are you ready to get royally fucked?" he asks with a smirk, and she moans in response. The vibrations on my dick as I push it into her mouth make me bite down on my lip. Fuck, that feels good.

I move in sync with Colt as he thrusts inside her pussy. Her hands are at her sides, fingers digging into the sheets as we fill her.

"That's it, take us. Take us both nice and deep."

She's gorgeous, a true vision with our dicks spit roasting her.

Once we're both buried balls deep inside her, we start to move in tandem. Over and over and over again as I tweak her nipples and Colt plays with her clit. We both pinch at the same time, earning us loud moans that almost make me lose my self-control. The sound travels all the way up my shaft and down my balls.

When I look up, I see Colt's eyes turning black, his teeth peeking out as his fingers dig into her upper thighs and turn black with long, dangerous claws. I don't need a mirror to know my eyes are red as rubies. We're both too close to losing our ever-loving minds with how good she feels.

"Now."

My command spurs him on; reaching over, he takes the butt plug and lubes it up enough to make sure she doesn't experience any unnecessary pain.

I know the exact moment he slips it inside her ass because she has a momentary slip of her breath, and her teeth come way too fucking close to my dick.

Except something about that excites me too.

Colt groans as he fucks her, and I know just how tight she feels with that plug in her ass. It's fucking heaven. Our girl loves anal and not one of us is sad about that.

Looking down, I watch as Colt rubs circles on her clit, making her completely crazed at the overload in sensation. Our bond allows us to know exactly how she feels, and right now, she's losing her fucking mind. I pinch her nipples once more, and I see the outline of my dick on her throat when she swallows it down.

Colt must see me because his gaze goes to her throat,

and then we're looking at each other.

Yeah, we're done.

"Come for us, baby girl." No sooner than the last syllable leaves my lips, Fallon is shaking, falling over the cliff, and Colt follows her over with abandon.

It's all too much for me. Taking care to pull out slowly, I bite the inside of my cheek to make sure I don't blow my load early. Colt pulls himself from her, along with the plug, and I move to bury myself in her ass. Her moans spur me on and I lose some of my carefully crafted control as she rides back into me, her tightness clamping around me. I reach forward and grip her throat, pulling her up so my chest is on her back and squeezing on her throat as Colt rubs her clit.

Her whimpers are almost my undoing. "Come for me again, Princess."

She shudders around me as I squeeze her throat some more before unloading inside of her.

"Holy fuck that was hot. This will literally never get old." Colt grins at us as we collapse on the bed beside him.

"What he said," Fallon pants, and I grin.

"Happy Birthday, Princess."

The siren has me out of bed in a heartbeat.

“What the fuck is that?” Colt growls, his Demon fully out as he crouches over Fallon’s body, protecting her against anything that might come through the door.

“That’s the red alert.”

“What‘s a red alert?” Fallon asks as I start to dress.

“It’s a Realm-wide alert. It means all fucking hell must have broken loose. The red alert can only come from Morgan and the guys directly.” I finish dressing and find them both following suit. “We need to get to the palace.”

“Maybe Fallon should stay here,” Colt says, and she glares at him.

“No fucking way, if something’s wrong, I’m coming.”

I don’t object, even though I want to. The palace is probably the safest place for her to be during a red alert. Adrenaline floods my system at the crazy thoughts running through my mind.

“Let‘s go,” she says as she pulls on a sweater and slides her feet into her boots. I look over at Colt, and he nods as he pulls his t-shirt over his head.

I can’t remember the last time I felt true fear, but the red alert has my hands shaking.

I take her hand in mine as Colt takes her other, and I can’t help but worry about what we’re going to find when we reach the palace.

TWENTY NINE

MORGAN

The howls wake me and have me scrambling from the bed. I've never heard Kaos make a noise like that, and my heart is in my throat as I whisper from the room after nudging Bryce awake. I appear in the hall where the children's rooms are, and the smell of blood is what hits me first.

No, no, no.

I rush toward Ares' room, and find him still asleep. Havoc is sitting at attention by the crib, but his howls match Kaos'. Once I've checked Ares, I rush into Mireya's room.

"No!" I scream, seeing Kaos broken and bleeding on

the floor. I know without looking that Mireya isn't in her bed. Whatever happened here, I hope that she got out, that she's in her hiding place.

I send out a flash to the guys through our bond, and they all appear in the room in an instant as I drop to my knees beside Kaos.

Caleb arrives first, and seeing the room, whispers away. I assume he's headed toward the safe room we set up for Mireya should something like this ever happen. The other three arrive shortly after. Malik disappears to Ares' room as I try to heal my oldest friend, all the while his dark blood pools on the floor around me.

Bryce and Killian place a hand each on my shoulders, lending me their strength and their power. I heal my friend enough that I know he'll survive and then reach out to Caleb. My hands shake as I wait for him to respond.

Fear roots me to the spot. This is why I waited so long to have children. I never wanted my enemies to have something to use against me. Kaos nudges my hand with his nose, and I close my eyes as he shows me what happened.

A team of six managed to get through my wards. They got into the room, and four of them attacked Kaos. Mireya ran, just like we taught her.

Good girl.

Two of them followed, but then everything fades. "It's

okay, boy, you did your best. Let's just hope the rest of the pack caught them."

"What happened?" Bryce asks as Malik re-enters the room with Ares in his arms and Havoc at his heels.

I tell them what Kaos showed me, and the anger that builds in the room is palpable. Havoc moves over to Kaos and licks at his wounds before nudging my hand too. He shows me one of the men entering Ares' room, but retreating when he saw Havoc.

The hound whines under my touch, but I stroke between his ears. "You did good. You protected him."

He curls around Kaos and whines as he tries to help Kaos heal.

Caleb appears in the room a second later, the look on his face frantic. "She's not there. I found one dead Demon torn up by the rest of the pack, but I can't find Mireya."

Killian disappears from the room while I fill Caleb in on what the hounds showed me. My fury knows no end, and my hands start to shake from my uncontrollable rage. I finish talking to Caleb when the alarm rings out across the level.

A red alert.

It will have gone to all levels.

Someone thought they could take one of the most precious things in my life from me, and they're about to realize that they seriously fucked up.

ABOUT THE AUTHOR

Sloane Murphy is the author of the international bestselling series, The Immortal Chronicles, as well as a range of other paranormal and contemporary romance. Sloane lives in Peterborough, England, with her husband & fur baby and over the years, she has developed an unhealthy appreciation for cheesy YA Films, cupcakes and bad pop music. She adores fairy tales, ballet and all things supernatural, drinks far too much coffee, and watches an ungodly amount of Netflix. When she's not busy writing, she can be found exploring the world with her husband and chocolate Labrador.

If you would like to send Sloane an email, you can reach her at sloane@authorsloanemurphy.com

Want to sign up for her mailing list? You can sign up HERE

Or come join her reader group on Facebook, Sloanes Little Monsters

facebook.com/sloanemurphybooks

twitter.com/SloaneMurphyBks

instagram.com/sloanemurphybooks

bookbub.com/authors/sloane-murphy

ALSO BY SLOANE MURPHY

THE SEVEN REALMS SAGA

The Shadow Walkers Saga

(Reverse Harem Paranormal Romance)

A Crown of Blood and Bone

A Crown of Smoke and Ash

A Crown of Shadows and Secrets

A Crown of Thorns and Lies

A Crown of Fire and Wrath

A Crown of Pride and Ruin

The Shadow Weaver Series

(Menage Paranormal Romance)

Witch's Curse

Hunter's Heart

Demon's Blessing

The Shadow Queen Series

(Reverse Harem Paranormal Romance)

The Shadow Queen

The Shadow Legacies Series

(Rejected Mates Romance)

Luna Rising

THE IMMORTAL CHRONICLES SERIES

(YA Paranormal Romance. Complete Series)

Descent

Crash

Soar

Rapture

BLACK WATER ACADEMY SERIES

(Upper YA/NA Paranormal Romance. Reverse Harem)

Marked

Chosen

Hunted

DARK FAE DUET

(Paranormal Romance. Dark Fantasy)

Summer Princess

Winter King

OTHER AUTHORS AT HUDSON INDIE INK

Paranormal Romance/Urban Fantasy

Stephanie Hudson

Xen Randell

C. L. Monaghan

Sorcha Dawn

Sci-fi/Fantasy

Devin Hanson

Crime/Action

Blake Hudson

Mike Gomes

Contemporary Romance

Gemma Weir

Elodie Colt

Ann B. Harrison

Printed in Great Britain
by Amazon

79493213R00235